ZOMBIE APOCALYPSE!

ACAPULCALYPSE NOW

WISH YOU
WERE HERE!

ZOMBIE APOCALYPSE!
ACAPULCALYPSE NOW

ALISON LITTLEWOOD

Created by STEPHEN JONES

RUNNING PRESS
PHILADELPHIA • LONDON

ROBINSON

First published in Great Britain in 2015 by Robinson

A CIP catalogue record for this book is available from the British Library.

ISBN 978-1-47213-588-9

Robinson
is an imprint of
Little, Brown Book Group
Carmelite House
50 Victoria Embankment
London EC4Y 0DZ

An Hachette UK Company
www.hachette.co.uk

www.littlebrown.co.uk

First published in the United States in 2015 by Running Press Book Publishers,
A Member of the Perseus Books Group

US ISBN: 978-0-7624-5813-4
US Library of Congress Control Number: 2015932761

9 8 7 6 5 4 3 2 1
Digit on the right indicates the number of this printing

Running Press Book Publishers
2300 Chestnut Street
Philadelphia, PA 19103-4371

Visit us on the web!
www.runningpress.com

Typeset by SX Composing DTP, Rayleigh, Essex
Printed and bound in Great Britain by CPI Group (UK) Ltd, Croydon CR0 4YY

Papers used by Robinson are from well-managed forests and other responsible sources

HOTEL BAKTUN

Where the magic never ends

BY INVITATION ONLY

Elizabeth Taylor, Frank Sinatra, Brigitte Bardot . . . all were part of the Golden Age of Acapulco, the destination of the stars. Now the Hotel Baktun brings you the height of luxury in an exclusive beach resort, right in the beating heart of Mexico.

Join us for the Grand Opening ceremony, graced by today's stars of screen and stage, and culminating in a special performance by rock legend Colton Creed. You won't believe your eyes!

We look forward to receiving you as our Special Guest as we usher in the revival of the glorious past.

Chapter One

IF MICK HALF-closed his eyes, the pyramid could almost appear to be real. The sun was behind it, the sky a deep, perfect blue, and it was easy to imagine that it was over 1,000 years ago, the monument rising high to honour the ancient gods of the land.

But it was not 1,000 years ago.

The pyramid's steps were a little too even and a little too high to climb. If it hadn't been cast into a jagged silhouette he could have seen that its walls were actually, in the main, windows; their purpose was to be looked out of, not at. If he'd been standing closer still he would have been able to see the balconies that wrapped around every level.

The structure was what he had learned to think of with disdain as a *theme hotel*. Still, its purpose was grand enough – to inject new life into tourism on this once-desirable stretch of coastline, to resurrect the ghost of its glamorous past.

Acapulco was once the playground of Hollywood stars, the gorgeous and talented and the fabulously wealthy. It hadn't been that way for a long time.

For a moment hope stirred in his chest, something that

at once surprised him and made him wrinkle his nose.

Somewhere, a power drill started up with a manic shrieking. A voice was shouting something, over and over: "Suntan, suntan!"

Where the magic never ends, he thought. That was how they were selling the new hotel, the words embroidered in small script across the pocket of the shirt he wore, just beneath its freshly minted logo.

The sound of the sea, soothing and always there, intruded on his thoughts, and he remembered that there was something real here after all. The final piece of the structure, the blocky shape set upon the pyramid's flattened top, was an actual ruin. It had been ripped from its place on the Yucatan shore, its heritage undermined by the mighty dollar, or in this case the English pound. It had been transplanted to this place, somewhere it was never intended to be. They called it the *Monumento que Canta*, the monument that sings, because of the way the wind was said to sound through it whenever the coast was about to be invaded.

There had been an outcry against uprooting it, protests in Cancun and along the Riviera Maya, no doubt witnessed by bemused and uncaring tourists. Now it was going to be the picturesque backdrop to a modern rooftop bar.

Mick shook his head. He did not know if the ruin's voice had ever been heard; now it never would be.

That voice came again, "Suntan!", this time raised and insistent, and he saw someone hurrying towards him. It was the head of food and beverages, the F&B as they called him, pale and sweaty and looking all too clearly as if he'd just stepped off a flight and landed somewhere he didn't belong. He also looked angry.

"Suntan!"

A sinking realisation swept through Mick. "My name is not Suntan," he said. "It is Iktan. Iktan Camal. It's a Maya name.

I said to them they could call me Mick. They have put it on my badge—"

"Whatever. Who the hell cares? There's a new load of painter and decs just arrived, and they want feeding." The F&B leaned over, resting his hands on his knees. His lily-white cheeks were turning red and Iktan briefly wondered if this was what a heart attack looked like. The man straightened. "They need a waiter. Get to it." He turned away, calling back over his shoulder: "And what's wrong with calling yourself Rick? Like in the film. The punters'll like that."

Mick frowned after the man's portly form. Another realisation washed over him and he muttered, "That's *Casablanca*, you *culero*. Not here. Not in Mexico." He sighed and started to make his way inside, heading past the empty hollow of the new pool with its unused waterslide. The sound of his feet was hollow against the new tiles, the gentlest of breezes failing to stir the fringe of ornamental palm trees, newly shipped in and set in planters made in the shape of a Maya headdress.

Outside, it was a steady twenty-seven degrees. Inside, the air-conditioning was turned up so high that it shivered the hairs on Mick's arms. Were the managers trying to bring their English winter with them? They should have taken the singing monument and stuck it on their hard, freezing coast. There it might have sung, with the cold breath of the north wind in its gullet and no one who would understand to hear it.

Soon the guests would arrive, dripping with jewels and leaving a trail of money behind them. Mick grinned at that thought, reminding himself that he'd competed for this job, had *wanted* this job. If he couldn't be rich, it was best to stick to the rich as closely as he could; that way, a little luck – and money – might just rub off.

His real name, Iktan, meant "clever", but that should have been the name they gave to his little brother. He was the smart one of the family, the one who would soon be leaving his job in a fast-food joint and going to college, a college that he – *Mick* – could now help pay for. Their parents, who still farmed maize in the traditional Maya way, had frowned when the boys had come to the city, although they hadn't protested; they knew how things were. Now he would show them he'd done the right thing.

Smiling, he passed through the hotel's main lobby, its Reception desk taking up most of one massive wall. Water trickled behind it down some roughened material meant to look like rock, as if a jungle waterfall had accidentally found its way into a grand hotel in a Pacific beach resort. A huge television was mounted on the wall off to one side, though it was switched off and silent.

And here, there were other things that were real: a glass case, no doubt linked to some fancy alarm system, was full of ancient obsidian blades, incongruously placed next to ear spools decorated with gold and turquoise. Another held a large bowl made of clay, its painted design almost entirely faded, alongside miniature human effigies, beads and pieces of a broken mask. There was also a tablet, carved with figures that Mick couldn't make out.

He shrugged as he passed it. Apparently, the owner of the hotel had insisted that everything in these displays was genuine. Mick wondered whether the man was happy with the result of his endeavours. The effect of the smartly painted walls, everything in new straight lines, the shining glass of the displays, was to make the real appear to be fake; almost as if it were in disguise.

He looked up and saw the name of the hotel writ large in a carved wooden panel suspended above the Reception desk: HOTEL BAKTUN. Its name had been taken from the Maya Long Count calendar, a period of thousands of years that some said was meant to culminate in the end of the world, not too long from now.

He turned his back on it. The floor, wide and grand and made of local tile, was covered in a fine layer of dust. Wood shavings curled among the detritus like maggots in flesh. Mick hurried across it, ignoring the blows of hammers and the arcing *tick-tick-tzzzzzz* of a welder, leaving behind him a trail of perfect footprints.

As he moved, a man approached, walking with his head bowed and his hand to his forehead, as if he were trying to obscure his face. Mick swerved but somehow the man barged into him anyway, knocking him aside with a shoulder that was hard and unyielding. Mick turned, but the man made no apology, did not even pause.

Mick shrugged. He wondered who the man was. He hadn't been wearing an apron or overalls or a paint-stained T-shirt. He wore a silk shirt and chinos – a manager, perhaps? But he hadn't seemed that type, someone strutting around with his head thrown back to watch everything that was happening, ready to bark out an order. He had seemed more like someone who didn't really want to be seen.

But there were legions of people in the hotel, all of them making sure it would be ready on time, and who the hell was Mick? A waiter, nothing more, with a name that didn't quite belong to him. He had no way of knowing if someone was there who shouldn't be. And yet – he *did* know. He sensed it, could almost smell it. But then, the man could be a sightseer, not from the lands of money and showbiz but from the city, and why shouldn't he come in for a look around? The relics of Mexico were here, not in a museum for all to see but encased in glass in a new hotel, positioned only for foreign eyes.

As if in answer to his thoughts he saw the F&B heading towards the front-of-house manager, who was beckoning him with an anxious expression on her face. They met near the Reception desk and looked at something she held out. It looked like a miniature television. Why didn't they just switch on the big screen? But they bowed over it as if they were keeping a secret. As Mick watched, the F&B covered his mouth; probably his favourite football team had just lost. Mick smiled.

Soon the hotel would be ready. Mick would be waiting on celebrities instead of an army of workmen, people who would, before long, melt back into the city from whence they came. The gates would close and the hotel would become an island, a law unto itself; a place for feasting, while without, men scrambled and fought and died for whatever pesos they could find.

He made his way down a corridor with bare wires hanging down from the ceiling and towards the kitchen. There, he paused. A window was set into the side of the building and from it, he could see the sea. That bright blue line spoke of freedom, and clean salt air. He remembered days splashing in the surf, he and his brother closing their eyes against the spray. He found himself smiling.

The hotel was a future, of a kind. But still, he couldn't help but see in his mind's eye the pyramid as it would appear from that shore, its lines too clean and too new, blocking out the sky. And somehow, he knew; if he were a Maya god, he would not be pleased by the sight of this new tower rising into the air. He would, in fact, be really fucking angry.

Chapter Two

THE CHAMPAGNE ON the flight hadn't been cold enough. Ten hours, and Louise – or Louisiana, as she insisted on being called, despite hailing from the outskirts of Leicester – hadn't stopped talking about it.

She had stopped talking now, though. So had Celeste. The taxi, a rattle-bone blue and white VW Beetle they'd picked up at the airport – the busy, echoing airport, "In with the cattle," as Louisiana had put it, just as if it hadn't been her choice in the first place – had finally pulled up outside the hotel.

The driver had been silent all the way, pausing only beneath an underpass alongside a line of other similarly painted Beetles, where he had stopped to buy, randomly and without comment, a whole block of cheese from a street vendor. He'd carried out his business through the car window without saying a word. He didn't speak now. He simply sat with one arm hanging out of that same open window, the one that had let in the dust and a draught that baked rather than cooled, and tapped the side of the door with his fingertips.

Celeste wasn't sure she wanted to move. People milled about all around the hotel, men in paint-splashed overalls carrying tools or wood or sacks of rubbish. An electrician appeared to be wiring a light above a carved sign which said HOTEL BAKTUN. No one came to help with their luggage or to open the car doors, and Louisiana tutted as she shoved hers wide, tutting again when it sprung straight back at her.

She flicked back her gleaming blonde locks and did what Celeste had come to think of as her "Ferrari exit". She swung out her long, long legs, knees pressed together, and set her Louboutins firmly on the ground before pushing herself up from the seat.

A dry cough from the driver pulled Celeste's attention away and she realised that, once again, she would be the one to pay. There was rich, she thought, and then there was *rich* – after a certain point, the wealthy never seemed to pay for anything themselves. Of course, neither did those for whom it was merely a masquerade.

She pulled some pesos from her Prada purse and pushed them at the driver, thinking there would be change, but he folded the notes without looking and slipped them into the pocket of his shirt before winking at her in the rear-view mirror.

She looked away. It was too hot to argue. She hurried to join Louisiana, who stood with her back to the car, staring up at the hotel. She'd donned her Chanel sunglasses and Celeste couldn't see her expression.

Celeste went to open the boot and started to lug the heavy cases from it, setting them on the ground. As she did so, she thought of what should have been – a private flight with all the other guests, being pampered all the way, instead of an early trip to a hotel that wasn't ready for them.

At least the others would join them soon, and she remembered the reason they were here. She glanced up to the very apex of the hotel, feeling, as she always did, a flush of pride followed by her usual pang of disbelief.

The Baktun had been shaped as a flat-topped pyramid, and later, when it opened, it would sing; or rather, her husband, Colton Creed, would. She could hear his voice in her mind, raw and throaty and with a resonance that had more than once made her shove him straight down on to their bed.

He was flying in by private jet from L.A. later, along with his manager, to suss the place out before the opening performance; because that was what he did. He was a professional. It was one of the reasons why she loved him, though she often found herself wondering why he hadn't left her behind when he was caught up in the whirlwind of success; why he had ever even looked back. She wouldn't have blamed him. But she had been by his side from the beginning and she was by his side now. *Running to keep up*, is what the little voice in her mind whispered, and then another voice cut in:

"Christ. What the hell have you got me into, Cele?"

Celeste swallowed down her frustration. *A free show*, she wanted to say. *Another chance to soften up your unctuous sugar daddy*, she could add. She opened her mouth to say something about a free pass to luxury, then closed it again. She could see Louisiana's point. The hotel was huge and grand and dramatic, its windows glinting back diamonds in the sunlight, but the bustle around it looked like chaos.

It was Louisiana who'd wanted to fly out early, to be here when the "boys" arrived. The fact that her friend had passed up a private jet only showed the depth of her resolve. Of course, Louise – *Louisiana* – would have a glut of private jets if she could only get a ring on her finger. She'd also have all the champagne she wanted, as cold as ice.

Celeste swallowed her disdain. She'd seen the tiny back-to-back terrace that Lou had come from, had met her beetle-browed and bad-tempered father. It almost made her see why her friend had clung so fiercely to Shelby Waxler, Colton's slimy producer, who was sixty years old if he was a day.

Still, Louisiana's odds weren't good. Shelby did not hold any particular disrespect for the sanctity of marriage; rather, he didn't seem to think it had anything to do with him. He liked his playthings and he liked them young. If Louisiana hadn't spent everything she had on surgery, her snub little nose, her doll-like Cupid's bow in its baby pink lipstick—

"For heaven's sake, leave those," Louisiana said. "Someone will bring the luggage. I can't get burnt." She shaded her face from the sun with her hand, then endeavoured to shade that hand with the other.

Celeste looked dubiously at the suitcases. The taxi was a rumble of dust in the distance and no one was near, but still...

Louisiana clipped away in her towering heels. With one more glance at their possessions, Celeste hastened to follow.

If the outside had been a mess, the lobby was worse: people milling about everywhere, the tiles filthy, broken old tat in dust-covered glass cases, no one to greet them and no one at the Reception desk. At least in here it was shaded and deliciously cool. Louisiana tapped her knuckles on the desk, then straightened, looking towards a huddle of people in some kind of uniform – navy shorts, khaki shirts – bending over something.

"Watching television!" she exclaimed. "While there are paying customers!"

Her voice carried easily and Celeste flinched, wanting to remind her that they were invited guests, not paying at all, but she didn't get the chance. One of the men had broken away from the huddle and was hurrying over.

"Pardon, ladies," he said. "We weren't notified—"

"You may bring our bags to our room," Louisiana snapped. "They're outside. Probably getting heat-damaged."

His badge said HECTOR: HEAD OF F&B. Celeste had no idea what that meant, but he said, "Of course. Our manager here will take your names—"

Louisiana held out a hand, stopping him. She turned to Celeste, her eyes glowing. "Do you hear that?"

Celeste had no chance to reply. Louisiana marched away, across the lobby and into a wide passageway, just as if she knew where she was going. Celeste stared after her. After a moment, she followed. Hector's voice trailed after them, so low she almost thought she'd imagined it: "You're feeling quite well – you flew in from London, didn't you? You're not sick…?"

Louisiana was standing on a wide-tiled patio that led down to a pool, overlooking the white-capped sea. She was in the full sun, regardless of the heat that beat down on their heads. After the shaded lobby, the colours were deep and rich. Celeste knew at once what her friend had heard, could hear it now herself quite plainly: the deep *thrub-thrub* of helicopter blades.

"There," Louisiana said, her sunglasses holding back her hair, shading her eyes with her hand, this time without complaint.

The shape, like a black hornet, was growing closer, stirring the soupy air. It was coming straight towards them. She felt a leap of hope – could it be Colton? But they were sending a limo to the airport, weren't they?

She looked around and saw an emerald circle of precisely cut grass away to the side of the building, marked with a crisp white H. She smoothed back her dark hair and glanced at Louisiana. There was no way her friend would miss this.

The sleek machine was almost above them, and coming in so low that she could just make out the pilot's impassive face behind his black sunglasses and headgear.

They watched it land, Louisiana grasping her hair in both hands and ducking as if she could avoid the blasts of warmth.

"I love the smell of chlorine in the morning," Celeste joked.

Louisiana never shifted her eyes from the man who emerged from the helicopter. He was wearing a rather old-fashioned black suit complete with a white cravat, his colourless hair swept back from his aquiline face by the wind stirred up by the rotor blades. He walked swiftly towards the hotel, his stride brisk and his back very straight, flanked by two broad bodyguards. "It's not morning," Louisiana murmured. "And anyway, the pool's empty."

Celeste didn't know what was more depressing, the fact that her friend didn't get the reference or that she'd found something else to complain about. Still, Louisiana didn't seem inclined to dwell on the state of the pool. She only watched the man as he entered the hotel through an unmarked black door.

"He didn't even look at us," Louisiana said. "We're his fucking *guests*, and he didn't look."

Celeste thought she was actually going to stamp her foot. "You think that's him? The mysterious owner himself?" She frowned after the figure. There was only the door, blank and closed again. It didn't even appear to have a handle.

"Of course." Louisiana straightened and looked around. "And his name's Moreby. Don't you know anything? He's supposed to be some distant descendant of *that* Moreby – the one who ran around London building occult churches and subterranean passageways and God knows what else. He died or maybe disappeared, I forget which, centuries ago. Funny really, though – this place is supposed to be built on top of a Mayan ruin, isn't it? Maybe the new guy's a chip off the old block. Now, where's that man? Ah – there you are."

Celeste had started at the name Moreby, but she turned to see that her friend was correct. Hector had indeed scurried after them. She wondered if Louisiana was right about the hotel's owner too. But then, her friend seemed to know everything about everybody that mattered; in other words, those with money or power or preferably both. Now here was Hector, come to usher her inside just as if she were a queen.

He led them back towards the patio entrance, babbling about how he didn't really do front of house but just for them he'd sort everything out personally and he hoped they had a lovely time. He shot little glances at Louisiana as they went, taking in her shapely legs, her pert breasts.

The glass doors stood open, but Hector went to a small side door and held it wide for Louisiana, taking in the back view as she went through, and then he handed the door to Celeste. She took its weight, wrinkling her nose, and let it fall again behind her. What was the point of making a fuss? It wasn't as if she really cared about such things. Although it occurred to her that, however tenuous Louisiana's grip on the superstar lifestyle, she was at least a damned sight better at it than Celeste.

Chapter Three

THEY COULDN'T HAVE built the hotel better. It was square, for a start, though Francisco Ramos couldn't really give two shits about what shape it was. What mattered was how far he would be from an exit at any given time, and for that, a square was just fine with him.

He'd already checked the outside. The idiots couldn't have made things any easier. Large central entrances were flanked by smaller ones, sometimes more than one. When the tourists came, many of the doors would be standing open all the time; none could surely be locked. He barely kept the smile from his face. Not even the sight of the helicopter pad outside – a *helicopter pad* – could wipe it off. The rich bastards deserved all they got.

The wages of sin, he thought, and brought the Saint Francis he wore about his neck to his lips, at once regretting the gesture. It had been automatic. The medallion had been given to him by his grandmother on his sixth name day, just weeks before she passed. He would not be parted from it, but still, the thought of God, or his saints, was better just now pushed to the darkest recesses of his mind. And no true member of *Los Fieles* would ever wear such a thing. There was only one saint they recognised, if saint she truly was.

But God liked those who seized opportunities, didn't he? That was what Francisco told himself. Even the church he attended – Our Lady of Solitude, the blue-domed cathedral in the *Zócalo* or old square – was originally built as a movie set before being adopted by the church. And no one else seemed to care about such things. He knew they'd been working straight through Holy Week to finish this place for the gringos, ignoring their obligations. Many had not even attended the Easter Saturday burning of the effigy of the Devil. Surely no good could come of neglecting such a thing.

He shook his head as he walked across the reception area. No one looked at him, but he raised his hand to his face, suddenly regretting the gaudy designer shirt he wore. He saw that someone was looking at him anyway, someone with the coffee-coloured skin and flattish features of a Maya. Francisco knew he should pass through quietly – easy in, easy out – but he couldn't resist barging the ignorant youth out of the way. He thought for a moment of pulling the pistol from the waistband of his chinos and blasting a hole through the stupid *huerco*'s forehead. He knew he could do it. He had done it before, without thought or feeling. It was easy to shut such things away. He'd had practice.

Deep breath.

He could see how grand this place was going to look and he reflected again on the stupidity of its owner, reputed to be a multi-millionaire. How could he own a piece of Acapulco, when it was all divided and claimed already? Why didn't he just pay his dues? Everyone had dues on this part of the peninsula, right down to the humblest fruit stall. They all paid. They knew, if they did not, that his boss – El Calaca, the Skeleton – would visit them while they slept, or possibly while they didn't; the outcome would be just the same.

Some of their enemies had the flesh stripped from their faces. Others – the lucky ones – were simply beheaded. Sometimes their heads were left at roadside shrines to *La Flaca*, their lady, until the *federales* came along and removed them.

There were many who would say that the drug cartels were ruining Mexico. Acapulco was a place that knew this all too well. Tourism to the city had plummeted in recent years, as rival traffickers fought each other for the lucrative coastal smuggling route. Heads had rolled in the streets. All the more reason the stupid foreigner who built this place should have known better. Soon, he would.

Francisco took note of the passageways and lifts and doors, committing them to memory. He couldn't mess this up. He was still earning his place, had to prove his worth. He looked longest at a narrow, plain black door set into the far wall before turning again. Rumour had it that the most splendid of apartments was not on the roof, as it should have been, but below the ground. The owner of the building, it seemed, was a basement guy.

He grinned, imagining this place full of the rich and powerful and completely unprepared. They were coming soon, gathering from across the globe to celebrate the hotel's grand opening – and Francisco would be waiting.

He thought for a moment of the ready market the wealthy visitors could provide for *Los Fieles*' product – he'd cut off his own head if there were not a few who'd appreciate a line or two, no doubt sniffed through hundred dollar notes. But that wasn't why he was here.

He headed towards the south side of the building, where there was a small, shallow pool, hidden away in one corner. It seemed as good a place to start as any. He turned down the main corridor, wide and hard floored and bare, a bright mural painted on the wall, and caught himself as he started to whistle. He would show that he could be trusted, not only with this but with many things, many responsibilities. *Los Fieles* were a cartel, but they were also a family. Francisco hadn't had a family since his parents ditched him and his grandmother died. Now he did. He wasn't planning on losing it.

It was almost too easy. He reached the wide double doors, topped with – they really couldn't have planned it better – two large portholes for peeking in. Inside the room was chaos: cubes in bright colours, a wall of painted shelves, tables with stubby little legs. He drew back, looking at the sign written across the doors: KIDS CLUB.

Francisco couldn't help but smile. This time, as he turned and walked away, he couldn't keep himself from whistling.

Chapter Four

ETHAN WARD JUST wanted to die. It had started in Departures, before they'd even found the ticket desk. Mum had taken too long to find the tickets and Dad hadn't shut up about it, making a show of taking them from her.

That was when Dad had noticed the connecting flight. He hadn't realised there was a connecting flight. He'd thought they were going straight to General Juan N. Álvarez airport at Acapulco, and apparently, if he'd known they were on such a cheap flight, with a *connection*, for the love of Mike, he might not have come.

Ethan had swallowed down the laughter that threatened to break out of him. It was Mum who'd entered the competition, Mum who'd won the holiday, a once-in-a-lifetime chance to see the hotel opening, with *Colton Creed*, for God's sake. Of course they were all going to come. They'd have been there if they'd had to walk across a field of sharpened knives.

It wasn't as if Dad was working; it wasn't as if he could take them on holiday himself. And now he could do nothing but moan, moan, moan.

Ethan pulled a face. He was fifteen; moaning was practically his job. But he remained silent and squeezed his little sister's hand. She hung from it, swinging her foot. Her current dream was to be a ballerina; tomorrow, he knew, it would be something else. Lily was only five. She'd spent the previous week wanting to be a horse.

Now they were in the terminal between terminals and Mum led the way to a row of plastic chairs that were bolted to the floor. An announcement sang out in rapid trills, words that sounded to Ethan like one long word that didn't make sense. He had no idea how they would know when to board their next flight. And then it would begin again, Dad complaining about the lack of leg room, how they should have been in first class – didn't they know they'd *won*, for the love of Pete, and he'd get a free paper and then grumble some more because he couldn't bloody read it.

Ethan got a tube of Smarties for Lily from the front pocket of her tiny wheelie bag, the one she'd insisted on bringing and then made her big brother handle: "Pullit, Eefun!" He didn't mind. He ruffled her hair as she settled back, swinging her legs, and he looked around.

Most of the people in the airport appeared to be Mexican. Some of the men had moustaches, like in the old spaghetti westerns his Dad sometimes watched on telly. An older couple stared into space, the woman wearing a cardigan despite the warmth that the clanky air-conditioning failed to dissipate. The man wore Jesus sandals with white socks underneath. English, then. Over in the corner was a tall, elegant-looking man: probably Italian. A young woman with pale hair and a tan – German? On his last holiday he had played at "guess the nationality" with a girl he'd met.

That was back when his dad had a job and a sense of humour. It had been fun, that year. Maddy was younger than him and the difference showed, but somehow she'd made him feel like a happy little kid anyway. He'd barely been out of the sea. He'd swum and sat around making friends and laughing. It seemed they all had.

"Ooh!" Mum said. She held out a guidebook to Acapulco. It had a bright sombrero on the cover. "Johnny Weissmuller used to live there. Did you know that, Les?"

Dad didn't answer.

"They buried him there. He had the Tarzan yell played as they lowered him into the ground. What fun!"

Ethan frowned.

His mother read on while Dad stared at the blank floor. "The city was flattened by a hurricane in 1997. The name Acapulco – it means 'Where the reeds were washed away'. Oh, that sounds a bit sad, doesn't it? There were thirty-foot waves in the hurricane. It wrecked the shanty towns. Lots of people died. Oh, it was called Hurricane Pauline, Ethan, like your auntie. Isn't that funny?"

"Hilarious, Sue," Dad muttered, while Ethan made some noise that could have been assent, could have been anything at all.

He turned to watch Lily, sitting at his side, her face absolutely focused as she stared into space. Mum was going on about ruins now, old pyramids and gods and serpents and sacrifices and a hundred other things that didn't matter. He frowned. He wasn't here for a history lesson. He was going to sit on the beach and play with Lily and make sure the two of them, at least, had a good time. And then he was going to watch the show and hear the Colt sing, and take pictures for Facebook to make all his mates jealous.

None of them would be able to believe it.

He ruffled Lily's hair again. She didn't notice. Her face was cherubic and her hair was golden and curling and it floated around her head like a halo. She didn't look like any of them. Ethan had sandy hair and Mum and Dad were both mousy. His sister was like something rare and precious and strange, and he found himself smiling as he looked at her.

She turned, as if she'd known he was watching all along, and her rosebud lips popped open. She regarded him with ocean-blue eyes. "Poopoohead," she pronounced, and then she twisted on her chair, eyes front once more.

Ethan burst into laughter. It startled Mum, who dropped her book, and even Dad looked around. Mum started laughing too, and Dad's lip twitched. Only a small thing, but it was there.

Lily raised one pale blonde eyebrow at Ethan, a quizzical look, and he couldn't help it – he dissolved again. He couldn't have explained to anyone, not even to himself, why it was so funny. But still, he didn't seem to be able to stop.

Chapter Five

IT HADN'T BEEN the easiest flight. They'd left London behind, the plane lifting and banking as if at once repelled and attracted to the ground, and Stacy Keenan could relate to that. With the back of her skull pressed hard against the headrest, she had thought of what she'd so recently left behind.

She had been all set to head-up security for the New Festival of Britain, had relished what that might mean, but before she'd even begun the preparations it had been snatched away from her, or rather, she had been snatched away from *it*.

The oddest thing was that her new boss was apparently some distant offshoot of the Moreby family, the same one that had built that church in south London, All Hallows, which had caused protests after being earmarked for a Festival site. By now, they'd be starting to excavate.

She gave a slow smile. She hadn't met her new employer. Her role didn't carry the kudos of the one she'd given up, but it carried other things: a suite in a five-star resort, endless days in the sun, all the burritos she could eat and tequila on tap. Most of all, more money than she'd ever imagined earning. And she didn't have to oversee the digging up of a smelly old graveyard.

All she had to do was keep the CCTV systems ticking, coordinate security for a high-profile launch event, and – probably the most difficult – babysit a few over-privileged rich folk while restraining herself from shooting any of them.

The flight out of Heathrow was full of them. Their voices echoed in her mind now:

"Mind my bag. That's Louis Vuitton. Doesn't she *know* that's Louis Vuitton?"

"But *Mom*, I don't like the blue candy, I only want the brown ones!"

"So typical, they said it would be private, this is just not good enough, is it, Charles? The seats aren't even full leather."

"Brr. This champagne is so *cold*."

Stacy had settled back in her seat that was only half-leather, accepted a glass of icy, freshly squeezed orange juice – she was a professional, after all – and closed her eyes. Shortly afterwards the turbulence began, but every time she'd awakened to those voices she had somehow forced herself back to sleep. It helped that no one had taken the seat next to hers. She could hear her fellow passengers, but only saw them in glimpses. Expensive tans and flashing watches, thousand dollar haircuts and sweaters tied around their necks, logos and labels showing, just as if they'd arranged them in a 360-degree mirror.

She barely awoke again until they came in to land. It was as if her brain had switched off for a while, mustering her resources before the job began. Excitement rose within her as she looked out on to a landscape of lush greenery, mountains and the startlingly bright sea. The deep blue and green were divided by the pale buff of cliffs or sandy beaches, a frill that caught the unforgiving morning sunlight.

Then the perfect curve of Acapulco Bay was there, its smooth sweep dotted with blocky white hotels. A thick, twisting peninsula jutted into the Pacific away to one side like the blunt head of a lizard. Stacy leaned in, her forehead meeting the window with a little bump that she hoped none of the fancy-pants guests had heard. That was where the new hotel was, wasn't it? Somewhere along the quieter north side of the peninsula, where rocky bluffs sheltered a small and very securable beach. Beyond that it rose away to the jagged clifftops that dominated that part of the coastline.

But she couldn't see the hotel. It all swept away from her as the plane began to bank, and for a moment there was nothing but sky. She half-closed her eyes against the burnished blue expanse as they began their descent into General Juan N. Álvarez International Airport.

It wasn't until she was on the ground that she realised she hadn't quite managed to escape the pull of London after all. She switched on her mobile phone in Arrivals – she could see the long snaking queues of the scheduled flight passengers on the other side of a large glass window, their faces bored or tired or irritated – catching sight of a little smiling girl, her head surrounded by a shock of golden curls and then she was swept away from it all and whizzed through immigration, to where a small fleet of luxury cars awaited.

As soon as she stepped out of the terminal, heat blasted her face. She began to sweat at once. That was when her phone began to beep.

She pulled it from her pocket as she showed her clearance pass to the drivers and stepped into the first car. She didn't wait for it to be full, merely urged him to hurry. As the Hotel Baktun's head of security it was practically her duty to arrive first, to make sure that everything was ready for its oh-so-special guests.

As the car left the shelter of an awning and heat stabbed through the windows, she looked down at her phone's screen.

There was the usual welcome to Mexico, information on networks and roaming charges, and then she stopped thumbing down the list because she saw it: the text intended for the security team for the Festival, the alert system set aside for emergency use only.

> To: All security staff
> Demonstrations at All Hallows festival site given way to violent protests – report to line manager as a matter of urgency for full briefing – all leave cancelled with immediate effect

She frowned, thumbing down the lines of text. Frowned some more. Then she opened a web browser and searched for *Hard News.*

Hard News Online
Wednesday, May 1, 1:15 PM
By Louise Gould

Concerns are growing today over the whereabouts of Janet Ramsey, the head of current affairs at *Hard News.* Ms Ramsey disappeared whilst investigating alleged breaches of safety regulations at All Saints Church in Blackheath, London, a controversial New Festival of Britain site where excavations were due to start this morning in the adjoining graveyard.

Fears were raised by Margaret Winn, a health advisor at UCH London, who had suggested that bodies uncovered from the site were being disposed of unlawfully, despite her concern that the area may have been used as a plague pit in the past.

One NFOB worker, a Russian national named Marek Schwarinski, had claimed that bodies or parts thereof were either placed in a skip by the church or simply dumped in the Thames Estuary along with rubble from the excavations.

Ms Ramsey failed to return from a late-night meeting with Mr Schwarinsky, during which she was to be shown around All Hallows Church and its crypt. At the time of writing, Mr Schwarinsky was unavailable for comment. When *Hard News* approached Mr Michael Brooks, the site manager employed by the construction company involved, he denied Mr Schwarinsky had ever arranged such a meeting, going so far as to suggest that someone may have been impersonating the workman, whose immigration status is now also in some doubt.

A source from within the Home Office has revealed to *Hard News* that Ms Ramsey's PDA was recovered from the scene earlier today. The voice recording of her visit speaks of "bodies stacked floor to ceiling", followed by the chaotic sounds of panic and, possibly, a personal attack, during which she was heard to call out Margaret Winn's name.

Official sources further indicate that Ms Winn is now a suspect in Ms Ramsey's disappearance, though Ms Ramsey had been heard to tell colleagues that the two were "old friends". Ms Winn's whereabouts are also unknown at this time.

All at *Hard News* are naturally concerned for the wellbeing of Ms Ramsey and are following up any leads that may lead to her safe return. Meanwhile, protests at the All Hallows site have escalated throughout the morning, following widespread rumours that demolition is continuing, not just in the face of popular opposition, but without proper planning regulations or safety and security protocols being in place.

Unsubstantiated reports appear to indicate the lack of control has in some instances led to outbreaks of hysteria, with members of the public reportedly biting and scratching each other…

Stacy sat back in her chair, full-leather this time, and it squeaked under her. The sleep she'd had on the aeroplane suddenly didn't seem to have refreshed her – she felt very tired. For a moment she thought of her mother, living near to the New Festival site in a small house on Blackheath Road. They hadn't spoken in years. If Stacy called to see how she was, if she'd seen anything untoward, her mother probably wouldn't even answer.

Loneliness settled about her shoulders. She missed London, suddenly and bone-deep, and then the car turned a corner and she saw the hotel. She knew it from the pictures and plans they'd sent to her, the blueprints and elevations and artist's impressions, but she hadn't imagined its scale. It was at once proud and blasphemous, a Mayan pyramid to rival them all, its bright modernity betrayed by edges that were too clean and too sharp.

Suddenly, it was all right again – whatever might be happening in London would surely be over by nightfall. The wilder reports would be crushed as they always were, and harsh reality would take their place. Perpetrators would be arrested, the fuss would live on for a couple of days' worth of screaming headlines, and then dullness would settle over the city once more. The vivid red of violence would fade to grey.

At least this place wasn't grey. Everything was made bright and vibrant by the morning sun. Relief washed over her. If she'd been in London, she would have had to deal with it all. It would have rested on *her* shoulders.

Thank fuck, she thought as she stepped out of the car, and then she froze and went back to her phone, tapping in a new search, something she ought to have done the moment they landed and had forgotten in the wake of the news from home.

Nothing major to report in Acapulco. No hurricanes on the horizon, no uprisings, no political unrest. All was at peace, all set for the coming celebrations.

The only dark spot on the horizon was the report of gastric flu aboard a cruise ship off the coast – a Russian-operated craft called the RFS *Demeter.* One of their VIP guests was arriving on that ship, wasn't he? Well, it couldn't be helped. He'd made his own travel arrangements; there wasn't anything she could do and it wasn't as if he could be her responsibility before he'd even reached the hotel. More fool him.

She shook away the problems of the world and started towards Reception. The lobby was full of bustle. Someone was mopping the floor while a waiter held a tray full of glasses, their sides slick with condensation, ready for the new arrivals.

She nodded in approval before continuing towards the desk, already deciding to keep the guests in the dark about events in London for as long as possible.

They were here on holiday, after all. Holidays and revels were nothing to do with the real world – there should be nothing to spoil the view. Making sure they had a good time was her first priority. That way they could spread the word. They could make the Hotel Baktun – and Acapulco – something magnificent, famous throughout the world, and people would see that she had done a good job. Yes, she would make sure they left here happy.

After all, she had always known that babysitting was all this was ever going to be.

Chapter Six

THE MAN EMERGED from a fold in the side of the cliff. He paused a moment, flexing his biceps, drawing himself tall. He was muscular yet lean and he wore only swimming trunks. A sigh rose, mingling with the sound of the waves crashing below, and the occasional *whoop* from the terraces that stretched around the almost circular opening in the cliffs.

He walked along the ledge until the rocky wall was behind him and there was only a sheer drop in front.

Shelby made a contemptuous sound in the back of his throat. Celeste gave him a look, but he didn't see it. Contemptuous or not, his gaze was fixed on the figure on the cliff.

The man stood there for a moment before drawing himself up on to his tiptoes. Suddenly, he leapt. Celeste gasped, leaning forwards as he twisted, once, twice, his arms wrapped tightly around his body, and then he snapped them out and down towards the water. Arrow-straight, he hurtled into the sea just as it swelled into an inlet, the waves surging and crashing with bone-pounding force on to the rocks.

Celeste put a hand to her mouth, half-raising herself from

her chair to see over Louisiana's shoulders. Her friend hadn't so much as twitched.

The sea receded. It looked hungry. It did not give back what it had taken, and then suddenly a cheer rang out as it *did* give him back, the man flicking an arc of spray from his hair before he raised a hand and waved.

Shelby made that sound again, half-snort, half-choke. "Easy as pie," he drawled.

Colton threw something at him – a beer mat. "They train for years," he said. "One chance. They have to time it just right so they have the right depth. If it's too shallow, they die. If the wave carries them on to the rocks, they die."

"Die, die, yada yada." Shelby mimed yakking mouths with his hands and Louisiana smirked and nodded, her head turned away from Colton. It was just like her, Celeste thought, agreeing with everything Shelby said, while conscious enough that it was bullshit to want to mask it from the world. It was only Celeste that seemed to see her true feelings.

Colton was still holding forth about the La Quebrada cliff divers, tossing his shaggy, prematurely grey hair back from his face. She loved it when he was like this, throwing his hands around as he spoke, as far from the reserved English as it was possible for him to be. His blue eyes shone with enthusiasm. Colton didn't have to put on airs, and it never seemed to occur to him to try. It was one of the things she loved about him.

He waved a hand around the vista and she scanned it once more. They were sitting at a cliffside café, opposite the diving platform. Despite its rocky situation there were people everywhere, filling the restaurant terraces at the El Mirador and Plaza Las Glorias hotels or packed into the public viewing galleries a little below. As she looked around, the tinny sounds of a radio started up; the chirpy clatter of a mariachi band. She suddenly felt glad that Colton had persuaded them to leave the Hotel Baktun for the morning. She hadn't expected it.

He'd arrived several hours after she had checked in, slipping into bed beside her, sliding his cool body against her heat, curling around her. *Colton*, she'd thought, though she hadn't said his name. She knew him by the feel of his hands, his skin. She was the only person who still called him by his full name. To his fans he was "the Colt". Shelby sometimes even called him "Hoss". To her, though, he was Colton, and he always would be. Then she'd felt the surprising fineness of his hair against her neck, his lips against her shoulder blade…

La Quebrada, she thought now. *Abracadabra. Like magic.* And she scraped her chair back a little so that the sun fell across her eyes, leaning back, listening to him talk. The sun was like liquid, bathing everything. It was like melting.

Shelby wore a linen jacket that was already hopelessly wrinkled. It was probably supposed to be that way; she wouldn't know. Louisiana, after calling Celeste on her room phone – "Going casual? Me too" – had appeared in a skin-tight designer dress, a gauzy wrap over the top, some diaphanous material that looked like flowing silver. It set off her baby features, her doll-pink lips.

"'Sup, chick?"

Colton's voice cut into her thoughts. She opened her eyes and gave him a lazy smile, remembering the slow, warm strength of him the night before. She could see by his half-amused expression he was thinking of it too.

"You guys!" Shelby protested. "Quit being disgusting. Anyone can see it, y'know. I mean for Christ's sake, you're *married*."

Celeste shook her head and laughed. Were they really that obvious? She reminded herself that they *knew* each other, were friends as well as connected by business, and she glanced at Louisiana, ready to share a smile. She couldn't see Louisiana's eyes through her sunglasses. She was sitting with her back poker-straight, her legs crossed at the ankle as if posing for a photograph. She stared straight out into the blue.

Celeste followed her gaze, over Colton's shoulder and out to sea. She admired the yachts scudding across the waves, the dazzling white flanks of a ship. Then she frowned.

"Isn't the port on the other side of the peninsula?"

Colton twisted in his seat, saw what she meant. "Maybe it's resting."

Shelby sputtered, raising his margarita, his lips wrinkling around the straw as he took a sip. "Resting? Don't you guys know anything? It's a cruise ship, is what it is. It's not being allowed to dock."

"What do you mean?" Celeste said.

"Don't crease your brow like that, sweetheart. You'll wrinkle. It's been quarantined. Some kind of food poisoning or something. Or legionnaires' disease. One of those. Apparently the thing's loaded with wealthy Russians – they'll probably get sued to hell. I saw it on CNN. That's the thing with Mexico, people – great TV. *American* TV."

Celeste pulled a face. She had heard of such things happening, could imagine the passengers confined to their cabins, little hutches without air, everything filling with the stench of shit and vomit. It stirred some memory buried deep, something she had studied at school; something about conquistadors sailing across the oceans to the New World, bringing all manner of diseases with them.

"It's no big deal." Shelby waved a hand airily, and Colton reached for another beer mat, throwing it in his direction. "What? So they're puking a little. At least they're on holiday, right, Hoss?"

Colton's lip twitched. "Let's hope so. Their quarantine's not up to much. My driver told me a little black helicopter's been seen dropping in on that ship. Said they lifted someone right off the deck."

Shelby wrapped his hands around his throat, speaking in a choked voice. "Doctor Death . . ."

Celeste didn't laugh. She couldn't help thinking of the man they'd seen arriving by helicopter earlier that morning. It was odd that he might be a descendant of Thomas Moreby. She'd heard a story once – a long time ago – about her own ancestry; an odd tale of elopement and escapes and duels, of a woman named Anna who was forced to give her hand to that very gentleman.

Anna Whitby had found him repugnant. She had run away. She had carried a child, born out of wedlock to the man she loved, and that child had given rise to Celeste's side of the family. Of course there were other stories too – ones about Moreby's plans to use his unfortunate wife in his vile occult rites, but Celeste hadn't given credence to any of them; particularly as some of the wilder tales had reported the woman being sacrificed, and indeed that her husband had been over 100 years old when she married him.

She was startled from her reverie by Louisiana's laugh, high and trilling and brittle. She turned to look at her friend, who was still staring out to sea. She didn't look as if she had made a sound, although Celeste still couldn't see her eyes. She sat there quite motionless, poised and beautiful.

A second later Celeste heard a slapping sound and Colton's grunt reached her ears. He sat with one hand clutching his forearm. "Fuck it," he said, shifting his hand, revealing a smear of blood. "Mozzie. Bloody little bastard."

Shelby let out his high-pitched laugh. "Don't tell me the big man's been brought down by a bug."

"Fuck you."

"Fuck you, fucktard."

"No, fuck you..."

Celeste zoned them out as they descended into a well-worn groove of banter. It was an old routine and she didn't need to hear it. She kept looking at Louisiana. Her face was still expressionless, but Celeste thought there was a tension about it that hadn't been there before. Louisiana was pale and stony as alabaster. And Celeste didn't need to see the expression in her eyes to know why her friend wouldn't look at her.

Louisiana hadn't been staring out to sea; all the time they'd been sitting here, she had been looking directly at Colton.

Chapter Seven

THE WOMAN STOOD with her back straight and her belly out, hands firmly placed on her hips. Her hair was piled high on her head, her lips thrust into a pout, slick and shining with red lipstick that had bled on to her skin. Her bikini was covered in tiny pieces of what appeared to be mirrors, and she looked as if she wanted to kill somebody.

Smoothly and without pause, Mick turned and headed around her, giving her a wide berth. His arms were laden with gleaming white plates. The buffet was piled high with good local food like beans, corn, green chilli peppers, tomatoes made into salsas of every kind and stacks of watermelons cooled by shards of ice. Here at the VIP lunch, no one wanted it. They wanted fancy food setting before them on silver platters. They wanted candles and soft music and rooms that weren't full of other people.

Still, at least most of the guests were fully clothed. He didn't know why the woman was even wearing her bikini; they were only now filling the pool. He could just hear the rush of water.

He glanced towards the window. The last hotel he'd worked in had had a NO SWIMWEAR sign in the restaurant. There was no such sign here. Perhaps no one had expected they'd need one. He glanced at the formidable woman in the mirrored bikini just as she turned to look at him, and something in his belly turned colder than the air-con.

She smiled the smile of a spider that had caught a fly, and raised a hand and beckoned.

Mick looked down at the plates he carried: veal, fresh swordfish, pizza and chips. They were for the table in the corner. He looked back at the woman and she narrowed her eyes and he knew that he *was* the fly, already cocooned in a sticky web, and he walked towards her, his expression carefully blank.

"My lunch," she said, her Russian accent strong. "Vere – ees – my – lonch?"

Mick sensed heads turning towards them just as he felt the heat draining from the food he carried. "A moment, ma'am," he said. "This section is not mine. Is Miguel's section. I will see about your lonch – lunch..."

Her eyes narrowed even further, to dark slits. She had shaved off her eyebrows and drawn them on again with a dark pencil. Her tan didn't look real. "Ma'am?" Her voice was thunder. "You are calling me *ma'am*?"

"I—" Mick floundered. He suddenly felt he was a thousand miles from home, on a different planet perhaps, one where he didn't speak the language and didn't know the rules. He remembered a piece of advice Miguel had given him: just bring them more drinks, even if they hadn't asked for them. "Er – *Miss*?" He braced himself. That couldn't be what she had meant. She looked fifty if she was a day. Her heavy bosom loomed towards him as she leaned in, and then she did something awful: she smiled.

"That ees better," she said. "Now – my lonch!"

He nodded, backing away. If it wasn't for the need to balance the plates, he thought he might actually have bowed.

He turned without looking at her again and made his way to the corner table. He had thought that the guests would be elegant, glamorous and polite. He'd imagined Brigitte Bardot lounging by the pool in a ballgown, flashing smiles towards him. Instead it was all spoilt clamour and complaints, everyone wanting to be first to eat.

He apologised for the wait, setting down the plates. Fish for her, veal for him, pizza for their little girl, who stuck out her tongue. She had golden hair, curling and unruly. He smiled at her and winked, saw the *amá* and *apá* swapping their plates from the corner of his eye. He turned to apologise again and the dad waved his words away. This time Mick bowed as he turned, and he heard the little girl as she began to wail in an American drawl: "Mom, this pizza's coooooold!"

He did not stop. He had to get back to the kitchen. There were more of them crowding into the room, filling the tables, all demanding everything at once. Bikini woman's voice carried over the rest – "My lonch!" – while others raised an eyebrow or snapped their fingers, and he made his way through them all, pushing through the swing doors to the service area, clean and cold and scarcely less noisy. He rested his back against the wall for a moment and closed his eyes, jumping when he heard a voice:

"You lucky *cabrón*."

"What?"

Miguel chuckled in his ear. "Idiot. You don't even know who that is, do you? With the kid." He twisted, holding plates high as he backed through the door, shaking his head.

"Ah – Miguel, the lady in the bikini—"

Miguel hissed through his teeth. "*La puta*. She can wait."

The door swung back and he was gone. Mick stared after him. He thought of the father's face as he'd dismissed him: and then he had it. He had grown his hair since Mick had last seen him. Back then it had been shaved, his head dirty and bloodied. He could remember quite clearly the irregular shape of his scalp, its planes and curves. He had been skinnier then too; he was dying that time, wasn't he? Dying of cancer. Before that, he'd been older. They'd wrinkled him up for that one. He'd been a teacher, had saved a boy from his evil twin brother.

His eyes widened. Did he see nothing? He'd watched the father so many times, up on the silver screen. He was a leading man, a *star.* And here, in the middle of normality, when they were just people who needed to feed, he hadn't even recognised him.

He went to fetch more plates, an incredulous smile spreading across his face. At least now he had a story to tell; and he'd only just started to work here. Maybe, for once, he had made the right choice. This place might be full of wonders after all.

Chapter Eight

From:	Ethan Ward <ethanward@aol.com>
To:	Maddy Wood <georgiegirl@hotmail.com>
Sent:	WEDS, May 1, 13:20 AM
Subject:	Guess who?

Hey Mads! Long time no hear. Remember me from Rhodes? I'm in Mexico now! It's all boring old people but at least THE COLT is going to be singing at this big do (jealous, much?!). I've been guessing where people come from, remember that? Anyway, better get off, I'm on dad's phone. He'd freak if he knew.

– ETHAN

PS: Belated happy birthday!!!

From: Maddy Wood <georgiegirl@hotmail.com>
To: Ethan Ward <ethanward@aol.com>
Sent: WEDS, May 1, 19:24 PM
Subject: Re: Guess who?

Jeez Eeth, it's been what, decades?! You luuuucky thing, can't believe you're going to see the Colt, is that right? Hey – I'm 13 now! Practically ancient. LOL! Lucky you got me – I'm on my uncle Jack's old laptop, he left it with us yesterday. Things are really weird here. People have been getting sick. There have been some kinds of riots or demonstrations. Did you know they've been digging up an old graveyard near here? Ew. It's supposed to have a plague pit underneath and some people are really really mad about it. I think it's gross. Whatever's going on, my mum and dad have made me stay in ALL DAY!!! Can you believe it??? Anyway, I wish I was on holiday! All we've got is just this stupid New Festival to look forward to, no Colt there, boooo!
Have fun.
xx

Ethan snapped his dad's phone closed and slipped it into the pocket of the jacket folded under his sunbed; he'd left his own in his room. Anyway, perhaps contacting his old friend hadn't been such a good idea. Maddy made him think of holidays, as if they were both still gawky little kids in Greece. He hadn't really thought about her being that much younger than him, but – thirteen? Is that all she was? And so proud of it, too. Anyway, he didn't want to think about old churches and dead bodies.

He stood at the edge of their patch of paradise, taking in the glinting pool and below that, down some steep little steps, the sea. There was a lad about his own age lying face down on a sunbed not far from theirs. Maybe he was more the sort of person Ethan could pal about with.

As if he'd heard Ethan's thoughts, the boy looked up through his wiry red fringe and he flopped over on to his back, pushing earbuds into his ears and closing his eyes. A moment later a tinny beat rose from them, so loud that Ethan could almost make out the tune: it sounded like "Loco in Acapulco".

He pulled a face, then looked instead at his dad. He had no idea why he'd stripped to his shorts – there were grey hairs on his chest, wavering in the breeze – and then insisted on sitting under a sun umbrella. There wasn't a bit of him that was exposed. Now he was snoring, softly but with no sign of stopping, the sound blending with the constant rushing of the waves.

There was barely a breeze to stir the air, but out on the sea, there were whitecaps. A pedalo tilted and rocked. Even from here, Ethan could hear the shrieks of its occupants. Despite the roughness, someone was swimming out there, their arms cutting smooth and clean through the water. He could smell salt and hot skin and what his mother called her coconut slather. He was stuffed full of quesadillas from the buffet and soon, when Mum thought he'd waited long enough after eating, he would swim.

Maybe sooner than that, if she fell asleep too. He thought she probably would. She'd had a glass of tequila with lunch, something she hadn't asked for but the waiter had brought, and Dad had been complaining so much she'd snapped that she was going to drink it anyway. There was a whole wall of tequila bottles in the restaurant. This one was pineapple flavour and she'd licked the rim of the glass when she'd finished it and started to giggle.

Ethan pulled a face just as Mum dipped her sunglasses and looked at him. "Now, sourpuss. Why don't you take your sister to the Kids' Club?"

"Aw, Mum, we were going to go in the pool." The water was a perfect turquoise, clear and rippling and glistening. A tall

slide, made to look like a Mayan serpent, its mouth open just above the water, waited. It didn't look as if anyone had ever been on it. Nobody was swimming in the pool. He might be the first; they both could, him and Lily.

"Not now, you're not. I don't want her getting her hair wet."

Mum settled back on her sunbed. Ethan could see streaks of the coconut-smelling slap on her skin. He pulled another face, one she couldn't see, and went to get his sister. Lily was sitting by Dad's seat, making her dolly dance through the air in front of her. He led her away, towards the big open glass doors of the hotel. As soon as he did, he heard the words: "It's just a minor security scare, sir. Yes, Heathrow is now closed. Yes, Gatwick too. I'm sure everything will be sorted out by the time you need to fly home."

He turned to see a woman in uniform talking to a guest. Ethan could tell the man was rich just by looking at him. It wasn't the clothes he wore; there was something about the way he stood. The woman was tall and wiry with short-cropped brown hair aggressively clipped flat to her head. "Of course there's no sickness, sir," she said in soothing tones. "Nothing serious at all."

Lily pulled on Ethan's hand.

It's supposed to have a plague pit underneath, he thought, then shook the words away. He smiled at his little sister and walked on.

By the time Ethan got back to the pool it was already full. They had started to play music, not Mexican stuff but proper dance music, and someone was taking drinks around on a tray, brightly coloured things with little paper umbrellas and swizzle sticks. Everyone was smiling. As he watched, a man with lobster-red shoulders climbed to the top of the slide, waved at nobody in particular and let himself go with a whoop.

Just then Ethan saw who was walking past the pool, one

of a small group in a little patch of sunlight that was surely intended only for them, and his mouth dropped open. He would have recognised his idol anywhere. He almost thought he could hear the rasping tone of his voice. It was the Colt. The Colt and a pretty girl, another stunning girl following, holding hands with some other guy. That one was older, but he was still a part of that charmed circle, one that was made for them and no one else.

He frowned. It was the Colt, but he didn't look quite right. He was stooping, for one thing. For another, his face was grey. He didn't look at all well and for a moment Ethan was overwhelmed with apprehension that he might not be able to sing.

Someone nudged him in the side and he almost cried out. He turned to see his dad, thankfully wearing his shirt again, holding one of those acid-coloured drinks. At least he seemed to be in a good mood. He sipped and grinned. "Did you see that? That guy must be forty years older than that girl. Cracker, eh? Lucky git." He turned to go back to his chair. "Fetch the bug stuff, would you?" he called over his shoulder. "There are mozzies about."

Chapter Nine

AN IMAGE APPEARED on the screen: a section of an aeroplane's fuselage, shattered and broken, half-submerged in a wide grey estuary. A rescue boat, a black rib, scudded across the water towards it. Smoke fogged outward, too heavy to rise. The image blurred momentarily as a fine rain began to fall and the camera shook.

Stacy glanced around. Guests were beginning to notice. They were approaching the television located in the lobby. She wished that the staff had kept the big screen switched off, but something like this – she didn't suppose it could be kept a secret for long. The guests would hear the news; they'd be shocked; they'd calm down and life would go on, exactly the way it always did.

The image on the big screen changed. Now there was a newsreader with red-purple hair fanning across her shoulders, her eyes heavy with silver-blue make-up.

"We can now confirm that Virgin flight VS001 out of London Heathrow was shot down over Long Island by US military jets at approximately 11:40 local time this morning, with what is expected to be a substantial loss of life. Although officials have not yet ruled out terrorism, early reports indicating that the pilot, Captain Prado, may have suffered some kind of illness prior to entering New York airspace remain unconfirmed. Simon?"

Cut to Simon. He is standing in front of the shoreline, his hair blown awry, his face damp with rain. He clutches his microphone closer to his chest, as if readying himself. "There are some crazy reports at this stage, Allegra, as ever in a time of crisis. The Twittersphere has erupted over a feed from someone purportedly on the plane known only as @BooBooBoy, whose last Tweet said simply..." He holds up a notebook with his free hand, "They're killing us all – eating us – this plane full of dead. *Help* me." Simon looks into the lens, his expression earnest. "Of course, at times like this we all need to focus on the facts. This plane is in a bad way – it's broken up, there's a debris cone spread over a significant area, and until we know what happened and why—"

He breaks off suddenly as cries pierce the air. A woman runs between Simon and the dock rail at his back. She leans over it as if she is about to pitch herself over. Then more people hurry past, shouting wildly, waving towards the river.

"Wait. Allegra, something's happening." Simon steps aside and the camera zooms in on the water. "Allegra! I see survivors. This is amazing news!"

He falls quiet as the screen fills with the estuary, dirty grey eddies swirling around the sinking metal. Then a shape can be discerned, flailing in the water, and then another. Heads. They are people's heads. They push out into the river, just as if it wasn't half a mile and they could swim to the shore. But the rib is closing in fast. There are three men in it and one of them leans out over the edge, reaching for somebody's hand. A survivor stretches her fingers towards him, the cold no doubt making her clumsy; and then their hands meet and suddenly she pulls hard, dragging her rescuer further down, closer to the water, and she cranes towards him as if to kiss that hand, that touch of salvation.

"Are you seeing this?" Simon's voice is eager. It is the voice of someone who hopes that a Pulitzer might feature somewhere in his future. "Allegra, are you getting this?"

"We're right with you, Simon. Great pictures. I – Simon, what's that?"

Carrying through the rain, a man's cry rings out across the water. The figure in the boat is struggling, trying to pull back his hand as if he's changed his mind, doesn't want to help after all. But the woman in the river – her hair bedraggled, grey as the water – holds on, not only with her hands, clamped now around her saviour's arm, but with her teeth.

The studio – the world – hears Simon's snatched breath.

The guests gathered in the hotel lobby crowded ever closer around the screen as more survivors are seen to reach the boat, their arms flailing just like the first. There is something wrong with their faces. The two men in the middle of the rib do not step forward, don't try to help. They almost look as if they are cowering, trying to get away from the figures in the water. One of them grabs for the control wheel as more drowning men and women reach the rescuer who is still held in place, halfway over the edge of the boat. They snatch him and rip at him and tear at him with their teeth.

"Was that blood?" Simon's voice is different now. No one answers him, but it doesn't matter; everyone must have seen the bright spray, the only thing on the screen that seemed to have any colour, that spouted from the rescuer's head as he was dragged over the side and into the oily grey water.

Stacy snatched glances at the pale, unblinking faces around her. She would get *shot* for this. She could get fired. She returned her gaze to the screen in time to see one of the survivors – another woman, her hair soaked with river water and madness – sink her teeth into the rescuer's neck. Blood gouts this time in a deeper crimson, and it drenches the woman's face. She shows no sign of disgust. She blinks her eyes clear, the white crescents shining, and then shrieks in hunger and triumph, revealing red-stained teeth.

"Did you see that?" asks Simon, his voice small and lost, not the voice of a man who could sniff a Pulitzer, not the voice of someone who knows what the hell he is supposed to be doing. "She looked..."

"Dead."

The voice was loud and terse and *there.*

Stacy turned to see a man, his clothes damp and salt-stained, standing in the middle of the shiny new reception area. He had left a trail of wet footprints behind him and suddenly she realised she had heard his approach, the soft *schloop-schloop* forming a background to the noise of the television. She almost thought she recognised him, but what mattered now was what he'd said, that single word that could drive panic into the hearts of all her charges; that, and making sure he didn't say it again. "Sir—"

"They're dead," he said. "All of them. Every...last...one of them."

"Sir, please don't say that. Anyway, there are clearly survivors. They were – moving." She indicated the screen, but now it showed nothing but the sky. She could hear the screams though, and hear the sound of people running, as if they were panicking just out of shot. As she watched, a new sound came and then she saw a jet, a *fighter* jet, screaming down too low and too fast towards the water.

"There were no survivors. And yes, they were moving. That's kind of the problem." The man stepped forward, holding out a hand for her to shake. Stacy didn't take it, didn't even want to touch it. "I'm Alec McClelland," he said. "I believe you've been expecting me."

Chapter Ten

INSIDE THE HOTEL were cold tiles, echoing noise, the dead sound of a blank TV screen. Outside were the somnolent buzz of insects, the high sweet sound of birds, happy shouts coming from the sea. Ethan ran across the patio and towards the pool, half-closing his eyes against the dazzle. His face was running with sweat and his scalp was burning. A couple of girls were trying to get into a brightly coloured hammock that had been strung from a wooden frame; they were not succeeding. Ordinarily, Ethan would have watched, but now he did not stop until he was standing next to his mum and dad.

He could see from the rise and fall of his dad's chest – bared again, those wavering hairs making him look oddly vulnerable – that he was still asleep. He wasn't sure about his mum. She lay there perfectly still, a thoughtful little smile on her face. He couldn't tell if she was breathing. Suddenly panic rose and he bent and shook her.

She spluttered into life, sitting up, her smile dissolving. "What on earth…"

"Mum, there's been a plane crash. In America. There are dead people."

"Whu— Well, we weren't on it, were we?"

Her face so comically spoke of half-sleep that part of Ethan wanted to laugh. Another part didn't. He took a deep breath. "No – you don't get it. They're dead, see. But they're moving. Dead people are coming back."

His dad sat up too. His eyes were glazed as he scowled up at Ethan, who felt a sudden stab of fear. Holiday Dad, the one who'd been emerging, had been nicer than the dad with worries and cares and fears. He hadn't meant to call that version of his father back. But Dad didn't say anything else; he looked lethargic, possibly even slightly ill. It would be just like him to manage to get sunstroke while sitting under a beach umbrella and spend the rest of their holiday grumbling about it.

Mum threw back her head and laughed. "Oh, he's funny. Isn't he funny, Lester?"

"Hilarious," Dad muttered, settling down again.

"We should go and get Lily," Ethan said. "We should do something."

Mum settled deeper into her sunbed, making non-committal sounds, and then she murmured: "I'd quite like it if the dead came back. It's a nice idea, Eeth. I'd get to see my old dad again."

"Mum, they – they're *eating* people."

"Oh, no, love," she said. "My dad wouldn't do anything like that." She settled back, her eyes closed, her expression sweet; as if she were focusing on days that had long passed.

In the pool, the red-haired lad he'd seen earlier hefted a girl on to his shoulders and threw her into the water. Spray flew high and bright as she shrieked, "Fergus! You—"

Ethan wrinkled his nose as his dad half pushed himself up from his chair. Dad's frown had deepened, as if he were lost in some problem, and Ethan waited for him to speak.

"You didn't get the bug stuff," he said.

Chapter Eleven

"I CAME IN on the *Demeter*," said McClelland. "The ship's adrift."

Stacy had tried to take him up to her office, but he'd insisted on staying where he was. Someone – a tourist, she noted, no one she could yell at – brought him a chair. Then a waiter appeared with a mug of steaming coffee, which McClelland had demanded black. Now he sat in the middle of Reception, staring at the floor. He patted at his pockets, as if he wanted a cigarette but couldn't find one, and he shook his head before he continued. "She was slowly moving south. I don't think the captain knew or cared, not any longer; no one really did."

"The food poisoning. It was that bad?"

"It wasn't food poisoning." He sipped at the scalding fluid. "I don't think anyone knows what it is, not yet. I didn't see it start. There were rumours. It was hard to tell. The ship's mainly catering for the Russian market – that's where the growth is these days, so I didn't always understand what they were saying. I'd only joined the thing in the first place to meet up with some guys from the Russian arm of a research company – New World Pharmaceuticals – about a possible business deal. I never got to meet them. People began getting sick. Someone told me it had started after their boss flew in by helicopter – well, it could have been true. I heard the thing landing a couple of times.

"Anyway, it wasn't stomach flu or anything like that. The first thing I saw, some guy burst into the casino and took a bite out of someone's face. Then *that* guy started attacking everyone else. There was a whole lot of screaming. I didn't see much after that – I got the hell out of there."

"This is pure conjecture." Stacy looked around. "If we could clear—"

"It's the truth," McClelland snapped. "I saw it for myself. Anything it touched – it spread. You get bitten, you get scratched, it's game over. The captain tried to keep some sort of order. We were asked to stay in our cabins, were told they'd bring food to us there, but food didn't come. I could hear people opening their doors. Then I heard them screaming."

"And you didn't try to help?"

"I didn't try to help." McClelland raised his head and met her gaze. His skin was pasty white but his cold blue eyes were bright and intense and he did not look away. After a moment, Stacy did.

"I didn't help. I wouldn't be here now if I had. Everything in my room was fixed down, but I managed to get the bed loose by unscrewing the bolts with the edge of a knife and I barricaded myself in. I was hungry. I could hear things I didn't want to hear. At first the staff had been there, walking down the corridors, shouting out what was going on in Russian, English and Spanish, but then they weren't around any longer. Other things were, though. They shuffled. They *sniffed.* They didn't even sound like people any more. They weren't people."

"The ship was quarantined," Stacy said firmly. "I heard all about it. It's a standard procedure for what is a standard event, so there's no need to frighten my guests, Mr McClelland."

She couldn't help glancing up at the television as she spoke. It had blanked out just after the jet had swooped down towards the estuary and now it was the dead colour of nothing at all. She remembered the screaming, wondered briefly what had happened to Simon.

"I think it was the captain's choice," McClelland said. "He'd told us we wouldn't dock until he'd contained the situation. That was what he said. Then there were no more reports. I think he must be dead too, now. Or maybe he's still out there, wandering around his ship."

"Mr McClelland, that's enough. I don't know what sort of sickness was on board that ship, but it's clearly caused hallucinations." The onlookers shifted uneasily. "I'm certain it's nothing contagious. I'll show you to your room and have you checked over by the hotel's doctor."

"You'll do no such thing. You'll start gathering weapons. Because they're coming."

Murmurs of alarm spread – *like a virus*, Stacy thought – among the gathering. "There's nothing whatsoever to suggest..."

"I broke out through my porthole. It was too small, but I prised the frame away. Amazing what you'll do when you're starving."

"We'll bring you something. Waiter..."

"No. I haven't finished yet. It was a long drop; I landed badly. It was cold, too. Who'd have thought that blue sea would be so cold? But I could see land, not too far off. I used the life jacket from my cabin and I started to swim. It was pretty rough out there. Not placid, these seas, are they? Not like you'd think. Anyway, after a while I reached a party of snorkellers. I tried to explain that I needed help, but they just kept shouting about how they needed to "kiss the Virgin". It's off Roqueta Island, a submerged statue, some Catholic thing. They think it's good luck if they can swim down and touch it. Anyway, I'd had enough. I just wanted to get on their boat and get to shore, make my way here. But this guy, he started yelling about how there was something weird down there, below the waves."

Stacy didn't reply. She should stop him doing whatever it was he thought he was doing, but somehow she couldn't. She wanted to hear.

"He said there were people walking on the bottom. People without any oxygen tanks." McClelland looked around as if for effect. "So I had a look. I wasn't even cold by then anyway. I was tired and I was starving, but I couldn't feel it any more. I borrowed a mask and swam down. I saw the Virgin, some great weed-coloured thing with her hands clasped and her eyes closed. And beneath that there was something moving.

"Down deep, where the water clouded up, but I saw them," he continued. "The distance made them look really pale, and it was like the man said, they had no masks or tanks; but it didn't stop them. Some had already started to bloat, but they were still heavy enough to stay on the bottom. I could tell from their clothes that they were from the *Demeter*, like me. One woman even had a ball dress on. It... billowed around her. There were pasty men in shorts and women and kids, still dressed for their holidays, and they kept on moving towards the shore as if they knew exactly where they were going."

"It could have been turtles." It was a young man's voice. Stacy couldn't see who spoke. "They've got kind of wrinkly faces," he said. "Leathery. That could have looked like tanned skin. And the way they move, kind of ponderous – that could seem like a person."

"It wasn't turtles."

"How do you know?" Stacy asked. She didn't like the note of urgency that had crept into her voice. She just wanted him to say, *Ah, of course; that's all it was.*

He didn't. "I know," he said, "because one of them was looking up at me. I don't think he – it – wanted to. None of the others did that. But this one's head was tilted right back, pretty much all of the way. I think it must have been because he didn't have much of a neck left. But he did have a face, and for a moment—"

"Then it was just divers. Free divers, trying to touch the statue."

"But they didn't touch it. They never stopped. They just passed her, the Virgin, sitting there under the water, praying, and they never even looked at her. Only one of them saw me, and I suppose the snorkellers, and maybe he decided it was too much trouble to try to reach us, or maybe he couldn't. Anyway, they just kept on heading straight towards the shore. As if they had a purpose. As if there was somewhere they had to be."

Chapter Twelve

THE TOP OF the pyramid was flat, and broader than it looked from ground level. There were a few canopied sunbeds and a bar constructed from glass bricks, backed by a blocky structure of old white rocks. That was topped by a row of carved cubes with deep slits in their surface, like smaller versions of arrow holes. It almost looked as if it were real, some ancient thing that belonged out in the open air, while everything else was cheapened by the brilliant sunlight, revealed as a gaudy show.

Blankets in terracotta patterned with diamonds of bright blue were draped over the bar. Clay pots, painted with suns and lizards and flowers of every colour, was arranged on either side. As if to underline the theatricality of the place, the whole rooftop was ringed by spotlights, all ready for the big event.

Colton stood in their centre, not yet lit by their glare but like a man lost among the attenuated giants.

Celeste went to him and took his arm. The top of her head felt as if it was melting in the heat, but she didn't care. She wasn't sure why anyone would want to be up here in the daytime, even closer to the sun than they already had to be. The whole area was baking. Surely, at any moment, the tiles must crack, the canopies burst into flame. Louisiana and Shelby didn't seem to mind – they were sitting out in the open, right by the rail that edged the roof, Lou's long legs artfully arranged.

Celeste didn't need to say anything to Colton. He walked with her, his steps clumsy, his head lolling as if it were too heavy for his neck. She felt a stab of anger towards Shelby. Shouldn't he be helping? Colton's face was coated with sweat, but she knew it wasn't from the heat; it was cold sweat. *He* was cold. He kept shivering, as if he were coming down with a fever.

"Colton, sit down," she murmured, guiding him to a chair. He did, resting his arm in his lap. He'd wrapped a bandage around it, but she knew what lay beneath. The skin around the insect bite was a mottled purple, as if he'd hit it against a rock. The centre of the wound was oozing with infection, weeping yellow tears, and a rash had spread out from it, travelling up his arm. Worse, the veins beneath the bruising had begun to blacken.

No one had said the words *blood poisoning*, but Celeste couldn't seem to get them out of her mind. She'd made him promise to see the hotel doctor and he had finally agreed, but only after they'd finished setting up for the show. He was a professional, after all. He wasn't one to shout and make a fuss over little things; he simply got stuff done. But Celeste shouted now, beckoning to one of the staff. "He needs some shade over here."

The portly little man – Hector – nodded, but he didn't yet move. He'd greeted them when they'd arrived for the rehearsal, but he'd shown no sign of recognising Celeste, had barely even glanced at her. He'd only had eyes for Louisiana – and for Colton. Celeste hadn't cared. She was used to it. Now, in turn, Colton didn't even notice the man. He just sat and stared at the table, his face waxy, beads of sweat standing out on his forehead.

"It's grey," he murmured.

"What was that?" Celeste leaned in closer.

"All of it. It was so bright, but it's fading. Everything the same colour. *No* colour."

"Colton, that's enough." She pushed herself up. "You need a doctor. Now."

He shook his head and looked at her as if he'd never spoken. "I'm fine, love. Just the sound check and we're done." He smiled, the expression almost, not quite, reaching his eyes. He shuddered as if a chill had ripped through him.

"Colton—"

"He's fine, sweet cheeks. Of course it's your job to worry, ain't that right, superstar? She's a doll. He's got a touch of – what d'you Brits call it? Man flu, right?"

It was a newcomer who spoke. He'd come to record the grand event for posterity a film-maker who'd introduced himself only as "Larry from New Ridge". Louisiana had apparently heard of him, had shaken his hand, saying something about the way he'd broken box-office records. When she'd asked whatever would bring him to this place, he had grinned and said, "What brings me anywhere? An obscene amount of money, babe."

He made a rectangle with both hands, peering through it towards the area that would be Colton's stage. "Perfect. Perfect! Maybe if we could hide that bandage though, right? Longer sleeves, yes?"

He swivelled, arranging himself between the spotlights. "You'll be right here. The fire dancers will be on each corner. I might even get one on top of that ruin, if I can. But you're here, dead centre. They'll see you for miles, Hoss. It'll be awe-*some*."

Colton pushed himself to his feet, using both hands. Some of his fingers looked swollen, rubbery.

"Does it hurt, hon?" Celeste asked.

He looked at her and, for a moment, his eyes were a complete blank. "Can't feel it," he said, and Larry patted him on the shoulder as if that was a good thing before leading him away. Celeste didn't like to see him go, being taken from her just like that. She didn't like the easy way the man had called Colton "Hoss", as if he knew him. Larry was right; it *was* her job to worry. She was getting pretty good at it.

A chair scraped back, startling her as Louisiana landed in the seat next to hers. "Dear *God*," she said.

Celeste sighed. She knew her friend was waiting for her to ask what the problem was, to draw it from her piece by dramatic piece. But she wasn't going to ask.

"Men," Louisiana prompted again, nodding towards Shelby, who held an over-casual posture at the far side of the roof, smoking a cigarette over the rail.

"You know," Celeste said, her eyes still on Colton as Larry put a microphone into his hand, "It's hotter than hell up here. It's way too hot and Colton's sick and I have absolutely no idea why they would call this the VIP area at all."

Louisiana let out an incredulous laugh. "Look around you, honey bun. You can see for miles, can't you? And if you can see them..."

Of course, she was right. This was a place to see and be seen, nothing more. At least when Colton sang, it would all be worthwhile. Everyone would see how wonderful he was and then they could all go home.

Colton was standing with his eyes closed, just as he always did before he started to sing, and his shoulders heaved in a deep breath. Without raising his head he began, the chorus from what he knew was Celeste's favourite song: "Love's Young Dream". It was softer than his usual stuff, a ballad, and they had a standing joke about it: she would ask if he'd written it for her and he would always refuse to say.

A whine of feedback cut through the words and Colton

broke off, his eyes narrowing in unaccustomed anger. Celeste frowned. Colton never looked like that, ugly with annoyance. It drove the worry deeper into her chest. Then he muttered something into the microphone, *It's not a warning, it's a beacon*, something like that, and she pushed herself up.

Louisiana's long fingers closed on her arm. "You shouldn't interfere."

"What did he say?"

"Oh, you know Colton. He'll be making it up on the job. Probably working on a new song."

Celeste subsided, thinking, *"Colton"? Not Colt, or Hoss?* But Louisiana must be right again. Celeste settled back and listened as the song began once more, the bit about kissing at the top of the Ferris wheel. She looked out into the distance. From here she could see for miles, right across Acapulco, and she took in the high-rise hotels dazzling in the heat, the apartments and condominiums belonging to the wealthy of Mexico City, their glowing white walls fading into specks before giving way to cool green mountains beyond.

"I wonder if that ship made it into port. I can't see it any more, can you? Good job that man escaped when he did." Louisiana appeared to have forgotten her spat with Shelby.

Celeste was only half-listening. "Who?"

"Oh, you know: rich guy. McCallahan or something. Businesses everywhere; give Branson a run for his money. He was in the paper the other week, one of *those*, you know, him with a gun, standing over the body of a dead lion. Or maybe it was a rhino. It went viral on Facebook. He claimed it was all Photoshopped, but still."

Something Louisiana had said sunk in. "Escaped? What do you mean?"

"Oh – there's some sort of trouble; didn't you know?"

Celeste only vaguely nodded. She didn't care what kind of trouble he might be in, a man who would kill a lion or maybe a rhino. She was only worried about Colton, the way the shudders kept ripping through him as he clutched the microphone and sang.

Chapter Thirteen

"DO NOT PROCEED to the airport before contacting your in-resort representative." The voice was small and tinny, but at least there *was* a voice. That was what Stacy told herself. It didn't really make her feel any better. She'd tried to make the call on her mobile, but its previously cheerful three bars had diminished to zero: no signal.

As soon as she'd got back to her office she'd used the phone to call the team she should have been heading up – Internal Special Security for the New Festival of Britain sites. There was no answer in the office that should have been hers. That hadn't been so bad. She could tell herself they were out, or that she'd got the time difference wrong and they were all snoozing in their beds. Somehow, though, she didn't think they were snoozing. Not since she called what should have been a twenty-four hour hotline for festival matters and reached only an empty buzzing.

She glanced up at McClelland as the recorded message began again. This time she'd tried the helpline for one of the major tour companies. "Heathrow and Gatwick airports are currently closed. We expect the situation to be rectified soon. Please do not proceed..."

Stacy put down the phone with a sigh. "It doesn't prove anything."

"You need to get with the programme, Miss—" he read the sign on her desk – "Keenan, before all hell breaks loose. I'm telling you, I was there. I've seen them. I've heard the screaming."

You stayed locked in your room, is what Stacy thought but didn't say.

"You need to gather weapons. It's what I'm going to do. They've closed the airports already. There's no getting out of here."

"Mr McClelland, I cannot allow you to do that. If there's a temporary travel situation we can handle it. Everyone who is currently staying here is a guest of the hotel, and we can take care of them until things resume. I should think that will be before anyone here is due to go home anyway."

"What are you?" he sneered. "Security or PR?"

She opened her mouth to speak and closed it again. It was something she'd already wondered to herself. Aside from chasing out a few nosey locals, she hadn't anticipated much trouble at the hotel. The systems were all set up already – extensive CCTV cameras, all linked to a suite somewhere in the basement that, she was told, someone would monitor twenty-four seven. She would be advised of any issues that arose. Her mobile's signal packing in was a bind, but they'd find a way. And there were weapons, although she didn't intend to tell that to McClelland.

"May I remind you that you are also here as our guest," she said. "I appreciate that you have been through an ordeal. I'm more than happy to contact the doctor and provide you with anything you need. But I will *not* have you running about this hotel causing a panic. If that is your intention, we may not be able to accommodate you. Do you understand?"

He didn't look away from her. His eyes were bright and

cold, and he stared at her for a long moment before turning on his heel and leaving the room. He did not slam the door. She looked after him, seeing only a narrow slit of empty corridor, and then even that was gone.

She went instead to the window. It overlooked the main entrance and the road that led towards the city, and she saw an odd thing – people were walking away from the Hotel Baktun. They were not just any people. All of them wore navy shorts and khaki shirts. She glanced at her watch; it wasn't time for a shift change. The people weren't sauntering or chatting to each other. One of them was running, a mobile phone pressed to his ear. She spun around and went to the door, slamming it behind her as she went out.

Reception was chaos. A queue snaked back from the desk, but no one was sitting behind it. A young man holding a tray was fending off questions with, "Please, *señor, señora*, I do not know."

"Where is everybody?" A slender woman in a gauzy dress covered in a bougainvillea print grabbed Stacy's arm. Her hand felt slick with suntan lotion or sweat. "Half the staff have left. Why? We want to order some food."

"I'll find out for you." Stacy glanced towards a glass door with MANAGER etched into it. The manager was from Acapulco and had extensive experience in the leisure industry, is what she'd been told; she hadn't yet met him. No one was queuing at the door and she wondered, suddenly, if that was because he had gone too, if everybody had. She forced a smile on to her face and said brightly, "I'm sure there's no problem. It's not long since Holy Week, you know. A lot of the staff have commitments. It'll all be back to normal very shortly."

A short, stout woman barged up to her, shoving her face up close. Stacy could see the broken veins threading beneath her skin, the hair jutting from a mole on her cheek, could smell her breath, laced with stale coffee. She forced herself not to recoil.

"The USA has closed its borders," the woman said. "It says so right here on my iPad. Closed them with Canada *and* Mexico." Stacy realised that the woman wasn't just angry, she was trying not to cry. "So what the hell are you going to do about it?"

"I'm sure it'll all be sorted out shortly," Stacy said, automatically and without a pause. "Just bear with me one moment." She touched the woman's shoulder in what she hoped was a reassuring manner and strode purposefully towards the manager's office. She reached for the handle, half-expecting it to be locked, but it was not. She walked in and pulled it closed behind her, leaning back for a moment against the glass. She jumped when it rattled – they had started to knock, loudly, on the door.

"Just a minute!" she shouted. She went to the desk. The office was, as she had suspected, empty. The desk was covered in papers, everything awry, and a half-empty mug sat in a puddle of black coffee. The phone was not on its cradle and she realised she could hear it, a high-pitched buzzing beneath the banging on the door. She picked it up, cleared the line and took a deep breath. She didn't need to have them come here, she told herself; she could merely ask if there were any problems, anything she should know.

She dialled the number of the *federales*, held the handset to her ear and waited. It rang. For a moment she thought there would be no answer, that they were all gone too, and then there was a clatter and it was answered after all.

"*Hola?* She said. "*Buenos días? Hola*?"

At the other end of the line, there was silence. Then came a faint noise, so soft she wasn't sure she'd heard it. She turned towards the door, yelled, "A minute!" once more, and the banging mercifully stopped. She focused on the silvery whisper of the phone line. Then she heard it again, a definite sound but not a voice; there was a soft shuffling and then a scrape, as if someone had knocked into a chair.

She stared down at the desk. Dread was creeping into her. It was as if it was spreading from the other side of the phone. She shook the thought away. It was only McClelland, that was all, McClelland and his crazy ideas; they were infecting her.

There was a louder sound, undeniable this time, and she gasped and pulled the phone away from her ear. She could still hear it anyway. It was an inarticulate moaning, hollow and protracted and *wrong*.

She stared at the handset and listened as the sound dimmed in volume and then was gone. She didn't put it to her ear again. She only replaced it on the cradle and stared down at the desk, as if it could provide her with an answer.

Chapter Fourteen

IT WASN'T AS if you could believe everything you heard on TV, Ethan thought. That was what Mum had said and he supposed she was right. Lily was at the Kids' Club again. She loved it there, loved the chirpy girls – Sandy and Lauren – who ran it, loved the other children, as whiny and demanding as they seemed to be. Ethan just hoped it didn't rub off on his sister.

He stood at the edge of the beach, scuffing the toe of his trainers in the sand, which was so pale it was almost white. He could see broken pieces of shell in it. The beach was fairly small and secluded, edged by cliffs, reached via a steep stair that led down from the hotel's pool area. Despite the descent, the sunbeds on the beach were full. Harried-looking waiters hurried to and fro with cooling wipes and iced drinks. It made Ethan feel thirsty just looking at them. The sea was choppy despite the lack of a breeze, the soft rippling further out turning to lively waves at the shoreline.

Under their fresh sound, Ethan made out a voice calling, "You buy, you buy," answered by an irritated, "No!" as a local man walked along the beach, his arms full of embroidered handkerchiefs for sale. Ethan wasn't sure how he'd got there; it probably wouldn't be long before the waiters chased him off the private beach. And who wanted embroidered handkerchiefs anyway? No one, it seemed.

He started to kick off his shoes. The whitecaps looked cooling, and the deeper blue of the sea beyond them beckoned. A couple drifted along in a pedalo; he could just hear their laughter. There was the steady *tock . . . tock* of a couple of girls batting a ball to each other, the water foaming at their knees.

Then he saw the flash of arms cutting through the sea, out where the sunlight sparkled on the water, and he realised that someone was more intrepid after all. There was a girl out there, past the pedaloes or any of them, slicing through the waves as if they didn't exist. He watched her progress, fast and even, closing his eyes against the dazzle. He forced them open, looked for her again. She wasn't there. There wasn't even a ripple where she had been.

He frowned, looking up and down the beach at the chilled-out faces, wondering if anyone else had seen. They weren't even looking at the sea. Should he call someone? But now he wasn't even sure he had seen her at all. Perhaps the movement had only been a fish, or nothing but the sun's play on the water.

Then he heard a sound that froze him. He turned, warm sand scraping against his feet, and he looked up at the hotel.

It didn't look so grand now that people were staying in it. Its balconies were edged with brightly coloured beach towels or bikinis hung out to dry. It looked just as it was, a theme hotel, and yet, something remarkable was happening. Somewhere, someone had begun to sing. He knew the song and he knew the voice. The sound drifted into the peerless blue sky, and Ethan's heart soared with it.

He pulled on his trainers and started to run. The steep stairway didn't give him pause; he didn't stop until he was standing next to his mum, shaking her shoulder. "Mum! Mum, it's him – it's the Colt!"

She shook him off, frowning. "That's not until tomorrow, love."

"He's singing now. Listen!" Ethan held his breath to hear better, although the music was louder now. He recognised the chorus of "Love's Young Dream" before a high-pitched whine cut it off. "Oh..."

"Calm down, love. It must just be a rehearsal or something."

Ethan didn't care if it was a rehearsal. If the Colt was there, and a rehearsal was all it was, there might not be anyone else around. He might even be able to meet his idol. "Mum, we have to go!"

"We're not going anywhere. Your dad's not well. He's been bitten." She settled down, tucking her hands behind her head.

Ethan was only half listening. "Huh – who by?"

"Not who. A mozzie, you eejit."

But Ethan was focused on the music again, grinning at the opening chords of 'Coming Your Way', before he felt a stab of consternation. He never had fetched the bug stuff; now Dad would no doubt go on and on about it. But it didn't matter. The Colt was singing again, his throaty voice reverberating through the air. Another high-pitched shriek cut through it, not the whine of feedback this time but a scream, some idiot down on the beach, and he tossed his head as if he could shush them. Didn't they *know*?

Thankfully, at that moment, the volume jumped up another notch. His mum made an exasperated sound, as did a woman a few sunbeds along; an Amazon of a woman wearing a mirrored bikini that shot back flashes of sunlight so bright it dazzled him. Ethan didn't care. He grinned. It was the Colt, here, *now*, and for once he couldn't think of anywhere he'd rather be, anything he'd rather be doing.

Another scream pierced the words of the song: some other

idiot who didn't know how lucky they were. And then this song too petered out. The sound seemed to hang in the air for a moment, half-full of promise, half of disappointment. Ethan tilted his head as if he could see where it was coming from. It seemed to be echoing from the structure right on top of the pyramid, the old one he could just make out; the one that looked like an ancient ruin.

He closed his eyes, savouring that final note as his mother said, "Ew, what's that?"

A moment later, he realised what she meant. There was a smell. He didn't know what it was but it seemed to go straight to his tongue, so that he could almost taste it. It was a mingling of musky rot and the bottom of bins and dead fish, a cloying smell, a *foul* smell, and he turned and saw the man standing at the edge of the pool.

He knew at once that he was the source of that terrible smell. His clothes were soaked and salt-faded, the colour leeched from them. Fronds of seaweed clung to his trousers and then Ethan realised that he wasn't wearing trousers, only shorts. It was just that his skin was the same greyed colour as his clothes, and it was bloated and waxy looking. Ethan blinked. What he'd taken to be weed were actually wounds, as if the flesh beneath had swelled until the man's skin could no longer contain it and had split.

He saw the man's face. His mind couldn't process what he saw. The face was like a grey sponge, and it looked as if something had been eating his cheeks. Ethan thought at once of fish, delicately nibbling, and he shifted his gaze to the man's eyes. *Undercooked eggs*, he thought. *The jelly of them*. His belly clenched and he bent over, but nothing came up.

The man stood there and water dripped from him. He didn't look as if he'd been for a swim. He looked as if he'd been in the sea for days, maybe even weeks, so that he had absorbed it, been changed by it, had made it a part of him. He stared around as if he didn't know where to begin and then a girl sitting not far from him – Ethan recognised her as the girl Fergus had thrown into the pool – rubbed her nose, pulled a face, looked around and screamed.

The man's head swivelled towards her. His whole body did. He took a step forward, a shambling, unsteady kind of step, as if his legs were somehow loose – *water-softened* was what sprung to mind. Ethan's mouth formed a word – *move!* – but no sound came out and the girl did not move. She only looked indignant as the man's approach took on a momentum of its own and he half-stepped, half-staggered towards her. Then her lips moved and Ethan read the words easily – *Get away from me!* – and the man fell full-length on top of her.

There were more cries of alarm, more screams. Chairs scraped back and another girl ran, tripped and fell. She got up and Ethan saw the blood dripping from her grazed hands. She didn't seem to care; she kept on going.

The man was writhing on top of the girl, his sea-fat legs entwined with her clean tanned ones, and she was screaming, higher and louder than anyone else. Ethan realised that the rest of the world had, for the moment, turned to silence. People were sitting up, abandoning their sunbeds.

The girl's screams turned to shrieks, a high, pained, almost inhuman sound.

A young man approached the pair. He looked angry; he was pulling back the sleeves of his shirt. When he got close, he stopped and took a step backwards.

The man rolled off the girl. He fell to the floor and a shred of fabric came away with him. Then Ethan realised it wasn't fabric but flesh, pale on one side, bloody on the other, and he looked at the girl and saw the gash torn from her cheek to her throat. Blood swallowed the wound so that he couldn't see it any longer. The girl had stopped screaming. She was still awake though, staring straight up as if the sun didn't bother her any more, and then she pushed herself up. Her expression was blank. She must be in shock. She looked out towards nothing – no, towards *Ethan* – and their eyes met.

She didn't look as if she was in pain. That was somehow worse, because she *should* be in pain, and yet she didn't even appear to be conscious of what had happened. It was as if it had all been washed away, along with everything she had been.

Ethan was cold right through. He shivered, saw the hairs stand up on his arms as he remembered the things he'd seen on the television, the ones he'd been told not to believe. Now he knew that a part of him *had* believed them. And it was happening; it was in front of him, not some horror in the dark but out in the open, in the bright sunshine.

Mum pushed herself up, her eyes bleary. "Whatever is all that noise?"

"I—, Mum." Ethan's throat was dry. Suddenly all he wanted was for her to get up and put her arms around him and tell him that everything was all right. But she didn't get up. She just tutted and started wadding a towel down to rest her head upon, and he reached out and grabbed her shoulder.

The waterlogged man was on his feet again, his head swivelling once more. And Ethan could see from the corner of his eye that the girl who had been attacked was getting up. He didn't want to look directly at her. He didn't want to see if she was still staring straight at him.

"Mum – we have to move." He shook her and she pulled away. Ethan stepped between his parents' sunbeds. Dad was still sleeping, turned on his side with his back to his son. "Dad, come on! We have to go now."

Slowly, Dad turned over, letting out a sound that did not seem voluntary. It was more like the noise that air might make as it escaped a dead body, and there was a whiff of a stale scent, like sour breath, with a faint hint of decay in it.

Ethan stepped back. He couldn't help it. This was like

something out of a film, like make-believe. He'd heard of people getting bitten and turning into the thing that bit them. But his dad *hadn't* been bitten, had he? Only by a mosquito, because Ethan had forgotten to get the bug stuff. Now Dad opened his eyes and turned them on his son. Ethan let out a breathy squeak; it was the only sound he could make. It was as if his throat had constricted. There was no air left. He could not look away from his dad. His eyes were the same kind of blank as the girl's had been.

Ethan staggered back, almost falling over his mother's sunbed, and he heard her huff of irritation. Distantly, he could hear more screams coming from the other side of the pool, but he didn't look away. Dad's eyes were following him, and there was something avid in their expression. It reminded him of a bird watching its prey, an eagle, perhaps; or a vulture.

Ethan reached behind him, started flailing for his mother. He found only empty space and then he felt her touch on his shoulder, realised she was standing behind him.

"It's all right, love," she said. "Your dad's not so well. Bit of an allergy, I think. Sunstroke, maybe."

For a moment, Ethan thought it might be true. His heart leapt. They were here to see a show, weren't they? Maybe this was a part of it.

Dad bowed his head, as if indeed he had a terrible headache from the heat. That must be all it was. And then he lifted it, and looked at his son. There was no recognition in his eyes at all. And then Ethan saw the way they had faded, as if they'd clouded over, his pupils shrinking to tiny black holes.

Ethan's voice shook. "He's dead, Mum."

She answered with a stupid trill of a laugh. "Don't be so silly, love. You're all right, aren't you, Les?"

A huge splash came from the pool, a fat belly-flop of a sound. The girl who'd been bitten was in the water. Blood coiled through it, dispersing to a pale pink, the kind of colour that Lily went crazy for, what she called *princess pink*. Ethan's stomach lurched as he thought of her, on her own and away from them all, but at least she wasn't here, looking at this.

There was a boy, about eight years old, at the top of the waterslide. The girl had seen him, was wading clumsily in his direction, sending more of that red spiralling through the water. The kid had seen her too, was staring down at her with an expression of horror in his eyes. He drew himself up, all elbows and knees as he perched there, and then he fell, not down the chute but off the side.

Ethan heard a sharp crack as something hit the hard-tiled edge of the pool, saw only a spray of water and the girl lurching forward, snapping her teeth together. For a moment, he was frozen. Then he heard Dad's voice behind him, but distorted and thickened. "Eeeeeee…" and then, a few seconds later, "Fuunnnn…"

No, Ethan thought, *it's not fun*, and he tried to run, pushing his mother ahead of him. She slapped at his hands, alarmed now, catching his skin with her nails. He could hear his dad moving, a soft shuffling, and he pushed harder. "Mum, for God's *sake*."

She pushed him back.

Ethan felt – actually felt – his dad's teeth closing on the back of his neck, but it was only in his mind. The pain did not come. He ducked anyway, snaking away from his dad as a clawed hand grabbed for him, closing on nothing. Ethan skirted his mother, trying to drag her with him, but she fended him off and then Dad's arms were around her.

Ethan backed off, guilt already spreading its cold fingers over him, and he saw that it was all right. His dad was kissing his mum, that was all. He was holding her close. There were screams everywhere, but Mum wasn't screaming. Her eyes were half-closed and it almost looked like pain but it surely couldn't be. Then Ethan saw that his dad was sinking his face

– no, his *teeth* – deep into her shoulder, and that blood was running down her chest.

She opened her mouth and she wailed. It spoke of love and hurt and disbelief, and yes, betrayal, and Ethan emptied his mind of everything but his sister's face as he turned and fled.

The hotel's doors were in front of him. Others were running for them too and a man knocked into Ethan, sending him stumbling. Someone grabbed his arm and he cried out, but they just steadied him, set him running again. Ethan did not look back until he was inside, a panicked crowd blocking his view of the patio, and someone slid the great glass doors closed behind them.

His mother wouldn't be able to get in. That was uppermost in his mind as he pushed his way back towards the doors and looked for her.

There were more of them now, the people from the sea. They shambled towards the hotel, dripping something a little too viscous to be seawater. When they drew near one of the tourists, they grabbed and held on and they *ate*. A woman with a towel wrapped around her was down, paddling her arms and legs like a child in a tantrum; an old man was clamped to her back. A waiter fended off a bloated mass of a man using a sun umbrella. He prodded at his side and a big wad of spongy flesh sloughed away and fell to the baking floor. The man didn't seem to notice.

And then Ethan saw that one of the sunbeds was still occupied after all. The red-headed boy, Fergus, was lying there quite calmly, face down, tapping along to the beat that was no doubt rising from the earbuds stuffed into his ears. Someone was lurching towards him, moving awkwardly, possibly because of the wound ripped in his side, the blood already darkened and clotting.

Fergus did not move until the thing was upon him. At first he looked irritated; then he looked surprised. After that Ethan didn't want to see his face any longer, although he couldn't help it. He saw his terror there as the boy flailed, his hair quickly subsumed in the brighter tones of blood.

Someone shouted, "Please everybody, into the restaurant," and it wasn't the way that Ethan wanted to go but he was going anyway, borne along on a tide of bodies, everyone making inarticulate sounds, words he couldn't make out or couldn't bring himself to understand.

Chapter Fifteen

EVEN AS THE dying notes hung in the air, they seemed to swell once more. Celeste hadn't wanted to miss the song and she relished the final sounds of it, echoing back from that odd structure they'd chosen to adorn the hotel's roof. Its old white rocks reverberated with the music, giving it back but somehow changed, as if it was now something older and infinitely more strange. *They should use that in the studio*, she thought, and then she rounded the corner of the bar and saw Louisiana and Colton.

She froze, still holding the tray of iced water in her hands. She'd been downstairs to fetch it for him, since Hector and another waiter were simply standing gawping at the show instead of doing their jobs. She'd had to traipse all the way to Reception since the bar up here wasn't fully stocked – she'd pulled back the gaudy blankets and found only row upon row of bottles of tequila. There wasn't even a lift that went all the way from the ground to the tiny rooftop lobby, unless one had been hidden behind the small black door that wouldn't open.

And she hadn't wanted to see Colton with that look on his face any longer, somehow concentrated but dazed at the same time. Now he was sitting at a table with Louisiana bending over him, her hand resting on the surface, almost touching his, whispering something in his ear. She was so close that Colton must have been able to feel the warmth of her breath.

Celeste couldn't move. It was already too warm, and now a fresh wave of heat washed over her. She had never had cause to doubt him. She had sometimes wondered if there were groupies, quick fumbles backstage she didn't know about and didn't want to, but then Colton would look at her in that way he had and she would put the idea out of her mind.

As she watched, Louisiana – *Louise*, she thought fiercely – shifted her hand to Colton's shoulder and squeezed, her long pink fingernails just stroking the bare skin where his shirt met his neck. Her baby-pink lips were still moving. She leaned in, closer, those lips glistening and ready, and then Colton jerked away.

Louisiana straightened, her face hardening, and she saw Celeste. For a moment her eyes shone with disdain; then the expression was overwritten with a smile.

"Thanks, hon," she called, nodding towards the sweating glasses on the tray.

All Celeste wanted to do was pick them up and fling the contents, complete with ice, in Louisiana's face. Perhaps she would see if her friend could still smile then. But Celeste didn't. Nobody moved, and after a moment the obsequious little man – Hector – bustled over and lifted a single glass from the tray and took it over to Louisiana. As he did so, he snapped his fingers, summoning the waiter to bring the rest.

There was a sound in Celeste's ears. It was high-pitched and somehow wrong, and it took her a moment to realise that it wasn't just in her ears – she really was hearing it. It was coming from behind her and low down, from the pool area, and under that, she could hear the sea.

In front of her, Shelby sauntered into sight. He was still

smoking, staying clear of Louisiana and Colton just as if he didn't care, and now she wanted to pitch the drinks at him instead, glasses and all, and then perhaps she'd take his head off with the tray.

Another sound rang out. This time she heard it clearly – a piercing scream that rose and wavered and went on and on. She jumped, slopping water from the glasses. "What the—"

"Ignore them." Louisiana dismissed the sound with a wave of her hand. "Let them scream."

"But—"

"It's just your fans, isn't it, Colton?" Louisiana reached out, saw Celeste's face, stopped just short of touching Colton's shoulder once more. Her nails hung there, painted and sharp. "They heard you and they all love you. Isn't that right?" She smirked, never taking her eyes from Celeste's.

For a moment, no one spoke. Celeste thought about the way it had always been: Louisiana's easy way with money, her radar for anyone who had it, her sense of entitlement. And Celeste's own clumsiness, the sense that she was always running to catch up. The wonder she had always felt that Colton hadn't simply upped and left her behind a long time ago. Of course Louisiana was right. She always was, wasn't she? People adored Colton. *Everybody* did.

Except the screams weren't right, were they? They didn't sound like the usual kind of fan screams: breathy, excited, deliberate.

She shook her head, pushing it all from her mind, and an odd fact surfaced. It was something that somebody had told her about the ruin on top of the Hotel Baktun – that it was an ancient thing, a genuine Mayan artefact, and that it was said to sing whenever the coast was invaded. She lifted her gaze to it now, emptying her mind of everything but its blank face, and she found herself smiling. She did not know why.

When she felt she could compose herself, she looked back at

Colton. He looked sicker than ever. His hair was matted and wolfish around his face and his skin appeared almost as grey as his hair. *As grey as I feel*, she thought, though she forced herself to smile at him, and then she saw that Colton was smiling back. No: he was baring his teeth.

Chapter Sixteen

THE HOTEL LOBBY was far busier than Francisco had expected, and he didn't like that. Surely the guests should be out by the pool or rubbing themselves with tequila, or whatever it was the lazy gringos did; they shouldn't be here, getting in his way.

This time he took care not to make contact with anyone. He kept his sunglasses on and his head down. He wore a plain white shirt and slacks, though his Saint Francis medallion still hung at his neck on its heavy gold chain. He needn't have worried about being seen, however. Everyone seemed to have other things on their minds.

There was a woman who looked like security over by the office, but she wasn't looking at him; she didn't seem to be seeing what was in front of her face. Nobody else looked at him either. They must have found something to complain about already; they milled about, alone or in huddles, talking in low voices. Possibly their televisions weren't working, or there wasn't enough hot water.

Then Francisco saw someone who made him stop in his tracks.

He was part of a group of men walking around the edge of the lobby towards a small, plain black door. Three of them wore almost identical plain suits. Their broad builds and impassive expressions were identical too, but the one in the centre was different. He wore a pale silk shirt over chinos and he walked with a swagger that only emphasised his skinny form. He was dark-skinned with cheekbones that could cut, and he had a shine to his skin that somehow emphasised the shape of the skull beneath it. Francisco was never certain if that was the source of his name, or if there was some other reason.

He smiled broadly as he went, flashing a row of shining gold teeth, and his gaze swept over Francisco. His stride never faltered, but something in the way his eyes gleamed told Francisco that here was a man who missed nothing. But of course, he knew that already. There was a reason why El Calaca, the Skeleton, had risen to the very top of *Los Fieles*. Actually, there were two reasons. The second was his utter lack of a conscience. He was a man who did what needed to be done without looking back, and that included meting out discipline to anyone who let him down.

Without thinking, Francisco bent to tie his shoelace. It didn't need tying and he cursed himself as he fumbled. His first instinct had been to hide his face. It would have drawn less attention if he'd simply carried on walking.

When he straightened, El Calaca had gone. Francisco swallowed hard, feeling the sweat trace a cold line down his back. He glanced around, knowing even as he did so that he was making everything worse. Maybe El Calaca was watching him; judging him. Francisco had seen the results of his judgements.

Anyone who got in the way of their importation routes, for example, might have their eyes put out or their fingers cut off, usually well before they actually died, begging for mercy – *Man cannot forgive, my friend, did you not know?* – and then their bodies would be dumped, usually somewhere conspicuous as a warning to others.

Francisco had seen what he'd done to one of the brotherhood who had dared to suggest within his earshot that El Calaca's skinny figure and gold teeth, his own presumably rotted away, were a sign of his being a little too friendly with their product.

Francisco shivered at the thought. It hadn't been so much seeing what El Calaca had done – he had been a little inured to it by then, at least – as the fact that, all the time he'd done it, his expression had never changed. Francisco remembered thinking that El Calaca's eyes had had the soul burned out of them a long time ago, but, more importantly, he'd remembered the lesson: that the worst punishments were reserved for their own – for those who betrayed him, or those who simply failed in their tasks.

And they would all be given to *La Flaca*, the lady of the *Santa Muerte*, who did not judge. She accepted all men and all women, taking them regardless of the way they had spent their lives, whether they had strived for good or evil; because all men came to Lady Death in the end.

Francisco felt the blood drain from his face. But he would not fail El Calaca. He was one of the family now. He had helped them do whatever they needed to do, and he had seen first-hand how their enemies must suffer. He had watched without comment as they had stripped them of their very faces, so that none in the afterlife might know them. He had watched, trying not to flinch, as they peeled back the skin from their foreheads, ripping it downwards, taking it strip by strip. He had seen the blood run red. He had seen what awaited beneath, the gristle and bone, the naked eyes staring up at him, suddenly so big...

These faceless ones, the *desollados*, had been the worst; or Francisco hoped they were. His hand went to the medallion at his throat and it helped, a little. The memories receded. And yet, one day he would have to give it up, this thing his grandmother had given him. He would be accepted instead into the *Santa Muerte*, the worship of *La Poderosa Señora*.

He let his hand brush the place where his gun was hidden in his waistband and resumed walking across the lobby. He had to do his duty. He looked neither to the left nor right, but he felt himself sweating, felt fear streaming from him like a beacon. Surely everyone must see it.

Then he realised that, no matter what the guests' complaints, nobody was answering them. The Reception desk was empty. His stride became a little more relaxed. Perhaps they'd made this easy for him after all, abandoning their posts while he walked straight past.

He entered the corridor that led towards the Kids' Club. There were worse things than death, he supposed. Sad things. Bad things, that could taint a place forever, would make sure that no one ever wished to stay in such a place again. Terrible things, in fact.

He smiled. The owner really should have paid. Everyone had dues, and if they were not offered, they would be taken.

Francisco walked a little taller, taking the laminated badge they'd given him from his pocket. It proclaimed him to be Ernesto Aguila, a member of the security team. In the photograph, he was not smiling. "Security do not smile," they'd said when they took his picture, and he forced himself to straighten his face as he turned the corner and heard the bright sound of mingled voices singing, "We are the happy kids," followed by a loud and ragged *clap-clap-clap*.

Chapter Seventeen

MICK SMILED AND slipped the pesos into the pocket of his shorts. He had got into the habit of running the coins through his fingers to try to count them before they chinked their way inside. Any notes were separated at once; those went into the pocket of his shirt. He felt guilty about it – they had been told to pool tips – but he was sure from the scarcity of notes finding their way into the staff box that the others were doing the same. Coins for the box; notes for his brother. That was the plan.

Already someone else was clicking their fingers for service. Lunchtime was over, but there was always more work. Now he was bringing brightly coloured cocktails to the basted bodies laid out in the early afternoon sun. It made Mick uncomfortable just to look at them. It was surely time to step inside, enjoy the shade and maybe a sleep. Drinking would make everything worse. He could see them burning in front of him, baking from the outside, dehydrating from within. For a moment he pictured them sitting there until they darkened and shrivelled like sun-dried chillies.

He could hear music, the rehearsal for the big show, drifting from the rooftop. At least he was down here, where it was a little cooler. He took an order for a tequila sunrise and a sex on the beach – so crass, these tourists, always talking of sex – and he glanced towards the pool as someone screamed.

He had expected to see a girl but it was a man running by, his hands clutching his belly as he went. He was only half-dressed. He was wearing the kind of trunks they called Speedos, but this man wasn't fast at all. He ran as if his legs were about to give out. Or as if…

With a start, Mick remembered another of Miguel's pieces of advice from when he'd been starting out. "If you don't like – just give them the water from the tap instead of filtered. Give them something else to think about, no?"

Mick tried not to let the laughter burst from his lips. Tequila sunrise, he thought. Sex on the beach. Coming right up: like this man's *lonch*.

The man hurried past the pool, holding his sagging belly as if he could keep its contents inside. He veered around some sunbeds, kept on going towards the toilets. And then he swerved again and Mick's smile faded.

Red. Red, smeared across the man's belly.

The sound coming from the rooftop faded. Another scream shredded the day.

Mick narrowed his eyes against the sun. Someone he recognised was staggering towards him from the direction of the pool. It was the woman from the restaurant, the Russian *Miss* in the mirrored bikini, but now a hole had appeared in her face. He blinked. The vision didn't go away. Where her pouting red lips had been was nothing but a hole, dripping bright blood on to her ample chest. Still her mouth didn't stop moving, and he saw that she was chewing on something: a sliver of raw-looking meat. Suddenly she sucked it inside that dark maw and her tombstone teeth, surely too large for her mouth, clamped down. Another line of crimson slipped from her, running down her chin as she ate.

Mick froze. He searched the part of his mind that should know what to do and came up blank. The woman was hurt, that much was clear, though he couldn't imagine how she'd sustained such a wound. He must get help.

It was only then that he saw – really saw – her eyes. They were holes too, pale ones this time, filmed over as if in death. There was no pain in them, only a blank hunger, an inhuman expression. Something inside Mick went cold, like air-conditioning, like sickness. He couldn't bring himself to move.

Then someone else screamed and Mick knew that it wasn't in fun, wasn't a part of their holiday; it was a cry of fear, and it was closer, as if something was coming towards him.

His tray clattered to the tiles and spun, setting up a loud metallic ringing. The woman in the mirrored bikini stopped at once. Her eyes snapped towards him. Mick's bowels turned to water. He couldn't look away. He could only will the noise to stop but it didn't, it just went on and on, and then somehow he snapped out his foot and stamped on the tray, quelling it with a single loud bang.

Despite the noise, no one else was looking at him. From the corner of his eye, he knew this was because they were staring at what was happening by the pool. People were scrambling to get away, tripping over sunbeds in their haste, tripping over each other.

A woman sitting on the patio turned to him and said, "What's going on?"

Mick looked at her, becoming slowly aware of the uniform he wore; the one that meant he should know what was happening and, more importantly, what everybody should do about it.

He shook his head.

She frowned and sat up, started pulling on a loose shirt. "My husband's in the pool. Is something wrong?"

Mick reached out to her, stopping just short of grasping her

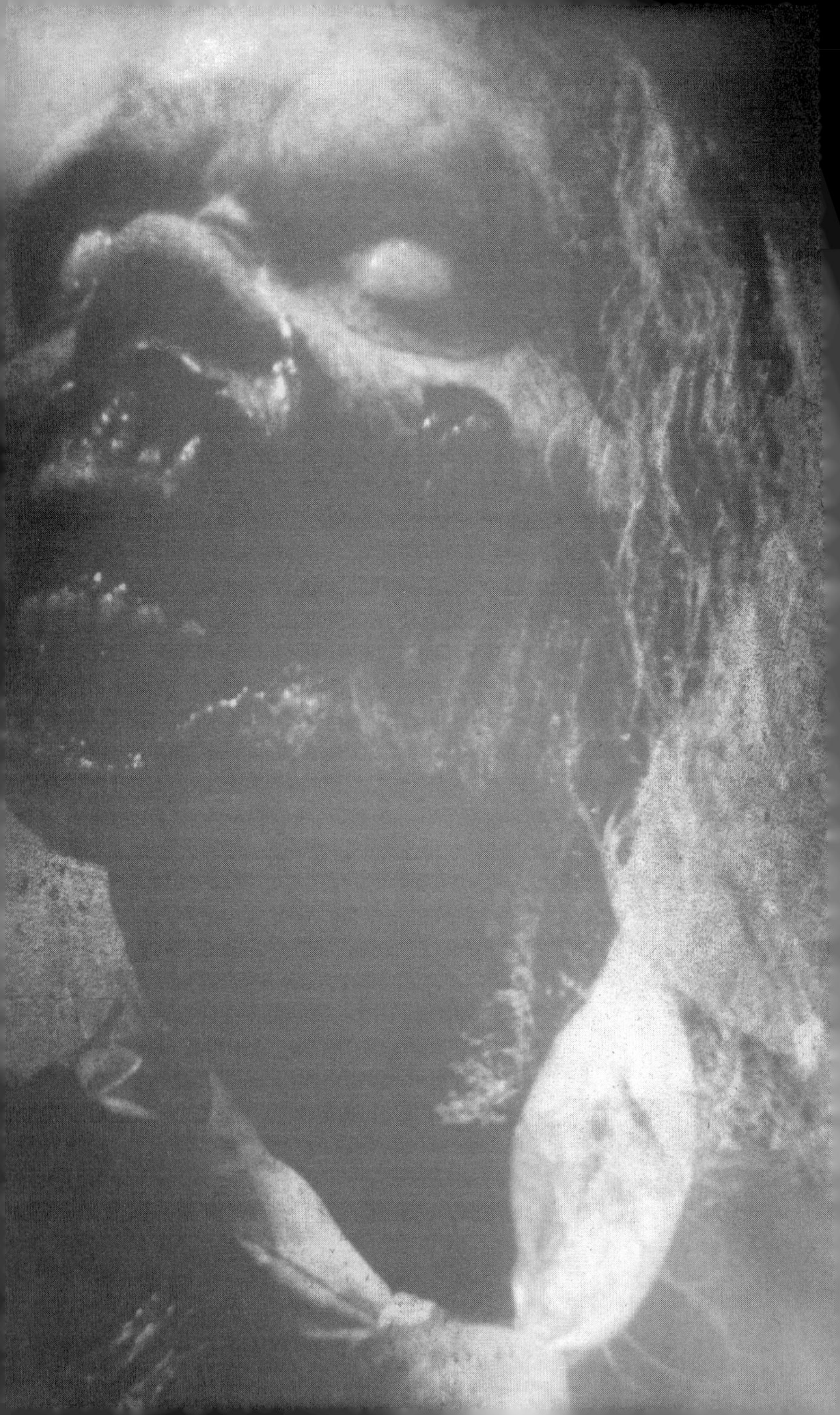

bare forearm when she turned and stared down at his hand. He did not know what was happening. He didn't know what to do, but he knew that he didn't want this woman to go down to the pool, towards that *Miss* with the blank, dead eyes. He looked up, scanning for her. He couldn't see where she had gone. He could only see that the pool was a chaos of splashing water that looked oddly pink in the afternoon sun. And then he saw there was indeed a man in it, half-swimming, half-wading through the water towards the steps to the waterslide, as if his life depended on it. He reached them and started to climb, looking back over his shoulder with wide, terrified eyes. The water was beginning to settle. A girl was in the water. She gripped what looked like a child's arm between her teeth.

"Gary?" His wife stood, shading her eyes. "Gary, is that you? What are you doing on the slide?"

"Please. Don't. I think you should come—"

She cast an irritated look over her shoulder at Mick as she walked away, and at that moment a short, stocky man smacked into her. She whirled about and fell. He didn't even look back, just kept on going towards the hotel. The woman didn't cry out, but Mick heard her bones meet the hard tiles. He winced.

Disease, he thought. There was a quarantined ship in the bay, wasn't there? Maybe they didn't have belly flu like everyone said. Maybe they had rabies. A new kind of rabies, that made everyone run and bite and go completely *loco*.

He peered down towards the seaward steps and the shimmering blue beyond, as if he could see the cruise ship out there now. He didn't see it, but he saw the figures cresting the rise that led from the beach. A moment later, he smelled them. It was like a garbage heap in the *barrio*, where only rats could bear to gather, feasting on the rotten leavings of mankind.

That smell told him everything. The future, the one where he got rich and his brother went to college, was not going to happen. Nothing was going to be the same. He knew that before he even saw the rotting faces, the sea-ridden corpses, the things the ocean had given back.

The first of them looked like tourists after a hurricane. There was a woman with a filmy dress stretched tight over her spongy flesh, grey skin showing through it, her straggly hair feral around her face. A man whose bare chest was slashed wide open, white bone gleaming through the clotted mess, where what looked like slithery black worms writhed. Another whose white uniform must once have been dazzling as he went about his ship. He stared dead ahead now, his eyes milky and running with moisture. There were children too. Mick couldn't bear to look at them. They came in a stinking mass, their steps slow and ponderous as if they were walking underwater, and yet their advance was inexorable. They shuffled and groaned. And the sun shone down on them, the dead and the living alike, and that was wrong, almost the worst thing of all. These things surely belonged in the depths, where the sun could never penetrate.

Mick heard an odd clanking sound and looked behind the horde of tourists to see what came after. His breath stopped in his throat. One of them was little more than a skeleton. It moved in an odd fashion, limping and hopping, and then the mass parted and he caught a glimpse of a wooden leg, and its skull grinned back at him. Another wore armour, the rotting leather breastplate loose and useless, a conquistador's morion helmet rattling around the bony head encased inside it. They were impossible and they were coming for them all.

Mick turned and ran for the hotel. It was the only thing he could do. He couldn't save those who lingered. He could only flee as if devils were after him – because they *were* – yelling to anyone who would listen to get themselves inside.

Chapter Eighteen

CELESTE TRIED TO remember the last time Colton had said he loved her. She couldn't remember when it had been, and that troubled her. As a waiter came to lift the glasses from the tray she carried, she looked at Louisiana's blank, pretty-doll eyes. She tried to remember when she'd last thought she actually liked her friend. They had known each other since they were knee-high to a grasshopper, as her mum would have put it. Their mothers were friends and so they had been too. She wondered if they would ever have spent time together by choice, and the saddest thing was, she couldn't be sure.

How many times had Louisiana and Colton been alone? The thought made something twist inside her. She knew Louisiana did not love Shelby. She loved what he represented: money, success, the lifestyle to which she would really love to become accustomed. If someone else came along who could offer the same things wrapped in a more attractive package, Louisiana wouldn't hesitate.

But Celeste trusted Colton, didn't she?

The tray went light in her hands as the last glass was lifted from it. Celeste didn't acknowledge the waiter. She was staring at Colton's eyes, trying to see the love in them, but she couldn't seem to see beneath their grey-blue surface. There was no warmth in them at all.

She shook her head, but her unease stayed with her. "Colton?"

He didn't give any sign that he'd heard. Celeste realised that, down below them, someone was still screaming. Maybe more than one someone. They must be playing some kind of game, but she didn't like the sound of it. She shivered, despite the heat. She wished they'd stop. She wished, for a moment, that it all would; that she and Colton were little more than kids once more, just starting out, sharing their rented flat above the chippy on the high street.

She still hadn't looked away from his eyes.

The waiter was at Colton's shoulder, just setting down the glass. The sound it made, a small tap, made Colton snap his eyes around as if the man had yelled in his ear.

Colton pushed himself away from the table. Celeste thought he was getting up but he continued to go over backwards and his chair tipped. He reached out – so fast – as he fell, grabbing the waiter by the throat, and they went down together in a clatter of chair legs and breaking glass. Colton was making an odd noise, moaning and wordless, and then there was another sound, that of ripping, and the waiter began to howl.

Celeste stepped towards them, but the howling only lasted for a moment. The agonised sound gave way to a wet gurgling.

Louisiana backed away, putting distance between her and them – *bitch*, thought Celeste, wasn't she supposed to care about him all of a sudden? Now she just looked green, as if what she could see on the other side of the table was making her sick.

Celeste hurried towards them. It was Colton who was ill and it was Celeste who cared, who would show her love...

The waiter pushed himself up. There was something wrong with his eyes. His shirt was pulled awry and a dark patch was spreading, rapidly, across his shoulder. It looked like blood. Celeste couldn't look at it. Instead she met his eyes and they were blank and lifeless as stones.

Louisiana gasped and staggered, stumbling against a table behind her. The waiter's head snapped towards the sound. Louisiana froze in place and then Hector quickly crossed himself and began to edge away.

The waiter stumbled towards him, reaching out with his hands clawed. He grabbed Hector's lapels and the portly man pulled free, letting out little gasps of terror.

Colton stood. He still had a piece of the waiter's flesh gripped between his teeth. He pulled it down his throat with a *schloop* and his throat bobbed as he swallowed.

Hector let out a cry with no words, "Aaaag," but Colton only had eyes for Celeste. She didn't like the expression in those eyes. Some light had returned to them, but it wasn't a good light. He looked crazed. He looked hungry. Suddenly, he lurched across the table towards her.

"Run!" Hector had found his voice at last. He rushed past Celeste, waving his hands in the air in panic. "*Run!*"

And she did. She turned and ran from Colton, the man she loved, not because of the champing of his teeth or the hunger in him, but because she had looked into his eyes and seen no love in them. She was no longer running to keep up with him; she was running away.

She heard a shriek behind her and she turned just as she caught up with Hector, at the glass door that led into the small rooftop lobby.

The shriek had come from Shelby. He was holding off the waiter with a chair, prodding him back, and then Colton charged in – *sunstroke*, Celeste insisted to herself, *he has sunstroke* – and Colton and the waiter, their movements fast but clumsy, went down once more.

Hector grasped for the door handle, flailed and missed.

Instead, his hand caught in Celeste's hair, pulling strands of it from her head. She didn't stop, just pushed the door open herself, hearing the clicking of Louisiana's heels right behind her. For a split second she thought of slamming the door back into her old friend's face, but behind her she saw Colton, coming for them again. Now his expression was terrifying. There was nothing left of her husband in that look. One glimpse told her that the man she had known was gone – *dead*, she thought, *he's dead* – and then Hector pushed her ahead of him into the lobby and he turned and slammed the door in Louisiana's face.

Celeste saw her friend's nose break. A gush of rich crimson spurted across the glass, and Louisiana screwed up her eyes against the pain. Somewhere deep inside her, Celeste felt a nasty twinge of satisfaction. She knew exactly how much Louisiana had spent on that cute little nose. But then Colton was there, at her friend's shoulder, the waiter was at the other, and they were pulling and biting and – *eating*.

Celeste's hand shot to her mouth. Red was all she could see. It was everywhere and Lou was screaming, but the sound was muffled because of the way her mouth was pressed up against the glass. Celeste could only watch as Colton got his hand around her neck, driving his fist into the wound he'd made. He got hold of something – it must have been Lou's collarbone – and he pulled, the waiter holding on to her golden hair and pulling the other way, opening his mouth wide, wider, closing his teeth around her forehead, and tugging back just as if her friend was a wishbone at Christmas.

The skin on Louisiana's forehead crumpled under the force of his teeth. *She wouldn't like that*, Celeste had time to think, *she'll get wrinkles*, and then Colton won out and pulled her away. He moved in close so that they were face to face and Celeste's insides went loose. Then Shelby dashed around the three of them as they fell writhing to the floor, shifting himself like a man half his age. He slipped into the lobby and hurried towards the stairs, dragging Celeste with him. She allowed him to do it, moving her away from the madness, the things she could not possibly have seen, blocking her view of her lover and her friend as they writhed on the ground together, Lou's screams gradually subsiding into low sobs and then a single hungry-sounding moan.

Chapter Nineteen

THE BUFFET TABLE was still laden. Ethan could smell the sour tang of vinegar, the sharper hint of chilli in the back of his throat. His mouth filled with saliva, but it wasn't because he was hungry. He felt sick. He stared at the numbed people standing between the white-clothed tables, seeing the shock he felt reflected in their eyes. One of the men sitting with his head in his hands was wearing only swimming shorts and he was soaked, dripping all over his chair.

Ethan could still see those things before his eyes, the bright splashes of blood. He blinked the visions away but still they came, people running, crashing full-length to hard tiles, the sound of it as their bodies gave before teeth and impossibly strong hands; their louder, ear-piercing wails of despair.

And his dad. His *mum*.

He shook that thought away. He couldn't face it. He had seen his dad kissing her, that was all, and he knew there had been something wrong about it but he didn't want to examine it, not yet. He scanned the room again and this time everything blurred. Now they were only people, going to load their plates and enjoy a holiday lunch, exclaiming about how hot it all was, talking of the food and the weather; nothing more. Nothing like those things he'd seen.

A man sat on the floor over in the corner. He'd helped himself to a bottle of tequila and now he upended it over his face. He kept on pouring it down his throat, even while it spilled down his chin and across his chest.

Ethan put a hand to his own face. He found his cheek was wet. He held out his fingers to examine the liquid, wondering if it was blood, but there was no blood, only tears. He shook his head. He couldn't remember the last time he'd cried.

He realised he could hear things. There was still screaming, though it was distant now, shut out. Someone closer by was murmuring "Jesus Christ, Jesus Christ", over and over. He looked around and saw a thin man on his knees, rubbing his hands together. Someone stood over him and, at the sight of him, Ethan flooded with relief – he was wearing a uniform. It was the one who'd told them all to get inside, to get away; someone who would know what to do.

An image of his mother rose in Ethan's mind, bringing a wave of guilt. What if she had needed him? She might even need him now. He closed his eyes. Dad had been *kissing* her, that was all. His mum hadn't needed him and neither had his dad, and the others – they were only ill, not evil. Someone really should have helped them.

He suddenly felt he was going to be sick and he grasped his stomach. A hand patted him on the shoulder and he jumped, turning to see a woman with dark shiny hair pushing a handkerchief towards him. He took it and she smiled, nodding. Ethan simply held it. He didn't know what to do, didn't know if he should run or just sit where he was and cry.

He wanted his mum.

He looked back at the staff member who stood among them. He'd make everything all right again. He would explain that everything was exactly as it was supposed to be, that it was all some kind of joke; just a part of the show, a publicity stunt for the brand new hotel.

Ethan's lip twitched. He remembered that he had heard the Colt singing and he felt the feeble stirring of old joy. It felt like a remnant of childhood.

Lily. The thought of her flooded his mind, and that was like clarity. He had to get to her. He knew that he wasn't all right, that he might never be all right again, but his little sister had to be. He straightened and stumbled towards the door, but that was when the waiter called out: "Everyone, please stay where you are. There is a little trouble, that is all. All will be fixed soon. Please! Sit. Eat."

Ethan looked towards the door. He couldn't stay here. Was he really supposed to help himself to tea and cake while the world went mad? He could still hear screaming, albeit muffled, coming from somewhere beyond the large plate-glass windows.

"Everybody wait, please. I will fetch someone."

There were cries of protest, some telling the man – it said MICK on his name badge – to hurry, some asking him not to leave them, one woman saying she'd report him if he dared to go. Everyone raised their voices, all speaking at once. And Ethan realised that beneath their palaver was another sound, that of someone knocking. No: someone was banging on the windows.

The restaurant was long and thin and took up most of one wall of the pyramid. Its windows looked out across the pool area and away to the sea. Ethan knew that some of them slid open but he didn't know which ones, and anyway it didn't matter, because the people outside were trying to beat their way through the glass with their hands, hands that were grey and skinless and dead. Some had their faces pushed up against it, as if they could simply walk through. One woman's cheek was shredded and her tongue pressed, swollen and wet, against the pane. She pulled away, leaving a cloudy smear on the glass, and she turned her head to look at Ethan. She didn't have any eyes but she seemed to look anyway, her head lolling as if she were nodding in approval. Ethan took an involuntary step away. He had to get out of here, grab his sister, hide somewhere deeper inside the hotel. Their room was on the third floor; they could go there, lock the doors and wait until all this had passed...

The woman who'd given him the handkerchief reached out and grabbed his arm. She appeared quite calm, but when he looked into her eyes, he saw the terror in them. "We're supposed to stay here," she said brightly. "They said so. You can stay with me, love. My name's Heather. That's my hanky."

Ethan looked down at the small damp thing he held. He realised it was one of the handkerchiefs the local man had been selling on the beach, this one sewn with a gaudy blue flower. It seemed that someone had bought one after all. He opened his fingers, let it slip to the floor.

"Your hand," she said.

Ethan didn't know what she meant. He only knew that the banging was getting louder. Glass was jumping in its frame. Then he heard a high splintering noise and a wide, white starfish appeared on one of the panes. The people – *no*, he thought, the *not-people* – on the other side redoubled their efforts. He could hear them groaning, a deep bass to accompany the percussive beats of their fists, and something inside him went cold. He tried to yank his hand out of Heather's grip, but she didn't let go. She looked at him, quite calm, but Ethan realised that something inside her had broken, that maybe it would never be fixed again.

"You'll sit here," she said, her voice conversational, "until they come."

He thought she must mean *help*, until help came, but somehow it didn't seem that way. She started to drag him towards a chair, her hand twisting and burning his wrist. She pushed him, her strength wiry and surprising, and he half-fell.

Ethan let himself go limp, spinning away from her, on to the floor. He scrambled away, grabbing something – the edge of a tablecloth – and he hauled himself up. Instead he spilled to the floor again, knives and forks clattering down on top of him. He grabbed one of the knives and held it in front of his face.

Heather's eyes narrowed. "Oh," she said, "you're one of them. One of *those* boys," and she stepped towards him as the silvery sound of glass shattering filled the air.

Ethan crawled along the space between the tables as Heather turned and froze. Behind her, the not-people spilled into the room. The stink of them quickly spread, and when it reached Ethan he could no longer pretend to have any doubts that they were dead. Indeed, some of them must have been dead for a long time.

Everyone turned, ran, cried out. A table was overturned and rolled. The dead made their remorseless way around it, their arms stretching out towards the living. Others were making their way down the side of the buffet, trailing their fingers in chilli and guacamole, recognising none of it, wanting none of it.

Then he saw the formidable woman in her mirrored bikini, one cup ripped and hanging loose – he wanted to look away and found he could not – and he saw the gaping maw where her lips had once been. She had grabbed a young man by his long curly hair, *hippy hair* his mother would have called it, and she pulled him towards her. His face was white and his own mouth was opened into a dark hole to match hers, but no sound came out.

The man grabbed at the nearest table and his legs pedalled, but he couldn't pull away from her. She yanked on his hair and he let go. The pair of them fell together into the buffet table and a large tureen yawed and tipped. It was full of chilli, the strong stuff that Ethan's dad had said could strip a man's tongue, and a big dollop parted with the side of the tureen with a *glurp*. It landed on the man's forehead and he closed his eyes tightly as it slid downward. Ethan wanted to look away but he couldn't move.

He saw the woman lowering her mouth – no, her *hole* – towards the young man's face. Her teeth were bared anyway because she hadn't any lips, but she drew back the shreds of skin that remained and bit down. Ethan tried to tell himself it was only the chilli, that she was licking it from his face, but the man started screaming almost at once. He kicked out but she had him pinned half-across the table, and as the kicks grew more frantic a brighter, fresher red joined the sauce already covering his skin.

Ethan couldn't think any longer. He ran, trying only to keep on his feet as others ran and shoved and screamed all around him. He didn't pause until he pushed his way through a door and stood in a corridor, listening to the cries in the restaurant as they grew shriller, always with the lower undertone of ravenous eating.

He blinked and looked around, and realised he did not know where he was.

The walls were different here, narrower and painted with some kind of mural, a line of shambling, blocky men. They reminded him of the photograph of a ruin he'd seen in his mother's book, the one she'd been reading at the airport – something he didn't want to think about now. These figures were brighter, not carved but painted in gaudy blues and yellows and reds. He knew he had never been this way before, but at least here, all was quiet. He turned very slowly and someone touched his shoulder. He almost screamed.

"*Shh*." The sound was barely audible.

It was the waiter who had been in the restaurant, the one who had made Ethan think that everything would be all right. Another man, thin, blond and blue-eyed, leaned against the wall behind him, as if trying to disappear into it. He looked terrified, his face white but with two hectic red circles patching his cheeks.

Ethan looked past them and realised where he was. It made him think of dead ends, of rats caught in a trap. He closed his eyes. He only opened them when the waiter tapped his shoulder once more. They were in the corridor that led to the kitchen. Ethan had wanted the lobby – he could find his way to the Kids' Club from there – but he hadn't been looking, had simply *run*, and he'd taken the wrong door somehow and now here he was, *trapped*.

The waiter put his finger to his lips again: "*Shh.*" Ethan scowled back. Did the man think he was stupid? He wasn't going to start calling out to those things. He peered back the way he had come, wondering if he had time to run down the corridor before those things came, and he saw the shadow that was creeping across the first of the lurching Mayan figures painted on the wall.

For a brief moment the shadow and the painting were almost perfectly aligned, their arms outstretched, one leg raised in a clumsy stride, and Ethan found himself straining his ears for the sound of its breath. But there was no breath. There was no breath because it was dead, the man was *dead*, but that wasn't stopping him taking another step down the corridor, and then another, and then he swung around the corner and Ethan saw his face.

The man didn't look like a monster. His face was almost whole, although his skin had a pallor that hadn't been there before. That was the first thing that struck Ethan. The next was that Ethan knew him. He had been in the restaurant with everyone else, perching on a chair while his wet swimming shorts dripped all over the carpet. Now it was blood that dripped from him – thin, watery blood – and then he half-turned and Ethan saw that he was a monster after all.

One hand had been de-gloved to the elbow, the skin dragged from it, and it was crimson, marbled with fat where the flesh had come away. It looked as if he'd been mauled by a shark, but the man did not seem to care. He moved like one of the dead men and his eyes were like theirs too, blank and with no humanity left in them. There was only hunger.

Ethan knew, when he saw those eyes, that the man was going to kill him. A few minutes ago he had been human, on holiday with his family, and now all that he had been was gone and only the monster remained. It was almost as if it had been there all along, lurking inside him, and in that moment it seemed like the worst thing of all.

The waiter – Mick – pulled on his arm, softly whispering: "Come."

Ethan allowed himself to be led away, keeping low as they ran down a corridor between metal cupboards and ovens, their feet too loud on the vinyl floor. Mick actually paused to reach out and switch off some of the burners as he passed, as if he were thinking of fire safety; as if that even mattered.

Ethan thought about sliding open one of the metal doors, climbing inside and closing it after him, but he knew from the relentless sound the thing made as it followed them that it would not stop. A simple door would not fool it. It would *smell* him. It would know he was there, drawn by its meat-hunger, and it would not pause until it had torn his flesh from his bones. Then he would be one of them.

That made him think of his mum, but in his mind she was like them too, her eyes pale and rimmed with yellow, and he let out a soft moan. The blond man pushed him hard and Ethan staggered, almost falling. Anger stabbed through him and he closed his hands into fists, realising that he was still gripping a knife, a useless piece of cutlery. He would need something bigger. Something sharper.

They turned the corner and saw only a wall covered with more cupboards and several large industrial fridges. There was no way out. All the strength went out of Ethan's legs in a rush. The monster was following them more quickly, shambling and rustling and knocking into things. There had been no point in running. Soon it would be upon them and it would eat them. And Ethan knew it would hurt, but then it wouldn't any longer, because after that there would only be blankness forever and ever.

Mick grabbed his hand, pulling hard. "There. Quick."

Ethan saw, with a surge of hope, that there was something there after all. What he'd taken for a blank section of wall was actually a small, featureless door, the kind that people might slip out of to smoke a cigarette during their break. They rushed towards it as a groan reverberated behind them. The blond man was following Ethan, still pushing hard, as if he wanted to get past him. Ethan stumbled, almost going to his knees. Mick's hand under his elbow saved him, and then the waiter struck out, hitting a small metal panel next to the door. A lock clicked open and they were through.

Ethan half-closed his eyes against the sudden blinding sunlight. Mick whirled, pushing the resisting door closed again. They were outside, not facing the pool but the side of the building, and they were screened by a line of extravagantly green and purple bushes growing in large white pots. It was oddly quiet, as if all sound had been cut off. Despite the sun Ethan felt cold, right through, but when he touched his face he felt oily sweat under his fingers.

He sensed movement to his side and turned to see the thin blond man hurrying away from them. He did not even look back before he reached the corner and was gone.

"Ass...hole," Mick pronounced carefully.

Ethan's hand shot to his lips, trying to keep a fat bubble of laughter inside, but it was too late. He glanced behind him in alarm, wondering if the monster had heard, just as something barged into the other side of the door with a muffled thud.

"Don't worry," Mick said. "It cannot get out."

It, Ethan thought, but he didn't say anything.

"We must go. Find help."

Ethan shook his head violently. "No," he said, "I have to get back in. I have to find my sister."

"You can't. They're inside. You must come away. We will find the *federales*."

Ethan did not reply. He didn't have to.

Mick sighed and leaned in closer. "They bite," he said, "did you see? You must take care. They bite or they scratch you and it spreads. You become like them."

Ethan met Mick's gaze, saw the earnestness in his expression, and slowly the knowledge spread through him: he was alone. His parents were gone.

Mick looked away, as if reading his thoughts. "I am sorry. I must go, do you understand? My brother is in the city. I must go to him." But he did not move. He just stood there, head down, rubbing the bridge of his nose. When he spoke again his voice was lower, resigned. "I will go with you first. I will show you the way, and that is all."

Ethan hadn't expected him to change his mind. He nodded vigorously.

"Then follow me. And keep quiet."

Mick crept to the corner of the building and Ethan followed. As he did so, he allowed himself to look down at last, not at his feet as he stepped across the baking ground, but at the back of his hand, to where the skin was broken by a long red scratch. He couldn't quite remember how it had happened. He only remembered his mother's face as his dad took her in his arms.

It spreads, he thought. *You become like them*.

He shook his head. She had scratched him before she'd been bitten, hadn't she? Before she became like the others. So it was just an ordinary scratch, something that could happen to anyone. It didn't have to mean anything.

He wondered what it would feel like if he was beginning to change. Would he be able to tell? Wouldn't there be – something?

He pushed the thought out of his mind, concentrating instead on his sister's face. Once he'd found Lily, it would be all right. He would know what to do. And help, by then, would surely have come.

He forced himself to walk quietly as he followed the waiter and saw what lay on the other side of the building.

Chapter Twenty

FRANCISCO CROUCHED DOWN behind a large case full of broken bones, holding the girl close. He listened hard. He had known there would be noise when they found her missing, but so soon? And this – it wasn't right. It was coming from outside for one thing, not from behind him; not from the Kids' Club.

He could feel the girl's gaze on him. Her hair, from the corner of his eye, was a golden halo. He turned to make sure that she wasn't about to start screaming, but she just stared at him with wide blue eyes and slipped her thumb into her mouth.

Crouching as he was, Francisco could feel his pistol digging into his lower back. He straightened and smoothed down his shirt. He didn't know what was going on, but he had seen El Calaca in the lobby and now there was screaming. The two things must surely be connected, although he didn't know how, and that was what worried him.

There must have been a part of their plan they hadn't told him. He didn't like the idea of that. He was a brother now, wasn't he? One of *Los Fieles*, the faithful. But then, perhaps they were only creating a diversion to help him do his part. Or maybe – the thought struck him now – his part wasn't the half of it. Perhaps it was Francisco who had been sent in to create a diversion for them.

The truth was, he didn't know; the family had kept it from him. And they hadn't even given him the means to contact them. He shook his head, hoping he was wrong. Anyway, he shouldn't have to contact them. Members of *Los Fieles* did not call for help; they simply did their duty. If he failed...

The girl pulled away from him and he yanked her back, his fingers reaching all the way around her upper arm. She started to wail and he yanked again, harder, and her eyes opened wide in shock.

He started down the corridor once more, pulling the child after him. Someone ran past the end of the passageway and he froze, but they didn't even look at him, just shot a glance back over their shoulder. Francisco reminded himself to walk as if he had every right to be there. He had a badge that proved he did. He straightened as he walked, pausing only where the passage opened out. He'd go across and he'd be outside. The car would be waiting for him. But in between...

Francisco couldn't work out what was happening. It was plain that something had happened because people were running, though they couldn't seem to agree on where to run to. Some still wore their scanty beach clothes and they dripped across the tiles as they went this way or that. As he watched, someone with bare feet slipped and went down, their face crumpling with pain as they hit the floor. No one stopped to help them.

Then came a muffled scream and everyone turned.

A woman with neatly bobbed grey hair and flowing white clothes was pressed up against a glass door, her hands spread against it, her face contorted with horror. Someone had slid the door on to its catch and no one moved to let her in. She grabbed the handle and it started to slide, and then someone did move. A balding man in a muscle shirt and shorts went and grabbed the handle on the inside, and Francisco realised that he wasn't helping at all; he was holding the door closed.

It wasn't his business. He had to keep hold of the kid, and anyway, he couldn't do anything that would attract attention. He started to tug the child away. All he needed to do was slip out of a side entrance and away. He was nearly there, and really, this couldn't have worked out better; everyone was looking in the other direction.

The woman screamed again and she turned, pressing her back to the door. Someone was walking towards her. Francisco couldn't see what the hell was going on but then they were on her, and he saw that there was something wrong with them; everything about them was grey and dripping and rotten, and they had seaweed in their hair and no face, *no face*, and they started to tear at her, not with knives but with their teeth.

There were more of them, all converging on the woman. She was on her knees and Francisco was glad he couldn't see her face any longer, because he could hear her pain. He had heard pain like that before, but here, in this open, shining place, he could not take it in. It was too big and too loud, her voice rising until it hurt his ears, and then she scratched against the glass with her bloodied hands and she half-pushed herself up.

Her once-white clothing hung loose and bloody, wrapped tightly around her body as if she were a bandaged mummy in some old film. She held out her arms as if imploring those inside to let her in. Chunks of flesh were missing from them. Her hands were bloodied stumps and there were no fingers left.

The others continued to tear at her. When Francisco wrenched his gaze from her terrified eyes, he saw them. His throat went dry; he almost let go of the kid. She had seen them too. She drew in a long breath as if preparing, and then she shrieked so shrilly it drilled through Francisco's brain. He snatched her up, shielding her face from the sight if only to make her stop, and he hurried back the way he had come.

When he reached the case full of broken and shattered things, he stopped and crouched down once more, letting his heartbeat slow. The blood was rushing in his ears so loudly he almost didn't hear the child's whisper: "Where's my mummy?"

He didn't answer, and after a moment she began to cry. Francisco blocked out the sound. He had to concentrate. There were exits everywhere, except now they weren't exits, were they? They were entrances. And those *things*...

Francisco took hold of the medallion around his neck and clutched it tightly, as if he could absorb the answer from the cold metal. As he did, the whole weight of his past seemed to press down on him. He had done terrible things and now terrible things had come to him.

He began whispering a Hail Mary, his lips moving rapidly over the words. He started as someone ran past, a woman with a young boy, herding him along. He heard the boy's question, his voice high and fluting: "What are they, Mum?"

Francisco stopped whispering. He felt cold all over. He shouldn't pray like this; he couldn't. He belonged to the dark now, to Our Lady of Death. He knew that he did, because he had seen his past looking back at him; he had seen their bloodied, peeling faces.

He had taken up the knife for his family. He had done whatever they asked him to do.

And now, before he could even be one with his brothers, their victims had returned for him. By the will of God, the *desollados* had come to take their revenge.

Chapter Twenty-One

STACY PULLED HARD at the door. It was plain and black and, according to the plans she'd seen, it opened on to a stair-well that led down into the high-tech heart of the pyramid, positioned not at its centre but in the basement. The control room was down there too, with a bank of CCTV screens that should show every part of the hotel. Everything she needed to see was there, and it struck her afresh how ridiculous it was that the door wouldn't open.

She let out a frustrated sound and stopped trying to insert her fingernails between the door and the jamb. The thing was locked and she was here, on the wrong side of it, and that was that.

The gun cabinet should be in the control room, tucked away behind another plain door, this one made of metal. It was so close, probably not so very far beneath her feet, but it might as well have been a hundred miles away.

A group of people stood close by, watching her futile efforts. They had moved with her like a cloud of mosquitoes. She sighed. She couldn't let them see her concern; she certainly wasn't about to show any fear. She had to *think*.

"Everyone, it would be best for now to return to your rooms," she said. "Please, try to stay calm." At that, from somewhere along the corridor, came the sound of glass shattering. Everyone moved a step closer to her.

"It's just the Day of the Dead, isn't it?" came a woman's tentative voice. "It's some kind of show, or something. Isn't that what they do here?"

"*Día de los muertos*! She's right. They're dressed up. It's – realistic . . . " The man's voice faltered.

Stacy drew a deep breath. She had seen people die. And everywhere, people were liable to panic. They'd trample over each other in their efforts to get away. That breaking glass – she glanced around. She couldn't see any of those *things* yet.

"*Día de los muertos* is in November." There was a clatter as someone dropped a bundle of wood on to the floor behind her. Stacy turned to see sections of broken timber, sharp and splintered and studded with nails. It was Alec McClelland. "Day of the Dead – it's in November. It's only just been Easter."

Of course, he was right. Stacy had heard there'd been arguments with the employment agency over people having to come in through Holy Week. She felt misgivings about that now; shook the thought away.

McClelland looked at her. "I said you need to gather weapons."

She scowled. "That's exactly what I'm about to do." She looked across the room, towards the glass doors of the hotel. Those *things* had been there before, but they did not appear to be there now. "You don't need to take things into your own hands, Mr McClelland. I'm in control of this. I'm about to go outside."

"Then you are a fool, Miss Keenan. And you are about to die."

The gathered people looked from Stacy to McClelland as if watching a tennis match. Stacy pressed her lips into a thin line, turned on her heel and walked towards the doors. Behind her was silence; no one followed. She did not look back.

The main doors were closed and she didn't plan on opening them. There was a smaller side exit, and she peered out of it. She could see the grassy banks that swept downwards from the side of the hotel towards the sea. A clean white H was carved into the grass and hibiscus swayed their orange heads in the flowerbeds. It was a picture of tidy tranquillity, until she looked at the brightly coloured hammocks that had been strung from a wooden frame on one side of the garden.

Something was hanging in them. No, there were two somethings, bundled like cocooned flies or a spider's eggs, heavy and sodden. Four of those things – *walkers*, she thought and did not know why – crouched around them, taking bites from whatever was wrapped inside.

Stacy blinked. Hair was hanging loose from one of the parcels. Something dripped steadily from it: blood. She grimaced, turned away, heard a voice at her ear. It was McClelland. "Human burrito," he said.

Her eyes narrowed in anger. He had followed her after all, to mock or to try telling her what to do, or maybe just to watch her die. "I'll thank you to keep back, Mr McClelland. Leave this to the official channels." *Official channels*. She was a head of security with no security guards and no guns, locked out of the control centre like a naughty child, and she hadn't the first clue what was going on.

He waved her onwards. "Be my guest."

She tossed her head in irritation. "I'm heading across that lawn. There's a gardeners' store. There'll be—"

He snorted. "You're going to keep those things off with a pitchfork?"

"I was thinking more like a machete."

He raised an eyebrow.

"There are bound to be some. There are coconuts here,

see?" She pointed upwards, trying not to see those things tucking into their meal from the corner of her eye. "Gardeners at hotels like these like that sort of thing. They use machetes to cut them open for the tourists, stick in a straw, and they get tips in return."

He leaned forwards and she waited for a sarcastic comment. It did not come. "You're right," he said. He met her eyes. "I'll come with you."

Stacy leaned in against the glass. She thought she could hear those things outside swallowing down flesh, a wet sound interspersed by the ripping of muscular tissue, then the sharp pop of a bone coming free of its socket. Then came the louder sound of wood striking wood. She jumped and turned to see McClelland selecting short, spiked sections from his heap of broken timber.

He came back, passed one to her. It was square and unwieldy and she could feel splinters jutting into her palms. She closed her hand tighter, relishing the discomfort, wondering how much worse it would feel to have that skin ripped from her, to feel teeth sinking into her body. She felt a wave of disorientation. Of all the things there were to fear in the world – disease, car accidents, even a bullet – she had never imagined this. She had never imagined the raw hunger of it: human flesh turned to nothing but meat.

"Okay?" McClelland's voice was soft, meant only for her, and that startled her more than his earlier pronouncements.

She nodded. "Follow me."

The heat that closed in as soon as they slipped out of the door felt like blood, warm and wet and somehow alive. Stacy kept her back to the building, sidling along it so that she was out of sight of the people within. They made her feel watched and that was a sensation she didn't need to feel; not until one of *them* saw her. She wondered briefly if she would still get that back-of-the-neck sensation if the eyes that were watching her were dead, and she pushed the thought aside.

It didn't make any sense, but then nothing did any longer. It was as if the world had been shunted into some parallel dimension, one where the dead walked under the sun and the living hid in the dark. Where movies became real and the watchers became – what? Victims?

She swallowed, feeling a line of sweat trickling down her lower back. "Over there," she said, pointing with the chunk of two-by-four she gripped.

"We can keep skirting the building, come in from the other side."

Stacy opened her mouth to protest at McClelland telling her what to do, then closed it again. What was the point? He was right. There was no way she wanted to head straight across the lawn. It would be suicide, right where everyone would be able to see, and she had an inkling that might just finish a few of them off. They'd seen enough already.

She led the way and McClelland followed, not saying a word. She wondered if, inside him, his thoughts were as disordered as her own. Just what had he seen on board the RFS *Demeter*? She tried to imagine being trapped in a cabin while dead things stalked the corridors, searching for prey. She couldn't.

Stacy stopped behind a blocky planter spilling over with creamy clusters of honeysuckle. She could smell their warm sweetness and the scent was of summer; of holidays and long evenings spent with an ice-cold glass of wine in her hand. She somehow felt nostalgic for the scent, even while it filled the air around her. It was as if she knew that everything had changed.

They had almost arrived at the corner of the pyramid. There was only a small stretch of lawn before they reached the store, a small wooden structure disguised by more planters. Someone had designed it all very carefully.

She could hear a shuffling sound, like dragging footsteps.

McClelland nudged her and she almost cried out. "Go," he said, and he led the way, his feet making no sound on the grass.

There was nothing else to do but follow, but Stacy couldn't seem to move. She forced air into her lungs, pushing herself away from the wall. She caught up with him by the small wooden door to the storage shed. A heavy, new-looking padlock hung from it. McClelland raised the wood he carried, ready to smash down, and she reached out and grabbed it.

"Wait." She bent lower, seeing that she was right. The padlock was in place but it hadn't been fully closed. Carefully – and quietly – she lifted it free and laid it down on the grass.

The door gave only a slight creak when it opened. It was dark inside the shed and it smelled of emptied plant pots, of green things, of the faint whiff of chemicals. There was a small window, but it looked as if it was made from clouded Perspex. Stacy pulled a cord just inside the door and a single bulb suspended from the roof began to glow. It cast deep shadows, highlighting the edges of various tools hanging from hooks on the wall: forks, spades, hoes, rakes. She eyed them with interest. On the other side was a rough pile of fraying rope, its bright colours snatching at the light. And there, on top of a row of cupboards at the back, was a machete, its blade dark grey and dull in the dim light.

McClelland strode towards it. Stacy reached out to pull him back, then realised he wasn't going for the machete after all; instead he picked up a half-empty packet of cigarettes that had been discarded on a shelf. She pulled a face.

He shrugged, then went instead to the rope, pulling on various strands as if testing it. It was a hammock like the ones strung outside and Stacy grimaced at the recollection of their grisly contents. It occurred to her now that there was only one way out of the shed, and that was behind them. They'd trapped themselves. They had better move fast.

She squeezed past McClelland, felt his muscular back

twitching as he wound the rope around his shoulder, and she took hold of the machete. She hung on to the two-by-four with her other hand. She could use that to keep them at bay while she hacked with the machete, couldn't she? She had a sudden image of herself sporting a sword and shield and it almost made her want to laugh. She realised she didn't even know if those things could be killed. They were dead already, weren't they?

"McClelland, how do you do it? Fight them, I mean?" She kept her voice low but she knew from the way he had gone still that he had heard. He did not reply.

Irritation, now familiar, rose within her. "You hid."

He still didn't move. Then he slowly turned, and despite the shadows she could see that his eyes were hard. "No," he said. "I survived."

And both of them jumped as something thudded against the door.

Chapter Twenty-Two

HECTOR RAN AHEAD of them like the cork bursting from a bottle and then skidded to a halt before they'd even reached the stairs. Celeste stopped dead behind him. She didn't know what he was doing, couldn't seem to gather her thoughts. She was running away from the man she loved, the one who needed help, but the image of his feral eyes wouldn't leave her mind.

Hector was hitting his hand against the small black door which presumably hid a lift. "Here!" he squeaked. "Come here!" The door didn't open.

"Quiet!" Shelby snapped.

"The shaft," Hector gasped. "We can force the door—"

Shelby pushed him hard. "Or just take the frickin' stairs, douchebag."

They headed down. Celeste had almost expected everything to have gone dark in the stairwell, but the lights placed at regular intervals shone steadily, showing the way. It was all normal, just like the stairs in any hotel, and she couldn't reconcile it with what she'd just seen. She had spent half her life feeling as if she'd stepped into a movie, with her superstar boyfriend and limos and beautiful things. Now it had all turned to horror.

Shelby started to pull ahead as they descended. The only sounds were the rushing patter of their feet and Hector, above them, gasping for breath. Then Celeste slowed. She leaned over the rail and said, "Shel... wait."

He had reached a corner and he looked back, exasperation written across his features. It struck her what good shape he was in for his age; that Louisiana, really, had been lucky...

She shook the thought of her friend away. "Shelby, I can't leave him."

"You what?"

"Colton's ill. He didn't know what he was doing. I have to help him, get a doctor."

He let out a hiss. "Honey, you go back there, you're minced."

"He... he wouldn't hurt me, Shelby."

He let out a laugh, glancing upwards at the way they had come.

"Sweetheart, that's not Colton. He's not in there any more. Don't you get it? He – he's a fucking zombie, for God's sake. Those things were eating people."

"No, I can't believe—"

"It doesn't matter what you believe. You fucking *saw* it. Look, if you want to do something useful, tell me you got your phone. I must've left my cell on the fucking table."

She held out her hands. She wore only a thin green cotton dress; she'd left her mobile behind too.

He sighed. "Right. Now get moving, before I drag you down here myself."

While Celeste stared down at Shelby, Hector caught up with her. He didn't pause as he passed, just plucked at her sleeve, more as if she were his mother who might save him rather than trying to hurry her along. After a moment, she followed.

At first, the stairs were narrow and walled in on both sides. After they'd gone down a couple of floors, however, they passed through a fire door and into a wider stairway. It struck Celeste for the first time how wasteful the pyramid's shape was in a hotel. The uppermost rooms were the most desirable, weren't they? That was where most hotels had their fanciest penthouse suites.

Here, the stairs wrapped around a central square well. And a sound echoed up it, one that made her wish for the protective closeness of walls once more. She leaned over the balustrade only to see Shelby's greying head thrust over the gap on the level below hers. There was nothing there, only the clean white rail wrapping round and round, but she could still hear that sound, eerie and distorted – a long, drawn-out keening.

It was Hector who was first to move. "I'm getting out," he said quite clearly, despite his shortness of breath. He kept on down the stairs to the next landing and pushed his way through the door and was gone, on to whatever floor of the hotel they had reached – ninth? Tenth? Celeste wasn't sure.

"Thank fuck for that," Shelby whispered. "On the other hand, I think he's right. We should get off these stairs. Whatever it is, it sounds like there are more of them down there."

Chapter Twenty-Three

ETHAN POKED HIS head around the side of the building, below Mick's, and looked out over the pool area. From here, he wouldn't have known there was anything much wrong. A woman in a wide-brimmed hat took hesitant, shuffling steps along the wet tiles, like someone who'd had too many tequilas. A cluster of holidaymakers stood outside the restaurant, looking in at the windows. A man sat atop the waterslide and peered down at the tourists in the water.

And then he made out the bloodstains on the shuffling woman's dress. The window, a short distance from the window-gazers, was shattered into gleaming monsters' teeth. And the man on the waterslide hadn't paused there to enjoy the sun pouring down on to his bared torso. He was clutching at the edges with white knuckles, as if he was afraid of the water; the water that wasn't even blue any longer.

But of course he wasn't afraid of the water. He was afraid of the people – or what had once been people – standing waist-high in the pool, facing the slide, waiting for him to let go. Another pawed at the ladder, too clumsy to climb. A woman and a child, along with a young couple – one with a strip of skin missing from his scalp and dangling at his shoulder – stood where the slide entered the water in the form of an open serpent's mouth. One of them patted at it, as if he wished he could climb it, or as if it were his pet.

Mick sighed. "We need to go back inside," he whispered. "We will just have to take a quieter way in."

Ethan nodded. A part of him wanted to stay where he was and simply give up. Those things had already got inside the hotel, had burst out of the restaurant. They hadn't had any mercy, hadn't spared anyone who got in their way.

He thought of Lily once more and anger rose within him. He nodded curtly and took one last look around just as the man clinging to the waterslide turned his head. Their eyes met. The man froze and then mouthed, "Help me."

Ethan's throat went dry. He couldn't look away. He could see the man's scalp through his thinning hair, and it was a deep unhealthy pink, not from any wound that Ethan could see but from the sun. His shoulders were a slightly deeper version of the same shade. The man was roasting alive and he had no sun lotion and no water to drink and no one to help him.

He looked down at the pool. It was pale pink, but clots of deeper red spiralled through it, and things he didn't want to examine more closely were floating on the surface. One of the objects was bobbing like an inflatable toy, but not like any that Ethan had ever seen. He realised it was an arm.

At the same moment he recognised it, it drifted within the notice of the woman standing at the foot of the slide. She reached for it, her hand splashing down uselessly. Ethan saw that she was pretty. Her hair was blonde and she had lovely bow lips and she grasped out again, pulling the sodden thing to her, and she lowered those perfect lips to the ragged thing and started to eat. Viscous-looking water ran down her chin. She did not stop to wipe it off. The man standing nearby tried to grab her meal and she let out an animal snarl and snatched it away. He followed. He grappled with her and she slipped, went into the water. She came up spitting and squalling, still grasping for her prize.

Ethan looked back at the man who was waiting at the top of the slide. They regarded each other.

Mick very gently took hold of Ethan's chin and turned his head so that he was facing forward. "Better that you do not look."

"But—"

"We cannot help him. We find your sister and we go."

Realisation swept over Ethan. There was nothing he could do. They had no weapons and they were outnumbered; all they could do for the man would be to die in his place. And he had to get to his sister.

It struck him how quiet everything was. There was no happy shouting coming from the sea, no sizzle of a barbecue or calls to the waiter to bring more drinks. There was only the steady beating of fists against glass and the indescribable sounds coming from the feasting at the pool.

When Mick starting walking again, Ethan followed. He did not look back.

Chapter Twenty-Four

AT THE SOUND of thudding Stacy leaped, not away from the outbuilding's door, but towards it. She hit it with her full bodyweight and it slammed closed just as a swollen, bloodied hand slipped into the gap.

She flinched at the sound of crushing bone and cartilage, but she didn't stop pushing against the door. The thing's fingers twitched, opening and closing like a starfish, and then the skin gave at the wrist and a yellowish substance spurted from it, splashing her bared leg. She cried out in disgust.

McClelland had somehow got himself tangled in the hammock and was trying to free himself. Stacy had dropped the machete and she opened her mouth to tell him, but he'd seen it already. He threw the skein of ropes to the floor and snatched it up, adjusting his grip. Stacy was sliding backwards under the force put upon the door from the other side. She couldn't help it. That thing was strong, much stronger than she'd expected.

McClelland nodded, a signal she understood at once, and she flung herself back and away. She crashed into the tools hanging from the wall and they clattered into each other, a rake falling to the ground with a metallic ringing sound. She reached out, trying to steady the rest, to keep them from falling and making more noise. At the same time she twisted, trying to see the thing – the monster – that stood in the doorway.

She had expected it to be a man, but she didn't know what it was. It didn't have a face. Only shreds of skin clung to the empurpled flesh beneath. This thing shouldn't be walking, shouldn't even be moving. Maggots writhed in its empty eye sockets and she only had time to think *they only feed on dead flesh* before McClelland stepped in front of her and swung downwards.

She swivelled and grasped for one of the tools hanging on the wall, but she heard the sound of bone splitting and turned to see McClelland's machete embedded in the creature's skull. The smell had been bad, but now it was worse and she knew she would be smelling it for some time, that it would embed itself in her mucus membranes, that it would stay with her long after she'd tried to block the sight of it from her memory.

The thing didn't stop moving. It turned, clumsy, and grabbed McClelland by the neck of his shirt, and she heard it rip.

A hole opened in the purple mess that had once been a person's face. It had yellowed teeth that were a little too long, a single silver filling flashing incongruously as it closed on him, but McClelland pulled back, wrenching the machete from its head. It gave with a sticky sound and he swung again.

The weapon found the groove it had already made and sunk in deeper. This time the effect was startling. The thing did not cry out, but it slumped to the floor with a wet sound. More of that foul-smelling ichor leaked from it, spreading outward and towards the door.

Stacy didn't want to think about stepping through it. She could still feel the putrescence on her skin; she didn't even want to touch it to wipe it away. The thought of doing so made her gorge rise.

"Out. Quick." McClelland paused only to snatch up the hammock and another object – he'd found a second machete at the back of a shelf – and he strode through the stuff, opening the door to sunlight and clean air. Stacy hopped over the body and stumbled outside, her hand across her mouth.

She doubled over, retching, hawking up a thin phlegm that only made her feel worse. Then she looked up and saw them shambling towards her, three of them – what appeared to have once been a family. The man's nose was streaked with sun-block that stood out brightly against his greying skin. His wife's sarong, half-untied, trailed behind her. The boy, no more than ten or eleven, still had bright orange armbands wrapped around his bite-marked skin. When he opened his mouth he revealed the clumps of meat that were caught between his teeth. He looked as if he'd been buried up to the gills in raw flesh, and judging by his expression, he was hungry for more.

Stacy's breath whistled in her throat. The sound seemed to come from a long way away. She remained frozen for a moment longer and then she turned and felt something being pushed into her hand. She wrapped her fingers around it and raised it in front of her. She was struck, suddenly and forcefully, with a sense of the surreal. Was she really threatening the guests she was supposed to protect – one of them a *child* – with a machete?

McClelland stepped to her side. He held his own machete, the strap wrapped around one wrist.

The three looked up, moaned, quickened their pace. Stacy could hear the boy's teeth snapping together.

"You know," McClelland said, "I think we might do better to run."

And so they did.

Chapter Twenty-Five

ETHAN AND MICK walked quietly down a long corridor. It wasn't like the public areas of the hotel. The walls looked as if they'd only had one coat of paint and the floor was covered in plain grey lino. Mick had said it was a service corridor and that it led to the other side of the hotel. He hadn't seemed too sure but Ethan had to trust him, because he'd lost track of the corridor's turns. Everything must have been orientated north, south, east or west, but it was narrow and claustrophobic and he couldn't seem to think.

Mick turned and put his finger to his lips, but there was no need to do so. They had kept quiet the whole way, though there had been sounds: distant bangs and the breaking of glass and, worse still, the screams. Ethan just wished they would reach somewhere, and soon. It would save him from the images that kept rising before him. Nothing made any sense any more. He couldn't believe in any of it; he surely must be dreaming. Soon he'd wake up and he'd be at home. That made him think of his mum, smiling when he went down for breakfast.

He'd dreamed about her too, hadn't he? She had been kissing Dad, or rather, Dad had been kissing her. There had been something wrong with that kiss, and he told himself it was probably because he hadn't seen his mum do more than peck his dad's cheek in a long time. Except he knew that wasn't it, not really.

Thankfully, there was a door ahead of them. It looked identical to other doors they'd passed, but Mick pressed his ear to this one and listened. Ethan couldn't hear anything at all. The noise of the door pushing free of the jamb made him jump.

On the other side was a tiny lobby, with more corridors leading away to the left and right and straight ahead. The space would have fitted into the main reception area many times over but they'd decorated it anyway, with another one of those display cases full of broken things. Ahead, Ethan could just make out the glass façade of a small gift shop. It held all the same sort of things as the tourist shops in the airport – bright weaving, colourful pottery, sombreros with little dangling fringes.

Mick gave a low whistle as he stepped towards the display case. He seemed to have forgotten the need for silence. "Look!" he said.

Ethan looked. Inside the case were fragments of pottery, ancient and dusty looking. There wasn't anything he wanted to see. Then he realised what Mick was looking at and his eyes widened.

There were blades in there, made of what looked like old, chipped black stone. And a bigger object, long and sturdy with smaller pieces of that same rock sticking out of it, leaning against the back of the case as if they hadn't known where to put it.

"Obsidian," Mick whispered. "It is glass from volcanoes, yes? Important in the Maya culture, in my culture. Before there was metal."

Ethan shifted his feet. What was the use of all that old stuff? The thought of going up against those dead, walking things with old blunt blades was ludicrous. They had to get moving, but Mick showed no sign of wanting to leave. He looked almost hypnotised.

He put out a hand and rested it against the glass. "It is a *macuahuitl*," he said, his voice breathy with awe. "They were used in ritual... in sacrifice. Or just in battle. Someone here is a very rich man, my friend. It was said there are none of these left – that they are only in pictures now."

"Mick, we should go."

He stirred from his reverie. "We shall," he said, grinning. "And this shall come too."

"Why? It's a stick."

Mick's look was incredulous. "No. It is a – what do you call it? A club. A club that cuts, see?" He indicated the pieces of sharpened obsidian set into its side. "My people used them against the conquistadors. They are said to be made so clever, that the pieces could never be pulled out or broken. Once, they used one to cut off the head of a Spaniard's horse with a single blow. Like a Maya chainsaw, yes?" He laughed.

Ethan didn't laugh – he didn't think he'd ever laugh again – but he stared as Mick slipped off his shirt and wrapped it around his fist. "I do not think the rich man will mind," he said. "We need it more than him. Anyway, this thing should not be here. It should be in a museum." He stopped and spoke in a lower voice. "Perhaps that is why. Perhaps the gods really are angry."

Ethan didn't know what he meant, but he knew to step away from the case as Mick drew back his hand. He didn't think that the glass would break, but it did; it shattered at once, flying into jagged shards. Mick knocked them away before lifting the object from the case. It was heavy and beautifully carved, and Ethan could see at a glance how valuable it was. He was surprised that there hadn't been an alarm, that the room wasn't suddenly flooding with security guards.

Mick cradled the artefact as if he barely dared to touch it, let alone wield it. He turned to face the left-hand corridor. "It is not far," he said.

Ethan's heart leaped at the thought of seeing Lily. She might only be moments away. He could get her and go. He might never see those awful dead things again. The thought that he didn't know where to go hovered somewhere in the recesses of his mind, but he pushed it away and started walking.

Mick's whisper was urgent. "Wait! Not so fast. You don't know—"

It was too late. Ethan hurried along the corridor as far as he could see, and turned around the corner.

Chapter Twenty-Six

"WE SHOULD GET ourselves into a room, kid," Shelby panted.

Celeste frowned. They'd worked their way around this floor of the hotel. It hadn't taken long because they were still near the top of the structure, where the pyramid was narrower. Every time they had turned a corner she expected to see Colton ahead of them. Maybe it would even be the old Colton, the one she knew; the one that used to have feelings, that used to whisper to her in the night, when he slipped his arms around her and held her close. Not that awful thing that wore his hair and face and eyes; the thing that was now empty.

"We can't," she said. "We have to get out, Shelby. We have to get to the ground and call for some help."

"That's exactly what we're gonna do, sweet cheeks. We'll get into a room up here – not ours, they're too far – and we'll use their phone. We'll call the cops and the fire brigade and whatever the hell else they've got out here. A priest, maybe. Yeah, that should do it. And then I'm gonna get on to the office and call a damned chopper to get out here and pick us the hell up."

Celeste stared at him. Why hadn't she thought of that? They had money. They should use it. And then the cavalry would come; there would be people with guns and doctors and nurses in neat white uniforms and they would make Colton better. Everything could be all right again.

Relief and gratitude flooded through her, and then she looked along the line of closed doors and it faded. Those doors were heavy, she knew. They opened using key cards, ones they didn't have, and she remembered how solidly the locks thunked into place when they were closed.

Shelby walked up to the first of them. "Piece of cake," he said, tipping her a wink, and he reached out and knocked.

Celeste almost laughed out loud.

When no one answered he went to the next and knocked on that too. Then the next. At the fifth knock, she heard footsteps padding across the floor. A moment later a woman appeared in the doorway, one towel wrapped around her body, another turbaned around her hair. She had white towelling hotel slippers on her feet. She didn't speak, just raised her eyebrows.

"Ma'am, we really need to use your phone."

Her questioning look changed to a scowl. "You what? It's a hotel. Go find one." She began to close the door in their faces and Shelby slipped his foot into the gap.

"Are you fucking joking? Do you know who I am? I – I'll scream." The woman's aggressive tone belied the sudden fear in her eyes.

Celeste grasped Shelby's shoulder and spoke as soothingly as she could. "I'm really sorry, but my – someone attacked us. I'm not sure what's going on, but we can't get to our rooms and we can't get down to Reception, so we'd really appreciate some help."

The woman opened the door a few more inches, then slammed it on Shelby's foot. He howled, pulling it back, but then he threw himself into the door. It flew inward and the woman stumbled, clutching at her towel as the other slipped from her wet blonde hair. She turned and ran for the bathroom and Shelby started after her, then stopped, standing there, letting her go. She slammed the door closed and Celeste heard the bolt shoot home. Then came the scrape of a window opening and the woman shouting, "Help me! There's an intruder in my room. Karen Gallagher, 938. Please!"

Shelby turned to Celeste and shrugged. "Good luck with *that*," he muttered.

Celeste wasn't really listening to his words. She crossed to the window that looked out across the balcony, on to a bright, sunshiny afternoon. She could see the road leading away from the hotel, though no one was on it now. Beyond that was the city. A plume of smoke rose and hung in the air above it, tainting the skyline of another beautiful day in paradise.

Chapter Twenty-Seven

STACY STUMBLED TOWARDS the pyramid, heading for the same glass door they'd left by. A man was standing on the other side of it and she suddenly knew from the way he was clutching the handle that he wasn't going to let them back in. When he saw her, though – or perhaps it was the expression on her face – he stood aside. He didn't help, but he didn't try to stop them as she opened it and waited for McClelland to squeeze through the gap with his bulky load before closing it again.

He let the hammock fall to the floor, keeping hold of the machete.

"That's it?" said an older man with a balding pate. "That's how you're going to protect us?" He snorted, turning to his girlfriend, whose orange perma-tan almost seemed to glow. "That's how they're gonna protect us."

"We're calling the cops," she said, addressing McClelland. "Soon as they answer, they'll be all over this. I had to leave my shoes by the pool. Do you know what they cost?" She turned to her sugar daddy. "Do they know what they cost?"

He patted her on the shoulder. "They will, sweetheart. As soon as my lawyer gets on this."

Stacy cleared her throat and they turned to glare at her instead. She tried to force a patient smile on to her face and found she couldn't. The memory of the faceless body on the floor in the shed was too fresh. She wondered why the guests couldn't detect that smell on her clothes, embedded in her skin.

"We'll take care of this," she said, because that's all she could say. "McClelland, there's an events room right in the centre of this floor – for parties and conferences and such. There are no exterior doors, although you'll need to barricade the internal ones. Please take our guests there and I'll sort this out."

He sputtered. "What the hell are you thinking of doing?"

"There aren't that many of them. I'm going after them. If they won't listen to reason – if they keep hurting people – I'm going to stop them." Stacy tightened her grip on her machete. In a lower voice she said, "Look, I can't get to the guns. There must be some malfunction in the security systems. But I'll find a way – it's my responsibility."

"The hell it is. You didn't come on board for this."

"You don't get to choose for me, I'm afraid, Mr McClelland." She gave a wry smile.

He shook his head, looked around at Sugar Daddy. "You're capable of running away all by yourself, right?" He made a vague gesture. "Inside's that way." He picked up the hammock once more, hoisting it over his shoulder so that it wouldn't impede his arm movement. "There. It looks like I'm with you, Miss Keenan."

She opened her mouth to protest but stopped. She could hear something. It was the flat sound of bare feet striking a hard floor, padding towards them, and then the group surged away from it, pushing her and McClelland back.

An old woman was walking towards them. It looked as if she was wearing a nightgown, though it hadn't been night-time – jet lag, perhaps? – and she still wore a lustrous string of pearls about her neck. A nimbus of white hair surrounded her

NO LIFEGUARD
ON DUTY

wrinkled, greying face. She did not hurry, just walked towards the group, looking around like a tourist at a buffet who doesn't know where to start. Then her hand darted out, so fast, and she caught a young man by his ear just as if he was the naughty pupil in class.

He yelled and started beating at her hand, but her grip was iron. She kept on pulling and though she was half his size and half his weight, he was dragged steadily towards her, twisting his face away from her snapping teeth. Ready for bed or not, the woman was wearing dentures. They were coming loose, *clack-clacking* against her soft palate, but it didn't slow her down.

Stacy started pushing people aside, but then the girl with the orange tan snatched up one of the pieces of wood McClelland had gathered earlier and ran towards the woman. She whacked her, full force, around the head, and the dull *thock* echoed from the walls.

The old woman did not let go of the man's ear, but her gaze swivelled towards the source of the attack. The girl wasn't daunted. She looked furious, as if she'd found the source of her annoyance about her precious holiday, her precious shoes. She swung back the length of planking she carried and this time brought it down flat on top of the woman's white head.

Stacy winced at the sound; she couldn't help it.

The old woman did not. She didn't even look surprised. Her free hand darted out and caught hold of Orange Girl's hair.

She started to scream, batting at the woman's hand. The crowd backed further away, making it plain they weren't about to get involved, and Orange Girl's boyfriend moved with them.

The old lady pulled her in close, as if she wanted to whisper in her ear. Instead she opened her mouth wide and the dentures fell to the tiles with a dull *clack*. Ignoring the pendant of drool hanging from her lips, the woman closed her mouth around the girl's head. Her jaws worked, while Orange Girl beat at her, bucking and jerking in her efforts to get away. The old woman seemed to tire of her efforts just as Stacy pushed free of the group and strode towards them. She let go of the man's ear – he staggered back, red-faced with embarrassment or effort – and the woman clawed her fingers into Orange Girl's face.

The skin gave with an awful juicy noise and blood, too bright, spattered everywhere. Stacy made an odd sound in the back of her throat. She froze. The woman started to gum the slippery red stuff, the girl screaming now, animal shrieks of distress.

A piece of her skin came loose with a sound that reminded Stacy of McClelland's ripping shirt. The old woman jerked her head like a seabird trying to swallow a fish. The red stuff went down, a tuft of hair going in last, protruding from her lips. She closed her mouth on it, looking around, her eyes gleaming white. She turned towards the man who'd got away and let go of the girl, who fell to the floor with a smack.

McClelland strode up to her, his machete raised. She didn't even see him coming. He swiped downwards and cracked her skull.

There was very little blood, but grey matter flew and people jumped away with cries of disgust. The woman went loose at once. She fell to her knees, her nightgown riding up, showing spindly pale legs riddled with varicose veins, and as she tipped forwards her skull gave up the rest of its contents. Grey pulp spattered on to the tiles like overcooked stew tipped from a pot. Stacy closed her eyes against the sound. It was like someone vomiting. Then the woman fell forwards, on to her face, mercifully covering her blank expression.

Stacy felt the ghost of sympathy, or at least the knowledge that she *should* pity this small, helpless old woman, even if she could not. Then, quickly, it passed. She looked down instead at the machete gripped in her numb fingers as McClelland bent and wiped his blade on the back of the old woman's nightgown. The metal clicked against her pearls.

He straightened and looked around. "I think you should all make your way to the conference room *now*," he said. That broke the spell that was holding them in place. They moved as one towards the centre of the building, some of them almost falling in their haste. McClelland called after them, "And pick up anyone – anyone safe, that is – on the way!"

Only Orange Girl's boyfriend remained. He stood there, head down, staring at what had been his lovely young girlfriend. She was still lying on the floor, and then, as if he'd called her back with his gaze, she started to push herself up.

Her arm didn't bend properly, as if it had been broken in her fall. That did not stop her. She used it anyway, the elbow deformed and elastic, and she pushed herself on to her knees and then to her feet. She looked as if she were hanging in front of them like a loose-limbed puppet.

Blood still leaked from her scalp and from the slit in her skin that almost reached her eye. It had spread through her hair, staining her roots, and for some reason that made Stacy want to laugh. She kept it inside, wondering how much expensive moisturiser the girl had rubbed into her broken skin, how much she'd spent on the tan that was now streaked with a brighter tone.

The girl raised her head and Stacy let out a dry squeak.

It was when she heard that sound that Stacy knew she was in trouble. It was the sound a frightened child might make and she wished she could take it back, but it was too late; it was out there.

Orange Girl's eyes weren't haughty any longer. All human expression had been burned away, leaving behind only hunger; unnatural, insatiable hunger. Stacy had no doubt that the girl was dead. Whatever the old woman had, it had passed on with her bite. Now it was too late. The girl's wound wasn't fatal, but somehow it had finished her anyway, and if Stacy didn't move she would soon be dead too.

The girl stick-stepped towards her and stretched out her hands, looking more than ever like a puppet.

McClelland hoisted the machete back over his shoulder, but Stacy got in first. She went in low but swept upward, and her blade buried itself in Orange Girl's face.

She wasn't orange any longer. A gaping wound opened from just above her lips, through her nose and across her cheek. A flap of skin fell open, revealing muscle and bone and gristle, a bright flash of whitened teeth incongruous amidst the congealed matter, and then Stacy struck again because the girl hadn't even moved.

Her machete rose and fell until the sound it made grew softer. Wetter. Stacy couldn't see, but she kept on striking down. When she stopped, gore was spread in a wide circle around her and the girl had finally stopped moving. Her head and neck and most of her shoulders were pulped.

Stacy realised she couldn't see properly because her eyes had filled with tears. She couldn't shift that image in her mind of the girl smearing instant tan over her pert little nose and her smooth cheeks. Now there was only this, and she couldn't bear to look at it any longer.

She turned away, towards a window that was filled with sunlight, and she didn't realise that McClelland had moved with her until she felt his hand on her arm. She jumped, raising her blade once more.

"Woah – easy, tiger." His voice was soft. He peered into her eyes. "You okay, Keenan? It's tough, the first time."

The first time? Stacy stared at him, wondering if he meant the man-woman thing in the storage shed or something else. Exactly how much had he seen on board the *Demeter* before sequestering himself in his cabin?

She took a deep breath, trying not to look at the blood

and brains plastered across the floor. "I'm fine," she said. "We should go through the restaurant first. Judging by the sound, it's where they got in. Most of them might still be there. We can confine them."

He lifted his hand from her arm as if she'd burned him, his expression resigned and perhaps a little disappointed. He reached for his pocket, busied himself taking out one of the gardener's cigarettes; then he pulled a face. "No fucking lighter. Got soaked." He looked down at the bodies. "I don't suppose..."

"No." Stacy half-turned away. "Anyway, those things'll kill you."

He looked at her, startled, and she found herself laughing as he let out a dry spurt of air. It faded quickly; she was still trying to shake off the things she'd seen. Then she said, "Just out of interest, exactly what *are* you planning to do with the hammock? Offer them a nice little sleep, or just strangle them with it?"

"Oh, I'm not going to use it to kill them." His grin was wolfish. "I'm going to catch one of the bastards. It's the first rule of hunting: know your enemy. Well, we will – as soon as we can get a good look at one of them. Right up close and personal."

Chapter Twenty-Eight

THERE WAS A child in the corridor in front of Ethan. It was sitting on a little blue plastic tricycle and it was dead. It had once been a boy, but now it was a monster and its eyes were pale and rimmed with crimson. It looked as if something ancient lived inside those eyes. It looked hungry.

Ethan heard Mick walk up behind him, but he did not turn. He had the feeling that something very, very nasty would happen if he did. He couldn't even look away from the boy. He felt half-hypnotised, though he knew the kid was fully aware and watching him, with fascination but without malice, as a cat watches a bird. Its lips popped open and a string of drool descended from them along with a hollow, shapeless sound.

Ethan's guts turned to water. From somewhere behind the child there came another sound, one he'd heard before: *clap-clap-clap.*

We are the happy kids, he thought, and he swallowed down his despair. The clapping meant life, didn't it? It meant the other children were playing in there. It meant Lily was safe. He straightened, taking a deep breath with the taint of rot in it. *Zombie stink*, he thought.

Mick, at his side, held the *macuahuitl* in front of him. The movement was half-hearted; he did not raise it. Ethan felt relief at that. The idea of watching the child be clubbed to death, being cut open with those black blades...

But then, the kid was already dead.

The boy leaned forwards, pressing down on the pedals. He grunted as he did so, the sound more like a death rattle than anything intentional. The tricycle began to move. It rolled towards them and stopped, the kid too clumsy to pedal properly, probably too clumsy even to extricate himself from the pedals. Ethan saw that the boy had an ear missing. He was also missing the two smallest fingers on the hand clutching the handlebars.

There came another sound as the tricycle moved again, followed by a metallic scrape as the child's feet jammed in the pedals. Then a softer *hhhhh* on a stretch of brightly coloured rug and the rumble of plastic wheels on tile and the kid seemed to get the hang of it, bending lower, baring his teeth as he picked up speed. *Brrrr... hhhhh... brrrr... hhhhh...*

Mick and Ethan shot each other a panicked glance. They started to back away, but Ethan realised he couldn't do that, couldn't just turn and run. He nodded to Mick as if he'd know what to do and he darted aside, sliding along the wall, his knees turning to rubber when the child leaned out and snapped at him with his neat little white teeth.

The boy's impetus carried him straight past Ethan and Lily's face rose in his mind, clear as sunlight. He hurried onwards, only glancing back when he reached the brightly painted doors with KIDS CLUB adorning the outside. He saw Mick fending off the boy, not striking him with the club but prodding at him with the end of it, keeping him away. The kid was trapped between the steering wheel and his prey and he couldn't reach, but he kept snatching at the air, his hands flailing, his nails skittering off the plastic trike.

One scratch, thought Ethan, knowing he had to move fast, and he burst in through the double doors and stopped.

All around him, faces looked up. Round, cherubic faces, smeared in what looked like jam, and what struck him first was the silence; a moment of perfect stillness before the first one pushed herself to her feet and toddled towards him, arms outstretched, just as Lily used to do before she grew steadier on her feet. He stepped back, fear threatening to smother him, and looked around wildly.

There was a whole cluster of children in the middle of the room and he realised that they were sitting on top of something. One of them stood, a boy of five or six, leaving a gap through which Ethan could see ribs and the purplish-grey of organ meats. His eyes widened as he saw a shred of T-shirt and realised it was *her*, Lauren, one of the girls who'd run the Kids' Club, who'd taken Lily's hand and giggled as Lily skipped along at her side.

Lily.

Ethan opened his mouth to call her name, knowing it was already too late. The boy was coming for him too, and more of them were standing, swallowing down their grisly meal, holding out their hands to him as if offering hugs.

Then he saw her and everything stopped.

Her golden curls were dampened and sticking to her forehead. Her little dress – the blue one, wasn't it? – wasn't blue any longer. She sat on the floor at the back of the room, by a stack of fallen building blocks. Her Mary-Jane shoes stuck out in front of her and waggled to and fro, in just the way she always did. Her eyes were no longer the clear blue of the sky and all the life in them had gone. The bottom half of her face was a mask of blood.

Ethan's gaze fell away from those terrible eyes and he saw the thing his sister held. It was a girl's hand, curled and grey and missing most of the flesh from its fingers. Lily waggled that too and the flat of the dismembered palm struck the floor – *clap-clap-clap*.

Blackness came down across Ethan's vision. It didn't matter any longer, none of it mattered. He was making an odd sound, couldn't understand how he was making a noise like that, and then he saw that the others were coming for him. They were so awful, so *wrong*, that he moved without thinking; he turned and ran, staggering through the doors and back into the corridor.

The kid had partly wriggled free from the tricycle and was leaning over the handlebars, snapping his teeth in anticipation. Mick struck down on the plastic as a warning, but the boy didn't even flinch. Ethan moved towards them on legs made of rubber and Mick's look of fear gave way to relief, as if Ethan could help, as if he was any use at all.

Ethan hurried anyway, not wanting to see him die. He gestured for Mick to go, just *go*. He couldn't find his voice, but he knew from the noises behind him that the children were following. Mick's eyes opened wider and Ethan knew he must have seen.

Suddenly the waiter was all purpose – he thrust the *macuahuitl* towards the boy's face, lifting it clear at the last moment, and then he kicked out instead. His leg whipped through the air and his shoe met the boy's skull with a dull *thwap*. The kid flew back, his teeth still snapping. His legs were still caught in the trike and Ethan heard the loud crack of breaking bone.

The kid immediately started wriggling to get free. Ethan didn't wait to see what injuries he had. The two of them ran back the way they had come, away from the horrors they had seen. As soon as they reached a door, Mick grabbed Ethan's sleeve and pulled him through.

There were stairs in front of them and Ethan followed as the waiter started up. The boy had no will left inside him.

All he could think of was his sweet sister, stinking of death and drowning in blood, her mouth stuffed full of the flesh of the living.

Chapter Twenty-Nine

FRANCISCO DRAGGED THE child behind him. She hung from his hand, dead weight, and he pulled harder. He didn't have time for this. He didn't have time for her tears and her pouty little mouth and her sulking. Everyone was alone in life, at least until they found their true family; the kid would discover that for herself soon enough.

He could hear the *desollados*, their moans echoing down the long corridors just as if they'd been designed to amplify and distort the sound. It seemed to be coming from everywhere and nowhere at once. But then, perhaps it was; maybe it was coming from the very walls, sent by Heaven itself to torture him. Perhaps, worse still, it was coming from nowhere. It might all be in his head.

He touched a hand to the gun tucked into his belt. That at least was real and could be counted on. He hadn't bothered to hide it with his shirt; he didn't want to get it caught in the fabric if he needed it in a hurry. The stupid kid didn't even seem to know what it was, had only stared at it with her eyes wide.

When he'd been little more than her age, he'd been living on the streets.

He shook that thought away. All he had to do was keep his head until he could get out of here, but the hotel, once he'd left the main passageways, was like a maze. He kept turning towards what should have been the outer doors only to find more internal corridors, zigging and zagging until his sense of direction was lost. This must be some kind of staff section; there weren't even any signs. If only he could get outside, or at least find a window…

The kid started to wail. He yanked on her hand and her whole arm jerked, her teeth snapping together. For a moment she looked shocked and tears sprang to her eyes. Then she opened her mouth to cry harder.

"*Silencio*!" His voice was harsh and her face screwed up in despair. Francisco bent to her. He hadn't meant to yank so hard. It felt as if he'd nearly pulled her shoulder from its socket. "*Silencio*," he said more softly, putting his fingers to his lips.

After a moment she subsided but the wailing went on, growing louder, and then a shadow swung across the wall ahead of them. Without thinking, Francisco pushed the child behind him. The shadow was lurching and swaying across the wall, its shape suggesting something human, the way it moved suggesting otherwise.

Francisco found himself holding his breath. Then it appeared, one of *them*, heading straight towards him, and he grabbed for his gun. It was heavy in his hand. He had used it several times and he'd even pretended he liked it, but he never had become accustomed to the solid heft of it. The grip was cold and rough against his palm. It had belonged to another member of *Los Fieles* before him; he'd seen that from the notches cut roughly into the grip, had wondered what they signified. He'd never allowed himself to think too deeply about it.

The thing lumbered down the middle of the corridor. He barely had time to register that it wasn't a *desollado*, that it had a face, when the gun bucked in his hand. A small red hole appeared in its chest. The thing seemed less surprised at the gun's report than Francisco. It stalled but it did not go down. No blood spread from the wound. It did not appear to be wearing a bulletproof vest – how on earth had it remained standing?

Francisco's mind blanked. It was impossible, wasn't it? The thing took another lurching step towards him. But of course, it did; he could see that it was not of this earth. He could see it in its yellow-rimmed eyes. It was the punishment that had been sent for him and it would not stop.

He took a step back, felt the small hands of the child wrapping around his leg. He let out an odd sound, feeling glad for a moment that his brothers in *Los Fieles* were not around – they would never tolerate a weakness like that – and he forced himself to aim and fire again, this time execution-style.

The thing's head disintegrated into a cloud of blood and bone and brain that spattered against the wall and began to run down it, leaving grey clumps and streaks of red so dark they were almost black. The body fell heavily to the floor and did not move.

So that worked, anyway. Francisco's ears still rang with the gunshot. For a moment it drowned out everything else, but then the girl's panicked shrieks emerged from the high-pitched sound. He turned and grabbed her, shaking her hard. All sound faded again but he could see her crying, and he raised his hand to strike her cheek.

His ears popped and he could hear again. He could hear that the kid was crying because she was terrified. He let his hand fall to his side, took a deep breath. He could smell something too, the sharp odour of an interrogation cell, and he realised that the girl was overcome; her bladder had let go.

He grimaced and forced himself not to pull away. He did not want to touch her again, but he wiped the tears from her cheek. "Stay here," he said. "You understand? You stay here."

He walked slowly towards the body lying on the floor. It didn't look so terrible now, not so much like something from another world. It was simply a man, someone who was running to fat and losing their hair. His face was relaxed, almost normal looking apart from the small bullet hole dead centre in his forehead. It had been a neat execution; a true death.

Francisco leaned in closer. There was something wrong with the picture, wasn't there? This man could never have had anything to do with *Los Fieles*. He looked like a tourist. He had the paunch and pale sagging cheeks of someone who spent his afternoons doing a crossword puzzle before pouring himself a glass of whisky. Someone who was leaving the middle years behind him, settling into comfort and obscurity – someone harmless. He was no drug trafficker or member of the *federales* who'd refused to take a bribe.

Francisco scanned down the body, taking in the spattered linen shirt, the shorts, the hairy white legs and the ribbed socks tucked into leather sandals. One sock had come down, was wrinkled around the man's pasty ankle. A gobbet of grey matter clung to it, gelatinous and globular.

Francisco shook his head. He could not understand what had happened. Dead things were walking and El Calaca, a follower of *La Poderosa Señora*, was here in the hotel. The things had to be connected – but how? And just what was it that El Calaca had done?

The girl started to stumble away, moving like one of those dead things, supporting herself with one hand against the wall. "No, no, no." Francisco hurried over to her, prising her hand away, grasping it in his. He led her back in the other direction, guiding her as they stepped around the man lying in the middle of the floor. It wasn't until they were past and he saw the glassiness in her eyes that he realised he should have shielded her from it. He could have spared her the sight of the twice-dead man.

"It's all right, little one," he said. "Come."

As she did, she stopped hanging back and clung to his hand as they made their way onward. Ahead of them, the corridor ended in a white door. Francisco gave the kid's hand a reassuring squeeze as they walked towards it. There was no need for her to know that he hadn't the first idea what lay on the other side.

Chapter Thirty

THERE WEREN'T AS many zombies as Stacy had expected. That realisation came as a relief, but it was followed by new concern. If they weren't here, then where the hell were they?

The restaurant looked as if a herd of bulls had stampeded through it. Tables were upturned and the floor was littered with shards of broken china, cutlery and tablecloths, and everywhere there was blood.

There was very little left of the bodies. She looked around for the remains of those who'd been attacked, but there were no remains. Neither was there silence. The rattle of wood against wood drew her attention to the farthest corner. A dead woman was standing there, almost naked and with chunks of flesh missing from her torso. Her skin was blotched and swollen and bruise-coloured with putrefaction. She pawed at a couple of tables, one lying on its side, the other roughly stacked on top of it. There was a boy standing just behind her and he too was grasping at the lowest table, as if trying to climb it. The woman's fingers caught under the top one and at once she began to lift it. With a shock, Stacy realised that someone was crouching behind the upturned furniture.

Their pale freckled arms brandished a chair leg, thrusting the woman back.

"Quick!" McClelland moved first, stomping through the mess, not heeding the noise he made. He unwrapped the hammock from his shoulder as he went, spreading the rope in his hands. Stacy hastened after him. The zombie woman hadn't turned, but soon she would.

McClelland called out, "Hey, in there! It's okay. We're coming to get you."

The woman turned. It looked as if half her face had been clawed off and one eye was nothing but a putrid hole. Stacy just had time to make out a broken, pink-painted fingernail jutting from the mess, and then she was moving, raising her machete as McClelland threw the hammock over the woman's head.

She barely reacted, just looked around as if struggling to process this new information, and she stepped towards McClelland. Her grey lips drew back from her teeth. He didn't move, just readied himself to try to grab the ropes, and Stacy jumped to his side and swung.

Her strike was more effective than she'd expected. The blade bit into the woman's neck, making a sound like old, rotten wood. There was hardly any blood and it looked the wrong colour, too dark and too viscous, and then the woman tried to turn her head and it tilted at an odd angle. It slipped to one side as her neck split around the weapon and finished up resting on her chest, still facing outward. She peered at Stacy with one rolling eye. Stacy pulled the blade free as McClelland shouted, "*No!*" and she struck again, severing the last of the skin and slicing through the vertebrae; the woman's head dropped to the floor and rolled.

Stacy stepped away; she couldn't help it. The headless torso collapsed in a heap.

Then the topmost table crashed down too.

A tall and skinny man emerged from behind it. He didn't look as if there was any strength left in him. His light brown hair was plastered to his head with sweat and his eyes were glazed over, so that for a moment, Stacy wondered if he was one of *them*. He clutched the chair leg like a baseball bat and swung, hard and fast.

The force of it connecting with the child's head made a loud *thwack*. The kid spun, his hands flailing, and then he was up again, faster than she'd expected. He circled the gangling man who'd hit him. Then he snapped out his hands and caught hold of the other end of the chair leg. In the next instant he'd pulled it out of the man's hands and hurled it across the room. It *pranged* off the far wall. He was strong, this boy. Stacy could see from the lanky man's face that he had seen it too, that unnatural strength.

Stacy braced her feet and swung the machete. The blow wasn't clean. She caught him half across one side of his face and a gaping wound appeared, but while it filled her with horror, it did not even give the boy pause. He did turn, though, and he came for her instead.

She slashed at him, and then again. She kept going and suddenly his skull gave way with an awful soft sound. Grey matter sploshed from it and Stacy jerked away, not wanting the vile stuff on her skin.

There was silence. McClelland stepped forward and stood at her side. All three of them regarded the thing that had once been a child. Stacy's hands started to shake. She couldn't seem to stop them. She was appalled by the sight of the small crumpled body in front of her. She had never come close in her life to deciding to be a mother, but she realised now that she had always supposed it would one day happen. Now she wasn't so sure.

She felt McClelland's hand on her shoulder. His touch was gentle, but when he spoke his voice was light. "That's nasty."

The tall, skinny man let out a spurt of air. "Oh, yeah," he agreed.

"But that thing—" McClelland's hand squeezed – "it wasn't a kid."

Stacy pulled away from him and doubled over to retch. After a moment she straightened and wiped her mouth. There was nothing inside; she felt hollow. She looked at McClelland, shrugged. "Not any longer, it's not."

The two men laughed. Stacy couldn't laugh. She felt as if she'd never laugh again.

McClelland went over to the other, larger body, and started disentangling his precious hammock. As he did, he glanced up at the newcomer. "Name?"

"Craig. Good to meet you."

The platitude had come so automatically, was so much a part of a world that seemed to be fast disappearing, that Stacy suddenly *did* want to laugh.

McClelland nodded. "You got such a thing as a cigarette lighter, Craig?"

The man nodded back. He took it from his pocket and tossed it to McClelland, who grinned. "You know, you look like you might be useful. You should come along with us."

Chapter Thirty-One

ETHAN FOLLOWED MICK down a new corridor. Everything was unearthly quiet but he still couldn't think. Each time his thoughts turned to what they were supposed to do next, he saw his sister's face, the way she had been in the airport – laughing over calling him a silly name. Then she was different, her blonde curls dabbled in gore, her beautiful eyes turned cold. His own eyes kept filling with tears and he let them fall. Mick was too busy looking ahead to notice and Ethan was grateful for that. If it hadn't been for the waiter, he would have curled up and died. He'd probably have sat down in the middle of the Kids' Club and let them have him.

If they had, would he be like them now? Wandering about, not a care in the world – like his mum and dad?

That was something else he couldn't bear to think about.

They made their way around the outermost corridor of the pyramid. This was a guest floor and it was lined with doors, all marked with room numbers. They hadn't heard a thing; it seemed nobody was home. As they approached the corner, however, there came the hushing of wheels on carpet.

Ethan thought of the kid on the tricycle and he stopped

dead. Something trundled around the corner: a maid's cart, laden with a rubbish bag and sheets and cleaning things, ordinary things for an ordinary day. Then the woman who was pushing it stepped into view and he saw that nothing was ordinary after all.

She was a Mexican girl of maybe nineteen or twenty, with a braid of lustrous black hair and neat, pretty features, but she didn't look pretty now. There was something wrong with her. She was deathly pale and beads of sweat stood out on her forehead. She appeared to be shivering violently. She wearily raised her head, as if it was too heavy for her to lift, and she saw them.

Her eyes were glazed but they did not look filmed over, like the others' had. She gave a slight nod, as if wishing them a good day. There was a bandage wrapped around her arm. Ethan could see the discoloured veins beneath it, radiating under her skin to the short sleeve of her blouse.

Mick put out an arm to stop Ethan, holding the club tightly with his other hand, but it wasn't necessary; he had already stopped.

A sound pierced the quiet, making Ethan jump; a high-pitched "*Eeeeeeeee* . . ."

He couldn't move. There were footsteps, running along the corridor around the corner, getting louder. He braced himself, preparing to turn and run, but there was no time. A man emerged, a portly fellow in navy shorts that didn't suit him and a khaki staff shirt with a name badge. A fire extinguisher was hefted on to his shoulder.

"*Eeeeeeeeeeee* . . ." he cried, his cheeks wobbling and pink, and the girl didn't turn but he shifted his grip on the extinguisher and swung. It connected with her head with a metallic *clang*. The girl crumpled like paper. She went down on to her knees and started to turn her head as he swung again, the blow landing full in her face.

Ethan heard the *crump* as her nose shattered, spattering blood – *real* blood – and her head flew back and he heard the sound as her neck broke. He would replay it afterwards, that sound, and he would try to tell himself that it wasn't right, that surely couldn't have been what he'd heard, but the sick crunch of bone would never really leave him again.

"*Eeeeeeeeee!*" The man pounded down with the fire extinguisher as she collapsed to the floor, a limp dead thing. He did not stop until her head was pulped, her brains spread around her like a pool of vomit.

A foul taste flooded Ethan's mouth. He retched but nothing came up, only a thin drool that he wiped away. He couldn't look at the girl on the floor. He somehow felt he should, as if he owed it to her in some way, but he still couldn't bring himself to do it.

The portly man turned to them. He looked them up and down and then he smiled. "Afternoon," he said, as if he were ... *a cleaner, come to do their room*, Ethan thought, and instantly felt sick again. "I dealt with her." The man pulled a key card from his pocket and waved it in front of them, as if they'd been waiting for it all along.

"We should get inside," he said, "don't you think? It's a master key. Pick a room! It's yours." He didn't wait for a reply but went to the nearest door. The edge of the man's shoe just touched the grey mush on the carpet and Ethan suddenly felt faint. He leaned against the wall. Everything was too much for him after all. He would simply stay here, stay until some crazy creature from the land of nightmare came and ate him. Maybe that thing would be his mum.

"My name's Hector," the man said, his voice cheery.

"I know," Mick muttered, but Hector didn't seem to notice as he pushed the door open, revealing an ordinary room with an unmade bed, bottles of perfume and tubes of make-up scattered across the dressing table.

Ethan looked at his friend. His face was closed, his lips pressed into a tight line, but when the door started to close behind Hector he reached out and grabbed it and ushered Ethan inside.

Hector had gone straight to the minibar. He took out the tiny bottles, set them on top and seized a little packet of peanuts, which he ripped open and tipped into his mouth. He'd stuffed the key card into the top pocket of his shirt and he took it out again, waving it as if it explained everything. "Master key," he said. "I can go anywhere. Anywhere!"

Ethan slumped on to the floor. All he wanted to do was lie on the bed and drift, let everything go, but Hector was standing next to it and he somehow didn't want to go near him.

Mick went to the minibar, took a bottle of water and handed it to Ethan. The boy didn't want it, but he took it anyway, nodding gratefully. He didn't know why the waiter was still with him. Hadn't he wanted to go and find his brother? But he'd stayed.

He drank some of the cold liquid and found it good. His head felt clearer at once, but he still couldn't make sense of anything. Had he really seen the things he'd seen? He opened his mouth, not sure what he was going to say, and then he said: "She was sweating – that girl with the trolley. Those things don't sweat, do they? Even in the heat."

No one replied. Hector plonked himself down on the bed, stuffing more peanuts into his mouth, spilling them across the coverlet. He stared at the opposite wall, as if they weren't even there.

"The boy's right," said Mick.

Hector sucked in a long breath. "Well, she would have been," he said. "She was turning."

"But she *wasn't* one of them. She wasn't even dead. Not until—"

Hector looked petulant; it was the expression a child might wear. "She would have been one of them any second. She would have killed us all. You should thank me."

No one spoke. Hector looked at them, anger and disbelief written on his face. And he froze.

At first, Ethan couldn't tell what he was looking at; then he knew. He glanced down to the bottle of water he held in his hand.

"You're scratched," Hector said. "You're infected."

Ethan put out his hand. The scratch – the last thing his mother had ever given him – was a red line across his skin.

"Out," Hector said. "Out! He stepped towards the fire extinguisher on the floor.

Mick held out a hand. "You don't touch him."

"I do! I bloody well do." Hector strode towards Ethan and dragged him to his feet, then started pulling him, not towards the door but the windows. "Throw him off!" he said. "Off the balcony!" He almost sang the words. He sounded as if he had lost his mind.

Ethan tried to shake him off, but the man's grip was like iron, and anyway, there was no strength left in him. It had seeped away, the moment he had seen his sister's face steeped in blood.

"You will stop." Mick moved around Hector, standing between him and the window.

Hector's eyes widened in disbelief. "You don't tell me what to do. Anyway, don't you see? He's one of them. He has to go. Off the balcony with him, see him fly..."

Mick raised the *macuahuitl*.

Hector looked at Mick with new interest in his eyes. Then he shifted his gaze to the *macuahuitl*, and his expression became suddenly greedy. He let go of Ethan's arm; it was as if he'd forgotten him altogether. He stepped instead towards the waiter, as if drawn by some magnetic force.

A sound rang out from somewhere inside the hotel, loud and unmistakeable.

They stared at each other. It came again – another gunshot.

"You see," Mick said, "there is enough death. No one else gets hurt, not here."

Hector shook himself, as if he'd been doused in water. "Well, I'm not staying. Not with him." He was all indignation, as if Mick had suggested he should eat a lizard. "There's no way I'll stay in a room with that. It's no good asking me to!"

He stalked towards the door, and Mick and Ethan met each other's eyes. Mick's lip twitched.

Hector turned and came back again, his haughty stride almost making him waddle, and he bent and picked up the bloody fire extinguisher from the floor. He hefted it on to his shoulder and dragged open the door to the corridor before pulling it hard with one hand. The door swung to, slowing before it reached the jamb; it *shushed* closed behind him.

A sputtering laugh escaped from Mick's lips. Ethan smiled back at him. It was a real smile, the first thing in some time that actually felt good, but that thought only reminded him of what he had seen and it faded. "Where's he going?" he asked.

Mick shrugged. "Who cares? He can go anywhere he likes. He has the master key, doesn't he?"

Chapter Thirty-Two

SHELBY SIGHED AS the woman in the bathroom began to pound on the door, as if they were keeping her prisoner. He sat down on the bed, a few inches away from Celeste, and she edged back from him, drawing up her legs and wrapping her arms around them. He'd pulled packets of sweets from the minibar, had crammed a Mars bar down his throat, and now he tossed chocolates into his mouth one by one. Celeste hadn't touched her share. She didn't feel hungry; she felt like she never would be again.

Outside, they had heard an inarticulate grunting followed by shuffling as something passed by their door. She had hardly dared to breathe. When it had passed Shelby tried the phone, saying something about getting a chopper to get them out, but he hadn't even got a dial tone. He'd been about to slam it down, but remembered himself, or perhaps that shuffling, and replaced the handset quietly. Celeste had thought of her mobile phone, probably spilled to the floor on the rooftop along with Shelby's. It seemed impossible that they should have no way of calling for help.

Shelby swallowed another chocolate, his Adam's apple

dipping. "Only the dead are eating well tonight."

Celeste roused herself. "They're not dead. They can't be."

"Of course they're dead."

The casualness of the way he said it, his acceptance, made her unaccountably angry. It was as if he and Louisiana had simply walked away from each other, with no harm done and nothing to bind them, as if she had no further part to play in his life. "You don't even care, do you? Lou wanted to *marry* you. Do you know that?"

He let out a dry spurt of a laugh. "Of course I did. Come on, Cele. You know what she was. Louisiana just wanted the money, baby. She wanted all of the money, and she didn't really care where she got it, you hear me?"

She stared at him, incredulous. Then she sighed. "She was my friend, Shelby. I know what she was. But... what does that make you, exactly?"

He regarded her, then threw back his head and laughed. "Oh, I know what I am, sweetheart. And believe me, introspection doesn't suit me." When he spoke again his voice was lower. "How about you, Cele? Do you want me to tell you what you are?"

She fell silent. She looked away, staring down at the patterned carpet.

"You don't? Well, why don't you tell me, honeybun?"

She drew in a deep breath. It was as if a chasm was opening before her. Colton had always been there; it was him who made everything all right. He would have put his arms around her and told her she was special. Now his arms weren't there to define her any longer. And all she could think of was her odd ancestry, so long ago: a woman who ran away from her husband to bear a child with someone else, his face a blank. The woman who should have been Thomas Moreby's wife.

"I don't know," she whispered. "I really don't know what I am."

"Well, there's your problem, sugar. Right there."

Shelby tossed another chocolate into his mouth. They sat in silence as, beyond the window, the sky began to change from the faintest of blues to the bloody hues of sunset. It took Celeste a while to realise that the sounds coming from the bathroom had stopped. She didn't even think about it; her eyes were closing. At some point she must have slept, at least until the door went crashing back on its hinges and Karen Gallagher came storming out.

Karen had managed to prise the shower rail free of the wall. It was pointing straight at Celeste's head, trailing its torn white plastic curtain like a pennant. She shrieked as Karen came at her, eyes open wide, her lips drawn back from her teeth. Celeste was half-dazed from sleep but she saw Shelby stirring, grabbing the thing nearest to hand, and he suddenly threw his chocolates in the woman's direction, as if that could stop her.

They scattered uselessly and Celeste threw herself across the floor as the pole passed inches from her face. Without thinking, she stuck out her foot and Karen fell over it, sprawling across the bed. Shelby grabbed the telephone, then one of the woman's hands, wrapping the cord round and round it. He grabbed her other wrist.

"Go!" he shouted, and Celeste didn't need telling twice.

Chapter Thirty-Three

FRANCISCO GAVE UP on dragging the kid down the corridor. He wasn't even sure that *Los Fieles* would want her any longer – it had all gone too crazy for that. Who would pay for her safe return? Her rich-ass parents were probably shambling around the hotel, hands outstretched, moaning for a good uncooked breakfast.

He stared down at her and she looked back at him. He realised she hadn't spoken in a long time. There was no comprehension in her face at all; even the fear seemed to have left her.

Francisco let out a sigh of exasperation and he scooped her up into his arms. Instantly, she wrapped her hands around his neck, as if it was the most natural thing in the world. He stopped dead. He wanted to prise her fingers away, and at the same time, he didn't. He tried to remember if he'd ever clung like that to his mother. If he had, he couldn't remember. What he mainly remembered was the time after his grandmother died; hard mornings on the street before the sun rose, sitting on the paving in ripped and dirty clothes. Sharing his bed with the rats in the *barrio*. Panhandling for small coins that wouldn't even buy a hot meal. Until *Los Fieles* found him.

The girl swivelled her head, her curls tickling his nose. He resisted the urge to smile, reminding himself that this kid had probably never gone hungry in her life. But then, she was probably hungry now. He whispered something in her ear – "Come, *niña*" – and he carried her along the corridor. He had no idea where they were going, but as he walked, one of the doors in front of him slowly opened.

His steps slowed and stopped altogether. Someone's head appeared, almost comically, halfway down the door, peering around it towards Francisco. It was a white guy, a tourist, wearing an open shirt and with a deep tan.

"Thank fuck for that," he said in an American accent, and Francisco felt a stab of irritation at him using such words in front of the kid. Then he wondered why it could even matter.

"I thought you were a zombie," he said. "You're not a zombie, are you? Come in, if you want. There's plenty of room."

Francisco went to the door and looked in. It was a narrow storeroom, lit by a single naked light bulb. The shelves lining each wall made it smaller still. They were stacked high with sheets that had never been slept in and fresh pillows smelling of their plastic wrappers.

"I'm Larry," the guy said. "Here to shoot a film. Can you believe that? Now look at this place. And I don't even have my camera." He laughed – he had a high-pitched giggle – and he clapped Francisco on the shoulder. Francisco looked down at the man's hand until he removed it.

"So, what's your story?" Larry said.

Francisco just gave him a look. He shifted his grip on the girl.

"You rescue her? You a hero, is that it? I should get my camera. I really should. No one's gonna believe—"

At that moment, a group of zombies came around the corner.

They looked like a mariachi band. They moved in a tight

group; all of them wore little black jackets with fancy white trim, and red kerchiefs were bunched at their necks. Francisco wasn't sure that red was their original colour. One had striped ruffles around his upper arms, and most were still wearing wide sombreros with tassels dangling from the rim. Their blank dead faces belied their party clothes, as did the gashes in their skin, their white staring eyes.

They saw Francisco and the girl – a handily packaged snack with blonde locks – and they started to hurry, stumbling into each other in their haste. One went down and started to drag himself along the floor towards them, some thin yellow substance oozing from his lips.

Francisco didn't think. He leaped into the storeroom, realising at once that he should have run instead. Larry pushed after him, blocking Francisco's way out, and he slammed the door closed. Immediately, hands started hammering against the wood.

Francisco swung the girl to the floor and went to help hold the door closed. The noise continued, a percussive beat that echoed inside his head, and he closed his eyes, could almost hear the relentless tones of "Canción de Mariachi" building until he wanted to scream. He thought they'd stop – surely they were too stupid to keep trying to break through, they'd get bored, go in search of easier meat – but instead the blows intensified.

The door jumped under his hands and he heard a splintering sound. He wedged one foot against it, leaned over and grabbed the nearest stack of shelves. Larry leaned over him, helping to pull, and the shelf tipped. Sheets spilled and they ducked under them, edging back into the even tighter space behind the angled shelf. The banging on the door continued.

The girl had sunk down on to a pile of pillows. She looked exhausted. Night was closing in and, impossibly, she looked like she was going to sleep. Perhaps that was how children like her responded to fear: by switching off, making it all go away. Francisco wished he could do the same.

The thought struck him that if he could get out somehow, he could leave her here with this man. Larry looked around and Francisco saw the fear written across his features and he knew that he never could. He had stolen her and now he was responsible for her. Like it or not, she was his.

He touched a hand to the gun at his belt and looked at the door. He already knew there were way too many of them. Lady Death had triumphed and these were her minions, the things she had summoned. But it wasn't glorious, like El Calaca had always told them. What was it he had said? That no one brings man closer to God than death.

Beneath the battering noise, Larry started talking. His voice was dazed, as if everything had caught up with him or he'd just woken up. He looked around at Francisco. "Where the hell is this place?"

Francisco shook his head. The obvious answers no longer seemed to fit. They were in a storeroom in a new hotel on the Pacific coast of Mexico – and yet they weren't. They were in a situation for which no one had a name. They had been caught halfway between Heaven and Hell, in a place that couldn't possibly exist.

Chapter Thirty-Four

CELESTE RAN. IN the distance she could hear the sound of hands beating on wood, but she kept on going; there would be another stairway soon, wouldn't there? Shelby caught up with her, his breath rasping. "There," he said, pointing, and she yanked open the door to the stairs. Shelby ran into the back of her as she forced herself to stop and listen. There was nothing.

"This is our chance, hon. Let's get the hell out of this place." He nudged her through and Celeste started down, more quickly than she'd thought she could on her shaking legs. She didn't stop until they'd reached the ground floor. As her hand closed on the door handle she felt her spirits lift: they'd soon be clear of whatever had happened. Help would come.

"Go," Shelby said, and Celeste tugged the door open. They practically fell through it.

Celeste couldn't think which was the best way to turn. She heard Shelby's breath catch in his throat – the sound of a man choking, or perhaps having a heart attack – and she whirled to see if he was all right; she saw the zombies filling the corridor behind him.

Her chest tightened. There were maybe ten or eleven of

them, and Colton was at their head. He was barely recognisable as the man that he had been. His grey hair was bedraggled with blood. His eyes had faded as if cataracts had spread over them, but they were rimmed with red. His expression was that of a rabid beast, and Celeste's insides turned to water as he approached.

She turned, almost tripping over her own feet. Shelby grasped for her hand, to comfort her or himself, she didn't know which and didn't stop to find out; she pelted to the corner and swung around it. There was an open doorway up ahead. Her own breath made a pained squealing as she ran, and then someone stepped out just beyond the doorframe – a tall man who was slapping the blade of a machete into his palm. Her heart quailed, but she knew what followed was worse, and so she kept running towards him, and he stepped aside as she and Shelby passed through.

Something rustled behind her and a moment later the door slammed shut. Hands started to bang and slap against it. Celeste fell to the ground, hitting hard tile, as someone gave a cry of triumph and Shelby said: "Jesus, man."

She pushed herself up, wiping her bloodied palms down her thin green summer dress, remembering only then that Colton had bought it for her. She turned to see what had happened and she gawped.

Colton was there, hanging upside down, suspended in what appeared to be a brightly coloured hammock. His damp hair dangled through the gaps. He snarled and writhed but couldn't get free. The man with the machete stood in front of him, one hand on his hip. There was a woman there too, in staff uniform, and a thin young man. More banging on the door told her that Colton's new friends had found themselves shut out.

"Right," the woman said to one of her companions, "We have one. Happy now? Just what do you plan to do with it?"

The man with the machete tilted his head. "I want to know what they *are*. We know they feed, but I want to know if they're actually hungry or if something else is driving them."

"What could that possibly matter?"

He shrugged. "It might. As I said, know your enemy. I want to know what really makes them tick. And exactly how much it takes to kill them."

"How do you plan to do that?"

Celeste wanted to know that too, but he didn't reply. He just gripped the weapon with both hands and raised it. She stepped forward and grabbed hold of his arm. "I can't let you do that. That's my husband." She looked at Colton, twisting in his desperation to get at them, his grey lips flecked with what appeared to be liquefying flesh. He smelled like something that had been dug up from the ground.

"That *was* your husband," the man said.

Shelby put his hand on hers. "He's gone," he said. "Colton's gone, sweetie, and if it wasn't for these dudes we'd have been a light supper, nothing more."

"But that's just it," the man said. "Do they really consume human flesh? Because, you know, they're *dead*. How the hell do they digest anything?" His expression was musing.

"I don't care," Celeste said. Tears rose to her eyes and she felt the sorrow that was waiting, threatening to overwhelm her. "You can't hurt him."

The woman was at her side. "I'm Stacy," she said softly. "That's McClelland, and Craig. You need to step aside now. Let us do what needs to be done."

"No, I—"

Shelby hooked his hand around her arm and started pulling her aside. Celeste shook him off, but as she did McClelland struck out with the machete, slicing across Colton's midriff.

Celeste cried out. Colton's skin split with the sound of ripping paper. He didn't cry out, didn't even react. He just stared out at her with those awful pale grey eyes, and he didn't flinch as a mess of blood and stringy intestines flopped down on to his chest and dripped across his face. He didn't move until the red-brown mess reached his lips and then he started to lick, suddenly desperate, sucking it back down inside him, and the wound at his belly flexed as more waste pulsed from it.

Small, interlinked bones – which looked like someone's fingers – fell through a hole in the rope and pattered to the floor. Then something else, something that looked impossible to swallow, though at once she pictured his throat working, his hunger, his *need*. It fell to the tiles with a thin, shell-crack sound, and she realised it was a piece of bone, the skin still clinging to it. It was somebody's nose.

Her legs gave. Shelby couldn't hold her and she sagged to the floor. She knew whose nose it was. She knew how much they'd dreamed of a nose like that, how much they'd paid for it to be that snub shape, and then blood dripped from the thing that was clinging to it by shreds of skin and she realised what it was and she couldn't help it – her hand shot to her mouth and she wailed.

It was an eye. It was Louisiana's eye, and it was looking at her. As she watched, more skin slid down across it, just as if her friend had winked at her.

Celeste's head swam. There was a foul smell, an *old* smell, but now there was a fresher blood smell too. She wished she could just pass out so she wouldn't have to breathe it any longer. She wouldn't have to look into that single blue eye. The edges of the world faded but immediately started to come back. She heard Shelby's voice saying, "There, it's okay," and she suddenly wanted to punch him right in his stupid smug face.

Another voice cut in: McClelland's. "Christ," he said, "so, they have an appetite; but shit, they don't digest well, do they?"

Someone else said, "I should take a picture."

Celeste slowly raised her head. Craig had pulled a smartphone from his pocket, was fiddling with the screen. He held it out in front of him and a white light shone from it, highlighting the brightly coloured rope, reflecting back from Colton's empty eyes. In the next second, a hand snaked through a rent in the rope and grabbed Craig's outstretched wrist.

He cried out and writhed, his struggles echoing Colton's own of a moment before. McClelland leaped forward but he was too late; Colton had pulled him in close, had latched on to his arm with his teeth. He began to chew, gulping something down, red matter slipping from his lips and falling to the floor to merge with the contents of his belly. He bit down again and twisted his head, ripping flesh from the bone. When he swallowed, more of it spilled from the wound McClelland had made, fresh meat pulped and purged, right in front of Craig's horrified face.

Then the door burst open.

Chapter Thirty-Five

"YOU KNOW," MICK said, "there is a story that says the world will end along with the Maya calendar. That when the current period, known as a *baktun*, is finished, that's it. There is nothing more."

Ethan shrugged. He couldn't muster the energy for anything else. Mick had waved him towards the bed but there was no way he could sleep. Mick was sitting on the floor, his back to the minibar, staring into the dusk. He still held the obsidian-bladed club in his hands.

"We have day-keepers who keep track of the days. Perhaps my people knew this would happen."

Ethan roused himself. "Then why here? Wouldn't the end come at one of the big ruins?" He remembered his mum, reading to them from her book about Chichen Itza and Coba. "Why isn't it at one of the Mayan places? There are no ruins here."

"You mean *Maya*," Mick said softly. "The Maya places. And – aren't there? The *Monumento que Canta* is here. That is Maya. It is also called the *Tumba que Canta* – the tomb that sings. Did you know that?"

Ethan shook his head, though he realised that he had heard of it. It was the thing on the roof, wasn't it? The one that was to have been the backdrop for Colton Creed's performance.

That made him think of the excitement he'd felt when he first heard his hero's voice ringing out above the hotel. He hadn't known that was all there was going to be. Now there would be no big show, no lights, no fireworks. At least he'd listened while he could.

Mick went quiet for a while. Then he said, "Do you think there is a god of death?"

Ethan closed his eyes. He didn't want to think of that. He just wanted to be a long way away, back in his old house with his mum and dad and his little sister, Lily no doubt coming into his room without asking and annoying him. He wished she'd walk in through the door now. He'd do anything to be annoyed by her again. Now it was almost as if he was the child, being lulled to sleep by a bedtime story.

"My people, we are Catholic now, but we still have the old gods too. We have statues of the *santos* – the saints – but we make our own offerings. Candles, incense. Chickens, sometimes." He sighed. "There is a Maya death god. Ah Puch, we call him, but he has many names. Hunahau, Kisin, Yum-Kimil. The Aztecs knew him too: to them he was Mictlantecuhtli, the grinning god of death.

"Ah Puch is a rotting corpse. Sometimes he wears the head of the evil bird – the owl. Sometimes he wears the eyes of the dead on his helmet. There is only one way to escape his notice."

Ethan stirred. "There is? What way?"

Mick half-smiled. "If he is by, you must howl," he said. "Moan. Scream. Ah Puch will think you are troubled by demons already. He will pass you by. If he thinks you are one of the dead, he will not drag you down to *Mitnal* – to the lowest level of Hell." He paused. "Those things out there – perhaps our offerings were not enough. Perhaps they did not like this place, using the sacred things this way. Perhaps it is only that they want the old days back again. In those times, there were human sacrifices. The chosen ones, they were thrown into the *cenotes* – the sacred wells. They could not get out."

It was almost dark, but Ethan could see him shaking his head.

"I do not think even that would be enough for these evil things," Mick continued. "I think sacrifices will only make them hungrier. Like gods who only want more, the more you give."

They fell silent for a while. Even though it was growing dark, the hotel was not still. There were noises: stirrings, banging, the distant sound of what might have been running feet.

Ethan was no longer sure Mick was still awake. He wasn't sure he heard it when Ethan whispered, "Those things aren't evil. They're us."

Chapter Thirty-Six

LARRY COVERED HIS head with his arms, crouching with his back to the storeroom wall as if he could shut out the sound. The door didn't show any sign of breaking. Francisco glanced at the kid. Her face had relaxed in sleep, her lips pursed like little rosebuds, blowing spit bubbles as she breathed. Francisco grimaced. He doubted he'd ever looked like that as a kid. He could never have been that innocent. He had always known what life was – something that could be snatched away from you at any moment, no matter how much you struggled. He was under no illusions about that now.

They could only hole up here for so long. The noise would soon attract others; perhaps it already had. There was no other way out. He'd looked for ventilation hatches or air-conditioning ducts. He had even knocked against the walls, testing their strength. They seemed strong enough. They would keep them trapped inside like rats in a cage until those things broke in and tore out their throats with their teeth.

That wasn't going to happen. Not to him, not to the kid.

Larry gave a noisy, drawn-out sigh. Francisco doubted he

knew he'd done it. His brash east-coast ways had evaporated. Even his healthy tan seemed to have faded.

Francisco took out his gun, slipped bullets from his pocket and made sure it was fully loaded. He wondered if its original owner had ever had to use it to shoot dead men.

Larry looked up at the sound. "You're not going out there?"

He nodded, once. "Execution style," he said. "That is what works. You stay back. Anything happens, you bar the door and take care of her. You hear?" He half-expected Larry to protest, but he didn't say anything. Francisco took hold of the shelving, got his weight behind it and pushed it upright.

The door slammed into him and he staggered. The sound of their moaning was louder at once, more *real* somehow, and they were faster than he'd expected. They came for him, the tassels of their sombreros jauntily swinging, and Francisco raised the gun and fired. The noise in the enclosed space was astonishing.

Francisco ducked away as a man's hand clawed at his eyes and he straightened, firing again, jerking with the recoil. He barely caught a glimpse of the man he'd hit – about fifty years old, bronzed skin, a grey moustache with something caught in it that looked like blood – before he fell. Others took his place. They crowded in towards Francisco without fear, as if they didn't know what the gun was. He barely had time to aim, but the next was close and he dropped him, though it was messier, the guy's nose exploding into blood and bone. The others trampled over their one-time friend in their eagerness to reach Francisco.

He fired again and again. They all looked the same in their mariachi outfits; it was as if he were caught in some awful video game, forced to destroy the same man over and over again. Then there was only one left. Somehow, he'd managed to keep the sombrero on his head. It wobbled in an almost comic fashion as he shuffled forwards. Francisco's aim was perfect as he pulled the trigger and heard the chamber's empty click.

The mariachi didn't hurry. This one was a little younger than the others. He swayed as he stepped forward and there was the clicking sound of bone on bone, as if his leg had been broken. It didn't stop him. It didn't even slow him down.

Francisco threw the gun behind him, put his hand to his back pocket, pulled out a knife and flipped open the blade. He already knew it was too late. The zombie was reaching for him with both hands. He slashed at one while pulling away from the other, anticipating the teeth that would close on his arm a second later, and then the gun fired again – right by his ear – and the zombie fell, Francisco's knife still embedded between the knuckles of its left hand.

Larry was holding the gun, his legs braced, as if he'd been doing it all his life. His eyes flicked aside and he said something that Francisco couldn't hear but that he could see: *It wasn't empty.*

Francisco sagged back against the doorframe. He reached for the medallion tucked inside his collar. It wasn't something he thought about; he brought it to his lips. *Thank you.*

When Larry spoke again, sound had come back a little, at least in Francisco's right ear. "I think we'd better move out. Someone's gotta have heard that." He stared down at the bodies arrayed outside the door. "Fuckin' zombreros," he said, and as he stepped over them he started to laugh.

Chapter Thirty-Seven

CELESTE STARED AT the horde pouring through the open doorway. She had known there were others, but not like this. The first of them was little more than a skeleton with a hook for a hand, and it stumbled along on a wooden peg leg that clacked against the floor. It had a faded bandana still tied around its neck, too loose now that it barely had any flesh on its bones. Another wore a clumsy metal helmet that flicked upward into a point at the front, some old-fashioned thing, no use now. Then came a large woman wearing nothing more than a mirrored bikini that was barely visible through the red-brown blood dried on to her skin.

There were zombies in shorts and zombies in thin dresses that clung to their misshapen forms, zombies with white bars of sunscreen still painted down their rotting noses and zombies in sun hats, their faces contorted with need. They were a host; and they were hungry.

Celeste froze as the skeletal zombie – a *pirate?* – reached out and speared Craig through the nose with its hook. It yanked his head back and she caught a glimpse of Craig's eyes, wide and terrified. The skeleton began to mouth at his face, blood running through its bony jaws, and it shook its head as if in confusion.

Its brain, she thought, *it's rotten, or it's gone*, and she did not know why that even mattered, but then Stacy grabbed her and whirled her around.

"Run!" she shouted, and Celeste got moving.

They ran, hearing the chaos behind them as chairs overturned. There came a scream and Celeste only had time to realise that Craig wasn't dead after all, that he had one last cry of pain left in him, and then they crashed through a door into the restaurant.

They weaved between fallen tables, trampling broken china, and then they were through and Celeste was gasping, not from exhaustion but from fear. She turned and looked back. Zombies were flooding inside, and she realised that they hadn't all come from the hotel or even the sea. Some of them must have been from the city. They wore suits, their shirts bloodied and their ties pulled awry. One had on a fast-food restaurant's uniform, while another looked like a bus driver, and pushing through the rest was a blank-eyed shoe-shine man, still with one hand stuck inside someone's half-polished brogue.

It got them too, Celeste thought, *it's out*, and then Stacy yanked her out of the way and they shoved the double doors at the entrance closed. McClelland took hold of a display case – the objects inside forgotten, needing only the weight of the thing – and Shelby helped him pull it in front of the doors. It started to slide at once as the tide of bodies began to hit the other side.

"That way!" Stacy pointed towards the reception area, the hotel's welcoming face, the one with corridors that led everywhere.

"No way! We have to get outside." Shelby grabbed Celeste's arm and started to pull.

"There's no time," Stacy snapped. "The control centre's in the basement. I have to get down there."

"Don't know what the hell you're on, lady. No way, José," said Shelby.

"Fuck's sake. Come, or don't." McClelland started down the corridor, hefting his machete. After a moment, Stacy followed. She only glanced back once.

Shelby spat on the tiles and then jumped back as the doors began to open. Arms thrust into the gap, all of them flailing and reaching. "Right, Cele. We've got to go."

He hurried to the glass doors behind them and Celeste looked out. It was dark but not pitch black; the air out there was thin and grey, as if somewhere a new day would soon begin. There was no movement. The door was on a latch, but they slid it open and in the next moment she was breathing the clean, cool air.

"The road," Shelby said. "We'll head for the port, find a phone, get someone to get us the fuck outta here."

Celeste thought of the monsters she'd seen wearing suits and ties, of what that meant, but she didn't say anything. She nodded and they walked hurriedly along the side of the hotel. A large H gleamed in the half-dark away to their side: the helicopter pad. She remembered how impressed Louisiana had been, how she'd prided herself on knowing everything about everybody. *Not now you don't*, she thought, and then they reached the corner. As soon as they did they heard the now familiar moaning and shuffling sound of zombies, wandering about the gardens.

"Back," Shelby whispered, and they retraced their steps. As they went the shuffling gave way to another sound, distant and lonely; Celeste realised she could hear the sea. It seemed strange, as if it were something that existed only in memory or in a dream she'd once had. Like her friend. Like Colton, wrapping his arms around her. Like holidays.

Ahead was the pool area, rimmed with the dark shapes of sun umbrellas and palms. She could just make out the waterslide – it looked almost as if someone was still atop it, ready to splash down into the water – and then she saw there were other shapes, ones that moved.

"Shit." Shelby caught hold of the back of Celeste's top. "Wait. We gotta think." For a moment he bent down, resting his hands on his knees. "I'm too old for this. All right, we're not going through the hotel. Fuck that. And those things – they're around the perimeter too." He straightened. "The beach."

"But those things came from there."

"Yes, they did, and now most of them have got wherever they're going. I hope." The set of his jaw was grim. "I can't see we've got any other choice, Cele."

She nodded her assent. They sidled along the very edge of the tiled area that led on to the pool, the place of sunbathing, of fun, of organised games and cool water and of waiters bringing good things to drink, and she swallowed down what felt like sand as she walked away from the place they had set out for so nonchalantly such a short time before. She glanced back once at the giant pyramid, its black shape looming over them in the half-light.

Chapter Thirty-Eight

THE HOTEL RECEPTION area looked worse than it had when Stacy first arrived. The floor was sprayed with broken glass and what looked like muddy footprints. Then she realised it wasn't dirt but dried blood.

"All right," McClelland said. "Where are we going? I don't think those things have followed. They might have gone after the other two."

Stacy didn't know how to answer that but she couldn't help but feel relief, followed by anger at her own selfishness. She drew in a deep breath that turned into a wavering sound like something a child might make.

"What's up? Stay with me, Keenan."

"Sorry. I haven't forgotten, that's all."

"The hell? Get this out if you have to, but we don't have time—"

"The hammock. It was me who cut it open. If I hadn't done that, if Creed hadn't got his hand through, Craig would—"

"You have no idea what Craig would have done. We saved him in the first place, remember? And it was me who wanted to try *talking* to one of those fuckers. Blame me if you want.

Now, focus. Where's this basement you talked about? Is it really that important?"

"It's where he is."

"Who?"

"The boss." She waved a hand around the devastated lobby. "The man who built it all."

"Fuckin' A, as our American friends would say. So what?"

"So . . . everything. Or nothing." She pointed across the lobby to an unobtrusive black door. "It's there. It's all down there: weapons, cameras, everything. I've seen the schematics. I was supposed to report in when I got here, but I found it locked. It's like the whole damn thing was sealed off. That was before everything went bad. I don't think that could be a coincidence."

McClelland rolled his eyes. "So what you're saying is, essentially – I'm in the middle of a horror movie, and we have to go down into the cellar?"

Stacy smiled in spite of herself. "That's pretty much it."

"Then lead the way, Macduff. If we're done with zombies and we're off to tackle ghosties and ghoulies instead, you can damn well face them first." He winked and she gave a short laugh. "Better," he said. "Now, I dare say this machete will make a dint in that door, don't you?"

They walked towards it. Stacy was already thinking about all the noise it would make and what that might bring, but McClelland didn't pause. He raised the weapon and slammed it down. The blade bounced off the door and he almost dropped it, cursing under his breath. A peeled slice of raw wood showed where the paint had been chipped off. He hit the door again and again, working on the wound he'd made in the wood. Stacy ducked as splinters flew. She glanced around. There was no sign of any zombies, but surely they wouldn't be long.

McClelland paused. He'd made quite a hole, and through it she could see a section of wall, not made of plasterboard but rough-hewn stone. Cold air spilled out, and for some reason she didn't like to breathe it in; she took a step away.

McClelland stuck his head in through the hole – she wanted to grab him, drag him back – and then withdrew. He had a dust-covered cobweb in his hair. "Okay, no keyhole this side, nothing I can see on the other, but it's locked as locked can be. Still, I think we can get in, don't you?"

He was right. The gap he'd opened was big enough for them to climb through. The trouble was, Stacy was no longer sure she wanted to. Going below ground, now – it wasn't just like another floor of the hotel; it didn't even smell like one. It was what McClelland had called it: a cellar. It might even be a trap.

"If we go down there, we might find there's no way out again."

"Or it might lead to Narnia. Or a secret passageway that leads to the sea." He grinned, almost nonchalant about it now. "And if this place has been sealed off like you say, it could be free of those things."

She stared at him. He only smiled back, and it was a natural smile, like something out of the old days. It made Stacy feel better. "All right, but we'll do it like you said. I'll go first."

"Obeying orders at last, woman?"

She slapped at his arm. Then she hooked a leg through the hole in the door and ducked backwards through it. She didn't like having that cold black space behind her, but it didn't take long before she was standing on the other side. She had been right about the air. It was stale and smelled of time passing and of the dark.

"Can you see in there okay?"

"Not really," she whispered. "But I can see the start of some steps and I can see the bottom, so there must be a light down there. It's just everything in between that's a blank."

He climbed through the gap in the door the same way she had, momentarily blocking out the light. It made the glow coming from below seem brighter still. Then he stood beside her and sparked something in his hand: the cigarette lighter. It didn't help much, only cast inky shadows over each irregularity in the wall.

He yelped and let it go out. "Hot."

"Idiot."

"Haven't even had a smoke. Lost the fucking cigarettes."

She rolled her eyes, put a hand to the wall. The after-image of the flame still danced before her, confusing her vision. She shuffled forwards until she found the first step. It didn't get any easier as she went down. The stairs were carved from the same rough-hewn stone as the walls, and they were irregular and treacherous. At the darkest part she paused, and the sound of McClelland following her ceased. She could have been anywhere at all. *In a nightmare*, she thought, *that's where I am*, and she took a breath of that musty air and kept on going.

It grew cooler as they went down. It seemed to take a long time before it gradually began to lighten and she could see where she was putting her feet. Why had they gone so deep? She hadn't noticed it was so sunken when she'd looked at the blueprints. She had wondered why the owner's suite was down here instead of up high, on top of the pyramid, but she assumed that was because he could book out the penthouse rooms for eye-watering amounts of cash. Now she wasn't so sure.

Finally, she reached the bottom. A corridor led away to left and right. It was lit by lamps set into the walls, the wiring strung roughly from one to the next. A few feet away was another small black door. It looked as if it might lead to a second stairwell or even a lift, but there was no way of telling and no discernible way to open it.

Despite how far they'd descended, the ceiling wasn't that high. McClelland stooped under it. Stacy felt as if they'd been buried deep, as if she was suffocating.

"Holy fuck," he said. "What the hell is this? A mystery Halloween tour for the kiddies?"

A cold feeling crept over Stacy. "I wish it was." She checked both ways and started walking to the left. The CCTV centre should be just down here. The gun room was directly opposite. But there were no more doors. Instead there was a corner that turned ninety degrees to the right, and another corridor identical to the last save for the frieze carved into the wall. It had a blocky design and looked very, very old.

"Is that Mayan?" McClelland hissed. His voice echoed back from the walls.

"That would be my guess."

"There's something seriously fucked up about all this."

She almost wanted to laugh. "Yup. You know, I don't know what the hell's going on, but this doesn't even match any of the hotel plans that I've seen."

"Jesus, Keenan, I—"

She put out a hand and stopped him. There was something wrong with the sound of his voice. It was distorted, as if another sound had mingled with his words. She listened and it came again; the low murmur of voices.

McClelland gestured down the corridor and she nodded. They started off again, trying to move quietly, their shoes gritting softly against the stone floor. There was another corner up ahead, and this time they paused before they reached it. McClelland tapped his chest – *me first* – and Stacy scowled, shaking her head.

He met her eyes. After a moment he shrugged and she stepped forward.

At first there was only the dark. Then the walls opened out into a large chamber, the high ceiling held aloft by square stone pillars. There were torches around the outside, the flames flickering and sending weird shadows dancing and leaping between them. She was put in mind of what McClelland had said about a mystery Halloween tour, but this didn't feel like that. She didn't even like to breathe the air. It felt wrong in her lungs, as if something had been living down here for too long; something evil.

She hid behind one of the pillars, feeling irregularities on the floor through the soles of her shoes. Lines were traced upon the stone, punctuated by round indentations that put her in mind of constellations and astrological charts. She sensed McClelland moving in close at her back. She couldn't see into the centre of the chamber; there was only darkness, thick and deep, almost like a physical entity.

Voices spoke within it.

"Are they in place?"

"It is just as you said, *Comandante*."

"Good." There was a smile in the man's voice, as if he were barely keeping down the laughter. "And the chosen one?"

Silence stretched throughout the space, like it was a part of the dark, or the dark was a part of it. Stacy couldn't help it; she took a step forwards, as if she were being drawn. Shadows shifted across her vision and she realised she could see after all: two figures stood in the centre of the room. Even in the dim light, she could see that they were both dead. They were withered and grey and should have been buried in the ground a long time ago; but then, perhaps they had been.

A thought struck her and her skin went cold. *They're dead, but they can speak.*

As if in answer, the first voice – the *Comandante* – spoke again. "You will make sure of it." There was no longer any hidden laughter in the sound, only threat.

The other speaker responded with a silent bow. Shadows ducked, wavered, danced around him. As they did, a third figure was revealed. No: it was not a person but another stone column, covered in some kind of carvings, a series of what appeared to be jars set into its side. There was a smell too, like desiccated herbs she couldn't quite identify. It didn't look as if it belonged in the chamber. The walls were grey, but where the flames flickered against the column glowed with the mellow gold of sandstone.

"And the fleas?"

"He calls them to him, though they are few, now. He's been... hungry."

"Ah." Then the first speaker did laugh and the sound made Stacy want to scream. It scratched inside her head, made her want to sink into the floor; it was as if it were mocking her.

"So he is. Well, no matter. The time is almost upon us. And as for those who listen at the door..."

Stacy felt McClelland grab her arm and she let out a dry croak. He started to pull her, hard, back the way they'd come. She heard the footsteps coming for them, echoing over her head and from the wall behind them and all around her. She stumbled along with him, his fingers digging into her arm, and then she thought she heard, "Let them see. Let them tell, let them spread our glory across the world..."

Then there was only more of that awful laughter, and Stacy knew that it wasn't any use; it had never been any use. They were caught up in some terrible plan, a trap that had closed around her from the start. It had been set before she'd even stepped on the plane, before she'd given up her place at the New Festival of Britain. And now they had been made a part of whatever was happening here.

Someone had been orchestrating everything right from the beginning, and there could only be one reason they'd been allowed to walk away – because no matter they did next, they couldn't possibly pose a threat to whatever it was that had been set in motion.

Chapter Thirty-Nine

THEY WERE SO short a distance from the hotel, and yet Celeste could almost feel they were in a different world. It was slow, walking across the beach in the dimness; the sand was deep and choppy, and soon it filled her shoes and made its way between her toes. The sun was just visible over the horizon. It gave little light, and yet the beach seemed to glow: it was paler even than the sky.

For a while the only sounds were their laboured steps. Shelby was breathing more heavily and Celeste was reminded of the age difference between him and Louisiana. Most of all, though, she listened to the sea. Its constant rolling was somehow reassuring. Out here, things were just the same as they had always been. The waves would keep on rushing in, the sun would rise, and everything would go on. She just had to hope they would go on too.

That made her think of Colton; it was as if she were betraying him. She pushed the thought away as Shelby said, "The path's running out."

There wasn't really a path to start with, but she saw what he meant. Ahead, the sand thinned. It became a snaking line that gave way to still-dark rock that rose away into cliffs. They kept on going, though, and then she saw there was a way after all. A narrow, winding path rose ahead of them between rocks that were shining from the sea spray.

They started up it, picking their way between large, fractured boulders. Celeste went first – that was the gentleman's way, wasn't it? So he could catch her if she fell – and she might fall. The surface was slick and wet. Small crabs clung to the lower rocks, skittering away as she approached. That was how things had always been, hadn't it? Mankind the alpha predator, smaller creatures running away before them. Now something else had come.

When she paused for Shelby to catch up, she looked back. There was only the gleaming beach, darkening in the distance; it was impossible to tell if anything had followed. The sound the sea made had changed as they rose above it. It seemed deeper, more resonant. She could still smell its briny tang, almost unbearably clean and fresh. The things she'd seen surely couldn't exist in such a world. They shouldn't be tolerated, not anywhere beneath the wide sky.

The path dried as they went higher, and their pace quickened. It didn't seem long until it opened up around them and they found themselves standing on the clifftop, which jutted out into the sea in craggy points. It was growing lighter and warmer, the rising sun spearing from behind low clouds that would soon burn away. Behind them, Celeste could see the Hotel Baktun, a jagged ziggurat assaulting the sky. She had expected it to have shrunk almost to nothing with the distance, but they hadn't gone as far as she'd thought; they hadn't escaped its pull. And then she looked down at the lovely glowing beach and saw it hadn't quite lightened after all. A lingering patch of night still spread itself across the sand at the base of the cliffs.

It was moving.

Her throat felt clogged with sand. She grasped for Shelby's arm and he swore. "Shit. We have to keep going."

The thing she'd taken for shadow was a ragged mass of the wandering dead. Now she was conscious of them, she realised she could hear them too – their constant wailing blending with the sound of the ocean.

There was a horde of them. The sight sapped the last strength from her legs.

Shelby shook her, got her moving. She turned her back on the monsters on the beach and started to run, and then both of them stumbled to a halt. There was a sound coming from ahead, familiar and yet impossible; impossible, because it was coming from the wrong direction, from Acapulco itself instead of the hotel.

"Oh, Jesus," Shelby breathed, just as the lie of the land ahead of them was broken by lumbering, lurching shapes.

Their moans were louder now. Individual voices rose and fell from the masses that came towards them. Behind them, the first of the horde from the beach crested the cliffside path. It was followed by a limping figure, swaying so badly it was astonishing it had managed to make the climb.

The rising sun lit its blonde hair. It took another step, almost fell and recovered itself. Celeste saw why. The thing was wearing just one towering shoe, one that she had seen before. It was a Louboutin, six-inch heel, peep-toe, black patent, purchased on Shelby's platinum card. She always had admired the way her friend could walk in them. She didn't look so elegant now.

Louisiana's other foot was bare and bloody. The worst thing, though, was her face, half of which was gone. One blue eye, faded almost to white, glared at Celeste. She bared her teeth and the hole that had been her nose and her cheek and her empty eye socket flexed, gaping around the hungry maw.

Celeste blinked and realised that the rest of them were

spreading out in a semi-circle. She whirled to see the zombies from the city doing the same, blocking their way. They had advanced more quickly than she had imagined possible.

"Run," came Shelby's voice in her ear. They did, but it was too late. The ring was closing around them. There was only what lay at their backs – a jutting triangle of clifftop and the endless, indifferent sea. They turned and ran towards it, already knowing there was nowhere to run to.

Chapter Forty

ETHAN AWOKE, KNOWING that he had dreamed and the dream had been terrible, but now it was over. It was the weekend – he wasn't sure how he knew that, but he did – and soon they would all go to the park. Lily always wanted him to push her on the swing. She never got tired of it, though he'd be bored inside a minute. Today he had a feeling he'd do it anyway, just to see her blue eyes sparkle.

There was a soft sound, a muffled tapping against glass, and he half-opened his eyes. Shadows flittered across his eyelids and he knew how he'd been able to tell that it was the weekend. The window cleaner was here. Mum always complained about how he would show up on a Sunday morning, and she'd shuffle about pulling her dressing gown ever tighter, pulling the curtains tighter too, while the cleaner moved from one bedroom to the next with his noisy cloth and his irritating whistle.

Dark shapes danced behind the curtains, tapping and rubbing at the window. It didn't sound quite right, but Ethan didn't know why and he didn't want to know. Still, he couldn't help but notice that the window looked too big. There were shadows all over it, not just in one corner where the cleaner moved his cloth. And no one was whistling. Instead, someone was moaning as if in pain.

He sat up. He realised that he wasn't at home and then the whole thing suddenly crashed in on him. Lily was gone. Mum would never complain about the window cleaner again because all she wanted to do now was eat him. He didn't know where his dad was. He pushed himself out of bed and walked slowly to the window. He reached out, hesitated, then drew back the curtain.

The dead were there. He was looking directly into the face of a middle-aged woman. Her greying hair was swept back under a green sun visor that cast her grey face into a ghastly light. *American*, he thought. *Americans wear hats like that.* And he looked at the rest: a hook-nosed man who snapped his teeth – yellowing, English teeth – silently, on the other side of the glass, and he looked up to see thick purpling legs in flat white pumps trampling over that man to get up, higher, and then stomping over an artfully shaved, slender, tanned man he thought was probably Italian, and the sadness struck him with full force.

Their shapes filled the window. They squirmed and struggled in their efforts to scramble over each other, to climb higher.

He heard a sound behind him but he did not turn. It was Mick, staring up in wonder. "Where do they all go?" he asked, but Ethan did not reply. They simply watched as the zombies swarmed over the window, drawn by who knew what.

The boy glanced at Mick. He had moved closer to the glass, was staring out at a young man on the other side. Ethan realised that there were locals among them too, men in thin shirts or pale jackets or fast-food uniforms. This one looked about eighteen years old and wore a fried-chicken restaurant shirt. And then he realised something else: the whole crowd of them was surrounded by a cloud of insects, like flies on carrion. They didn't seem to trouble the zombies very much.

He opened his mouth to say something to Mick, but closed it again. He saw from Mick's expression that he wouldn't even hear him. He was just staring deeply into the eyes of the youth, as if he could see something beyond their flat surface, the snarl on his lips.

Mick abruptly stepped back and turned away. "We should go. Leave this place." And Ethan understood, although Mick's voice was so choked and muffled that he could barely make out the words.

Chapter Forty-One

STACY REELED AS she hurried along the stone corridor. There had been no surveillance cameras, no guns, none of the clean, straight corridors and offices she'd been expecting. Nothing was as she had been told. Instead there had been that voice, dry and like the soughing of the wind over sand; she could still hear it. It had wormed its way inside her like an infection. And all she could think was that Moreby had been running this all along; but the Moreby she had seen was dead.

For how long?

McClelland reached the top of the stairs, standing to one side to let in the light, and he waited while she clambered through the gap in the door. She realised too late that she hadn't checked what lay on the other side, but thankfully there was nothing; only freshly painted walls and the first rays of daylight streaming in through the windows.

It even smelled different up here. As she breathed, her memory of the basement was already fading, like something from a story she'd once read.

McClelland clambered through after her. She blurted out, "Did you hear them? They were *talking*."

"I heard."

"That means...McClelland, they're intelligent. At least some of them are. They were as dead as dead gets, but they were still talking and...and they were *planning*. Do you see what that means?"

He nodded. "We're fucked."

She opened her mouth to protest, then she closed it again.

He took a deep breath. "So, there are two types of those things. The first kind are shambling, clumsy, nothing but hunger. But they're being run by—"

"The *other* kind."

"Yup. That about sums it up. Not sure it helps us much."

She shook her head in despair. "It doesn't. I really don't know what else I can do." She looked around at the abandoned space, the blood-stained floor. "I don't think there's anything left."

He reached out and stopped just short of touching her. "Of course not. We should get out, hole up somewhere safe. We can wait till this passes, and then—"

"Then?"

"Rebuild on whatever's left."

For a moment, she couldn't look away from his eyes. It was as if he'd known it all along and had only been waiting for her to see it too. But there was something else in his look, a kind of warmth she couldn't bear to think about.

She shook her head. "But...I sent a whole load of people to find the conference rooms. And they went, because I'm wearing a uniform and I made it sound as if I knew what the hell I'm supposed to be doing."

"All right."

"All right what?"

"All right," he repeated more softly. "We go and get them. We'll do as you say. You're the boss, right?"

"But that's just it. I'm not. I don't know what the fuck to do."

He half-smiled. “You’re doing okay, Keenan. Though I think we’d better hurry.”

She nodded as, somewhere, there was the crash of a door flying back on its hinges. A moaning sound followed, echoing from the walls and across the room as the first of them pushed its way in.

Chapter Forty-Two

CELESTE AND SHELBY ran, away from the monstrosities that followed, the sun in their faces as if it was mocking them. There was nowhere to go. They were caught on a narrowing spit of land jutting out over the sea, and the sea was all that waited. It seethed and writhed beneath them, reflecting back the pearlescent light of dawn.

Celeste could hear the dead behind them as they followed. She didn't look at them. She was afraid that, if she glanced back, she would see Colton. If she did, she might go mad.

Shelby's hand grasped for hers, his damp fingers closing on her hand as he stumbled to a halt. They were at the edge. This was all that remained – a jagged black line of rock, the ocean below, and behind, only teeth and pain and oblivion.

For the first time, Celeste wondered what it would be like to be one of those things. Perhaps it would be better. She might not feel the ache that Colton had left behind. There would no longer be any fear. And the pain, after all, would not last forever.

It's grey, he'd said. *All of it. It's so bright, but then it fades.* She closed her eyes and the rushing of the sea filled her mind. Then Shelby's hand pulled on hers.

When she opened her eyes again the zombies were up close, standing in a ring. She wondered how she hadn't known from the stink of them; the air was suddenly rotten. And yet they didn't attack, not yet.

Louisiana was in the front line, looking at them with her one blank eye. There was no recognition in its expression, no memory, nothing of her friend left. Suddenly Celeste didn't want to be one of them; she didn't want that at all.

One of them stepped forward. Celeste did not recognise him. He was tall and slender and she could quite clearly see the shape of his skull beneath his skin. His cheekbones had broken through and they caught the morning light. He drew back his lips in a parody of a grin and the sun glinted from his golden teeth.

Celeste took a step back and Shelby's grip on her hand tightened. The ground under her feet felt unstable.

"*Señora*," the zombie said in a rasping voice, and then, impossibly, he bowed. "My lady. I am come to bring you home." He held out his hand, his movement courtly, just as if she were at a ball and he was asking her to join in the waltz.

Maybe he is, she thought, glancing around at the dead faces, the blank features. *The Dance of Death – isn't that what they call it?*

Shelby drew her tighter to him. He shivered, as if he was cold. Celeste didn't feel anything at all; she had nothing left to feel. There was only horror at this thing, this travesty that was so clearly dead and yet spoke and moved like one of the living.

My lady, he had called her. She had no idea why.

But it was as if he could see every thought passing through her mind. He gave a slow smile, revealing those gold teeth once more. "You are *La Poderosa Señora*," he said. "Our Lady of Death. You will come with us and we will worship you. They all will."

Celeste inched back. Her stomach lurched as the ground crumbled.

Chosen, she thought. *He chose me too. Like Colton.* But it didn't feel like that, not at all. This man exuded age from his bones. It was as if he had brought the past with him, a long distant past of escaped responsibilities, and she found herself wondering what it was that Thomas Moreby had had in mind for his wife – the one who had run away. Was it Moreby who wanted her now? And was this merely his skeletal servant? She had no way of knowing, and anyway, it did not matter.

Shelby pulled his hand free of hers and he twisted around. He stared down at the drop before him, the sea caressing the rocks below. Celeste almost smiled as she remembered the cliff divers. He had said it was easy, hadn't he? It seemed so long ago. He obviously didn't think it was easy now. He shifted his feet, as if that could help. She saw him clench and unclench his hands.

"Together, then," he whispered.

She opened her mouth, but she never answered.

Shelby jumped.

So fast. He fell so fast. There was only a space where he had been and then he was below her, getting smaller, his hands flailing and his hair blown back from his head, and she gasped and shuffled right to the edge, peering after him.

At first there was only the sea, but then she realised she could see him after all. His body was broken. He lay face down, but she could see from the strange way his back was twisted over the rocks that he would not breathe again. A wave came in and lifted him, one arm floating free for a moment before he was laid gently down once more. He lifted and fell, lifted and fell. Seeing him move like that, she almost expected him to push himself up, to stand and wave at her; but he did not.

There was a voice at her back, a low, hissing, insistent voice. "It is time, *La Flaca*," it said. "You must come with us."

She turned to see the skeletal man. He had stepped towards her and his hand was still outstretched, ready to take hold of

hers. She couldn't bear the thought of touching him. His eyes were yellow and gleaming, and they were like Colton's: no warmth in them, no warmth left in the world.

And yet there was nothing else for her now, only his hand and all that it promised. Maybe they wouldn't even hurt her.

We will worship you. They all will.

She glanced aside and saw Louisiana's ruined face. She looked as if she could not wait to tear out Celeste's throat with her teeth.

In the next instant, Celeste turned and leaped.

In that moment, she was free. The air rushed around her and she held out her hands for the joy of it, the light, the weightlessness, the way she could let everything go at last, and then the water was rushing towards her and she fell to meet it.

It closed over her head in a cold shock. There was noise in her ears, and chaos, and she found she had reserves of strength left in her after all; she fought against the pull, twisting, one foot striking rock, pain spearing up her leg. The taste of salt was strong on her tongue and it stung her eyes. She struck out, trying to reach the surface, and then she did. She gasped for breath, finding nothing she could hold on to.

She blinked hard, coughing water from her lungs. She spread her arms across the swell as it lifted her and let her fall again. Unlike Shelby, she had cleared the rocks. The cliff was a dark shape above her and a man's head, looking down, was the only thing to break its outline. She thought she caught the bright glint of gold in his mouth as he smiled.

Then a hand, beneath the waves, grasped her ankle.

She opened her mouth to scream and water flooded in. The hand was already pulling her down. Her cry turned into a bubbling choke and she kicked out, catching something beneath her. For a moment it loosened its grip and she gasped in air, but then there were hands all over her, grasping at her legs, their fingers sliding against her wet skin, tangling in her dress. She beat at them, finding nothing she could grasp. There was only the slippery skin of men long drowned and the sea closed over her head to claim her.

She opened her eyes, ignoring the stinging pain. There was worse pain, she knew that. She could feel it beginning, as teeth clamped down on her thigh, on her fingers, and then she saw someone's face thrust up close to hers: a girl with flowing golden hair. Her cheeks were dark-veined and her eyes pale, and she leaned forward and took Celeste into a loving embrace, opening her lips to reveal sharp white teeth.

Celeste fought. She couldn't help it. She knew there was no reason to it, but then, there was no reason left in the world. She struggled and as she did, she stared upward at the morning sun. She could see it still, through the first pale layers of water.

As they dragged her down to whatever realm they had found for themselves, her summer dress billowing up around her like a drifting shroud, she thought she had never seen anything more beautiful.

Chapter Forty-Three

AT FIRST, WHEN Francisco had held out his hand for the gun, it had looked as if Larry wasn't going to hand it back. Then he met Francisco's eyes and he passed it over. The bodies lay at their feet and Francisco darted glances at them as he reloaded the weapon, but they did not so much as twitch.

He tucked his gun back into his waistband and looked for the kid. She was awake, but the dark circles under her eyes made her face appear almost bruised.

"Well, kid," Larry said, "we better get movin'."

The girl looked back at him and she did not speak. Francisco felt a stab of guilt. If she had been silent so long, it was surely because of him. He should have shielded her better, kept her from seeing the things she'd seen.

She stepped towards Larry, lifting her little Mary-Jane shoes over a dead mariachi's leg. There was a kind of pain in seeing her go. Larry held out his hand, ready for her to take it, but she didn't; instead she stumbled to Francisco's side and wrapped her arms around his leg.

He stared down at her. For a moment he couldn't see and

then he rested one hand on her head, just lightly, as if in fear that she might vanish at any moment.

He looked at Larry and nodded. "We get outside," he said. "I have friends in the city. My brothers. They will help us." He wasn't sure what they would do with the kid, but then, he'd find a way. She was his responsibility now – he wouldn't let her down.

Larry nodded and Francisco led the way down the corridor. He didn't think he'd been this way before but it felt right, as if things had aligned for him and he was going the right way at last, doing the right thing.

He reached the corner, holding the girl back, peering around it. Slowly, he let go of her hand. A woman stood there, trying to walk into the wall, or that was what it looked like. She was blonde – so many of the guests had been, hadn't they? Blonde and skinny, trophy wives for rich men. Of course the child was blonde too, but that was different; she was more like an angel.

This one had a single fake eyelash clinging to her greying lid. Shining lipstick – if that's what it was – was smeared around her mouth and across her chin. This thing wasn't from Heaven but from Hell, and he raised the gun and fired before she had the chance to move towards them. Her head opened and she dropped.

Violence. That was the only thing that El Calaca had said conferred power. It was the only thing the faithful had ever needed. For a long time it was all that Francisco had needed. And he needed it now, just a little longer, at least until they got away. After that ... he glanced behind him at the blue eyes peering around the corner, and things he hadn't felt in a long time stirred inside him.

He would be a better man now. He would be better for *her.* He touched a hand to the medallion, making his promise – not to *La Flaca*, the twisted saint of *Los Fieles,* but to his namesake. Perhaps, in some way, to his grandmother. If he got out of here, he would no longer be a weapon of the gang, there to do their bidding without thought or question. He would learn to be human again. He would learn to feel things again, if only he could get away.

He reached out to take the child's hand and he heard a sound, footsteps coming towards them from around the next corner. He shifted his grip on the gun and raised it once more. The footsteps grew louder; he eased back the trigger.

There were two of them, a sandy haired boy and a waiter. Francisco moved quickly, levelling his aim at the boy's forehead, squeezing just as his eyes opened wide.

He released his grip on the trigger just short of blowing the kid's head off, but he did not lower the gun. The boy didn't look dead, but he didn't look quite alive either. He seemed dazed – sick, even.

He took aim once more, just as the Maya waiter called out, "No!"

Francisco nodded once, lowered his aim. The kid still didn't seem quite right. He was staring down the corridor towards them but he hadn't said a word. Then he fell to his knees.

Francisco realised he wasn't staring towards him at all – he was staring at the girl. As he watched, tears began to spill from the boy's eyes. Francisco spat. It was nothing but a weak kid who'd lost his mind.

He heard an odd sound behind him and he jumped violently, just as if he were a kid himself, one who was scared of the dark. He twisted around to look at the source of the noise and he saw something strange. The little girl wasn't silent any longer. She was standing quite still, her face crumpled, her hands grasping at nothing, and she was crying too.

Chapter Forty-Four

THE DEAD MEN were so clumsy and yet they moved so fast. Stacy raised her machete and struck, dodging their grasping nails and hungry jaws. All she could see was the semblance of what they had once been: an older man still wore the floppy sun hat his wife had probably bought for him so he could read the newspaper by the pool without tiring his eyes. A woman with impossibly shiny coiffed hair, only slightly awry, had crimson smeared across her perfectly even teeth. And there was someone else she thought she recognised, not from this place but from numerous DVDs she'd watched over the years, his skin still smooth but horribly grey. Up close, the smell was unbearable – the stinking rich were now just stinking.

She couldn't take her eyes from the zombie who had once been the toast of Hollywood, as he snaked a hand in under her machete. She struck down, but too late. She couldn't get a clean cut and she opened the back of his hand, revealing decaying meat that did not bleed.

McClelland dived in towards her, his own blow almost taking the film star's head off. Another strike did the job. "We have to go, *now*!"

Stacy was half-dazed. The dead were filling the space with their stench and their hunger. She had only tackled those in front of her; she hadn't realised there were so many. Even as she backed away, she saw it wasn't any use.

"Stairs!" he said, and they pelted across the room towards them.

There was no way they could make it to the conference suite, not without leading all the legions of Hell straight to it. "We'll head up and lose them, come back down another way," she said, even as she leaped up the steps two at a time. "Then we get the others and get out."

"If there are any others left."

He sounded reluctant, and she had a sudden flashback to her first impressions of the man. Back then, she'd only wanted him to shut up. She remembered the way he'd met her eyes when he spoke of barricading himself inside his room until the danger had passed. Would he really stick with her now, if he had the chance to do that again? But he'd come this far. And anyway, maybe he had simply seen something she hadn't. Maybe he was right – the Hotel Baktun was overrun. It was lost, and anyone who stayed here would be lost too. Still, if she had to, she knew she would go after the others alone.

The sound of pursuit changed as the horde reached the bottom of the stairs. Their moaning rose in pitch as their quarry pulled further ahead. There was more shuffling, the soft noises of bodies fallen and crushed beneath the feet of those who came after, no one stopping to help anybody else, any human kindness long since faded away. Perhaps there was no room for such a thing in the world any longer.

For the first time, it occurred to Stacy that she didn't have a plan beyond getting away from the hotel; that maybe there was nowhere left to go.

She didn't look back – she could not afford to stumble. She simply ran.

Chapter Forty-Five

ETHAN FORCED HIMSELF up from his knees and ran towards his sister. He dropped to the floor next to her, pushing the hair back from her forehead, looking into her face, kissing her cheeks. It *was* her. His Lily with her own sweet eyes, blue and full of tears, not cold and blank and soulless.

He threw his arms around her and pulled her to him. He sobbed into her shoulder. Somewhere at the edge of his thoughts was the knowledge that this had brought him back to a world of trouble. It mattered again if he lived or died. He *had* to live, because he had to take care of her; and yet that would mean helping her to understand, to try to explain to her what had happened to her mum and dad, even if he couldn't really fathom it himself.

As if in reply she pulled away from him, her fingers tangling in his hair, and she said, "Mummy?"

But Ethan was becoming conscious of other things. It was as if he was waking up, properly, for the first time in a long while. Mick was standing nearby – if it hadn't been for him, Ethan would never have found Lily. There was a taller fellow a short distance away, and in front of him was the Mexican man who'd had hold of his sister's hand, before he pointed a gun at Ethan's head...

He drew back and looked at the man's face. He didn't look very old but his eyes, somehow, looked much older. There was a kind of blankness in them, for all he looked fully aware of everything passing before him. He was thin and his face had tough lines to it, lines grooved from his nose to his lips, which had a downward turn, as if he rarely smiled. He did not smile now. He only looked at Lily, as if he didn't quite understand what she was, and then he leaned over and took her hand and pulled her to her feet.

Ethan stood too. He caught Lily's other hand, kept tight hold. He looked into the man's face. "Thank you," he said. "She's my sister. Thank you for finding her."

The man frowned. He did not let go of Lily's hand. He seemed barely conscious of holding it.

Ethan forced a smile. "I've got her now," he said. "We'll be okay, now we're together again."

The man shook his head. "I... I took her," he said. "There is supposed to be... money. That is it. I cannot just give her back."

Ethan frowned and pulled on her hand. "There is no money," he said. "What do you mean? Anyway, who cares about money now?"

"El Calaca will be angry." He dipped his gaze from Ethan's. "We took her for a ransom. I must keep her here."

"The fuck?" The taller man interjected in a strong American accent. "Francisco, what the hell are you on, buddy?"

Francisco lowered his head still further. Then his hand snapped open and Lily turned and hugged Ethan's leg so hard he thought she'd never let go. He let his hand settle in her hair. It felt dirty and clammy, but he relished the touch of it anyway; he had thought he would never feel it again.

He sank down beside her. "It's all right, sweetie," he whispered. "I'll look after you."

He glanced up only when Francisco stepped away from them. Ethan wished he would go, but at the same time he didn't want to let him out of his sight. Money? Ransom? He had no idea what he'd been talking about. They weren't rich, never had been. They wouldn't even have been here if Mum hadn't won the trip in some stupid competition, stranding them here, miles and miles away from home. He suddenly longed for their own house, its little rooms, its warm smells, and he rested his chin on Lily's head so that she couldn't see his expression.

"Mummy?" she asked again, and he closed his eyes.

"I am sorry," Francisco whispered. "I...I make some mistake. I thought she was someone else. It was all a mistake, from the beginning. I thought—"

"I don't know what you thought, buddy," the American said. "But enough craziness for one day, right? We should get out of this place. It's all gone bad here."

Ethan was still looking into the Mexican's eyes. Now they had an odd shine to them that was almost – but not quite – like tears. "I'm taking Lily home," he said. "I'm not sure how, but I am."

"You do that, kid." The guy nodded. "For now, how about we stick together? I'm Larry."

"Mick." They started shaking hands, just as if everything was normal, as if the world they had once known had formed around them again.

"So we need to go down," Mick said.

Larry nodded. "As soon as."

"Are you ready, Ethan?"

Mick gave a smile so heartfelt and yet so sad that Ethan felt tears welling in his eyes again. He blinked them back. "Mick, didn't you want to head into the city – to find your brother?"

Mick froze. He still looked at Ethan but he didn't speak, and then, almost imperceptibly, he shook his head. "We go."

There was nothing more to be said. Ethan adjusted his grip

on Lily's hand. His own fingers felt hot and slippery but he did not let go. They got moving, Larry and Mick first then Ethan and Lily, and the strange man – Francisco – behind them. Ethan didn't like not being able to see him, didn't like the fact that the man could be watching his sister, but at least he seemed to have subsided.

Safety in numbers, he thought, and that was when the zombies stumbled around the corner and saw them, and he realised who they were, and his heart failed within him even as Lily caught her breath and cried out with joy: "Mummy!"

And it was. It *was*.

Their mother looked the same as she always had, except that she was dead. She looked as if she wanted to scoop them up and hold them close and never ever let them go. His dad, just behind her, had the same intention shining from his eyes.

He could see the marks his dad's teeth had made in his mother's throat. There was white stuff in there – something stringy that looked as if it was holding everything together – and red, and purple, and her skin was grey, and the sight of her eyes gleaming so blankly made him want to close his own eyes and shut it all out, forever.

She was coming for him. She was coming for them both. They would be a family again and this time no one would part them, not ever. For a moment he found himself wondering what that would be like and then a shot rang out, blocking out everything else.

He could no longer feel Lily's hand in his. He couldn't feel anything. He tightened his grip and she cried out and he realised he was still holding it after all, that Lily was still there, her hand warm, still *alive*.

He stepped back even as his mother rocked on her feet. A new hole had appeared, this one in the centre of her forehead. It looked small and black and round and it did not bleed, but she swayed once more and then she fell, forwards, towards them.

Lily shrieked and Ethan pulled her back, stepping between her and this new horror, covering her eyes. He heard the sound as his mother hit the floor, the soft slump of dead weight with nothing left inside it, the louder crunch as her nose broke against the tiles.

Someone shouted something – "For Christ's sake, move it!" – as another shot rang out.

Dad, Ethan thought, and he tried to feel fear but there was nothing left, only sadness and a huge, overwhelming tiredness. He swung Lily up into his arms and pressed her face into his chest.

He turned to see Mick stepping in with his club. He swung it in a wide arc, burying its greedy knives into a teenage girl's neck. Then he dragged it towards him, and Ethan heard the ripping sound it made. He remembered what Mick had told him – *Like a Maya chainsaw, yes?* – as the girl's head toppled from her neck and rolled across the floor.

Francisco shot the man behind her. He was already lolling to one side, but in the instant before he fired Ethan saw that the wound was old; a large chunk of flesh was missing from his torso. What appeared to be shark's teeth were buried in the wound. He looked as if he'd been taken by the sea a long time ago. His skin was bloated and so foul that its miasma filled the air, making Ethan want to choke, but suddenly the way was clear.

They moved as one, hurrying towards the end of the corridor. There was a stairway leading down, and it looked empty. It was easy – surely it was too easy. Still, when Mick started down, Ethan followed. Lily was a warm heaviness against his chest and his arms were tiring already, but he knew he'd never let go again. He drew level with Mick as he reached the bottom, the others hurrying at their heels, and he heard his friend's muttered curse as a new corridor came into sight.

There were more of them down there. They were maybe

ten feet away and all of their faces were turned towards the stairs, as if they were already savouring some delicious scent.

A wild scream cut the air. It sounded like a woman in hideous pain, and then he saw someone running towards the zombies from the other direction. She didn't appear to be in pain – she just looked angry.

Flame blossomed in front of her. Ethan narrowed his eyes against the brightness and when he opened them again he saw the slender blonde woman, her hair looking damp from the shower and half-wrapped in a towel. Another towel was wrapped tightly around her body, tied in place with a frayed telephone cord. In one outstretched hand she held a cigarette lighter. In the other was a can of hairspray.

She pressed the button on top of the can and where the spray met the lighter it burst into a jet of flame that shot towards the zombies, who had turned, smelling fresh meat. A boy who had been nine or ten when he died caught it full in the face. He staggered back and Ethan smelled it at once, like a charring barbecue, and he grimaced even while realising how hungry he was. The thought was quickly followed by nausea.

The zombies didn't even pause. They showed no fear of the flame or of anything else. The woman screamed again, in anger or in fear, Ethan wasn't sure which. She raged towards the zombies, sending more flames flying towards them, and an old woman's clothes caught in a *whoosh*, going up like paper, engulfing her head.

Ethan looked at the boy to see the skin dripping from his face on to his brightly coloured T-shirt – WE ARE THE HAPPY KIDS emblazoned across the front. His hair had almost gone, and black and livid red patches covered his scalp. His eyes suddenly appeared too large, fatty globes in his hideous face, and then one popped in a burst of viscous liquid.

Ethan cried out in disgust. He could not look away. The boy was still upright, although the blonde woman had moved on, was playing the flames up and down a man's chest, trying to get him to light. She did not see the boy as he turned and seized her from behind.

She screamed again, not in defiance this time but in pain, as the kid sank his teeth deep into her arm. Her finger must have clamped down on the button because flame continued to jet out, caught between them as he moved in close. His face was crisp and blackened, still licked by flame as he buried it into her flesh. She screamed again, this time in horror as her own hair caught. The smell was intolerable. Rotting, dead things, sweat, fear and now the acrid choking tang of burning hair spread through it all.

Lily began to cough against Ethan's chest and she wriggled against him. He shifted his grip to keep her from falling.

The male zombie the blonde woman had tried to set alight buried his face in her belly as she slipped, her legs flying from under her, the hairspray rolling across the floor. She went down and the zombies were upon her, biting and tearing. Ethan only had time to wonder if it was any better to be eaten by a zombie on fire before he was running again, Mick pointing the way with his club, past the writhing, smoking heap into air that was, if not clean, at least better.

They kept on going. Ethan didn't know if anyone was leading the way or if it was a rout, if anyone even knew which way they were heading any longer, and then Larry skidded to a halt outside a wide double door which had the sharp ends of nails sticking through it – not in any regular pattern but haphazardly, as if a cactus had grown straight through it.

Everyone stopped too, and Ethan jumped when Larry banged on the wood, the noise of it shocking, and he shouted: "Hey! In there!" He banged louder, rhythmically, with his fists. "You in there. Let us the fuck in!"

Francisco leaned back and booted the door. There was a splintering sound and he kicked it again, careful not to put his foot straight through the sharp end of a nail, and the door flew inward. Lengths of timber that had been roughly nailed to the other side scattered; a barricade that would surely have given way before the slightest onslaught.

They stepped into the room and a ring of frightened eyes looked back at them. No one spoke and no one moved. They only watched each other, as if each side was waiting to see what the other would do.

Chapter Forty-Six

STACY AND McCLELLAND sprinted up the stairs, holding their machetes before them. They charged through the door that let on to the first floor, seeing a host of other doors lining the corridor ahead of them, each one bearing a room number.

"Wait!" McClelland's voice was low and yet urgent. She stopped, glancing back towards the stairs. "Hear that?" he whispered.

She did, still ready to run; but she realised an odd thing. The zombies hadn't followed them on to the hotel corridor. They were still heading upwards.

"Can't they smell us or something?" she whispered back.

McClelland grinned, making a show of sniffing his armpit. "Not me. Can't speak for anyone else."

She rolled her eyes.

They hurried to put distance between themselves and the zombies, before they could realise they had missed their prey. McClelland paused, frowning. "It's a pity we can't see outside. We should get into one of these rooms."

"*No.*" Stacy fought to soften her tone. "Look, we have no

idea what's in there. There's no need to go poking around when we don't have to."

"What, like in a basement?" He raised his eyebrows. "Knowledge is power, isn't it?"

She remembered the way he'd caught Colton Creed, the way they'd lost Craig, and she shook her head.

"C'mon, Keenan. We should check it out, at least. Look – that door's not closed properly."

All she could think of was the *Demeter*, the way he had hidden himself away while the plague spread around him. "McClelland – Alec, please. We can't stay here."

"Who said we're staying? He grinned, but it faded when he saw her expression. "Woah – take it easy, okay? It's not like we're checking in." He leaned in close to the door, listening. Then he pushed, taking its weight. "Come on."

Inside, the room was chaos. Empty packets of nuts were strewn across the floor, as if someone had worked their way through the minibar and then started on a maid's trolley. Empty bottles of water had been thrown into the corners. A suitcase lay open, disgorging its clothes, and the bed was rumpled. At least the room was empty, but there was a sound coming from outside the windows. McClelland went over, and Stacy hissed as he yanked open the curtains.

The other side of the glass was clouded with smears of blood and grease and rot. The sun streamed through it all, creating a mockery of a stained-glass window, yellow and red and purple interspersed with glimpses of the clear blue sky.

She realised that some of the shapes were moving outside. There were two of them on the balcony, a man and a boy, both zombies. The man was stretching upwards, his palms sliding through the mess on the glass, as if it were a giant finger-painting. Then he caught hold of the boy and thrust him against the window, as if he could climb over him.

"Shit. It's just like I said." Stacy bit her lip.

"What is?"

"Oh. I – I highlighted it as a security issue. It doesn't matter now, I suppose. I pointed out that anyone could jump down on to a balcony below theirs, maybe break into the rooms that way. But it's not so easy to climb up."

They watched in silence. The dead boy kept pushing the man off but then he slipped, falling to his knees, and that was enough. The man put a foot on his shoulder and hoisted himself against the glass, his palms squeaking through the mess, and then there were only the shadows of his legs and the sound of scrambling coming from somewhere above.

"Jesus – look," Stacy said.

Heads began to appear over the side of the balcony. There were four of them. Their moans were muffled by the glass and they didn't appear to see Stacy and McClelland, frozen, staring out; they just kept on trying to climb upwards.

A clatter rang out, not coming from outside but somewhere much closer.

McClelland and Stacy jumped and stared at each other. Then they turned to face the bathroom door. It stood half-open. No other sound came, but slowly, McClelland began to move towards it, his machete ready in one hand. With the other he pushed the door wide.

Stacy followed, trying to leave him enough room to swing the blade. What she saw was a perfectly ordinary bathroom, shining and new, with a mural of hand-painted Mexican tile. Toiletries were placed beside the sink: electric toothbrushes, expensive-looking moisturiser, an intricate perfume bottle she didn't recognise.

Stacy stood in the doorway. She could see the side of the bath, but she couldn't see what was inside it. A white plastic shower curtain had been drawn across. She knew there was someone there, though, by the soft-edged shadow that showed through the thin material; the darker oval where the plastic clung to a damp thigh.

McClelland stopped dead. The tip of his machete was shaking. Stacy went to his side, putting out a hand, gesturing for him to wait. She caught hold of the edge of the curtain. In the next moment, she drew it back.

A naked woman stood there, her flesh the colour of an ageing bruise. Her hair frizzed about her head as if she hadn't brushed it in a long time, and her eyes were whited over, the pupils contracted to tiny black points.

She reached out for McClelland, not looking at Stacy or the machete. She only wanted him. Her hands were open, welcoming him as if he were her lover, ready to enclose him in her cold embrace.

McClelland didn't move. It seemed as if he were hypnotised as the woman began to open her swollen grey lips, revealing a dark gap in her teeth, a lumpen tongue. Then he did move. He swung the machete in and down, but there was no room. The blow caught her across one arm and she did not even pause.

Stacy dropped her own weapon and grabbed the woman's wrist, feeling spongy flesh shifting against the bone as if the whole thing would slide off like a rubber glove. It gave McClelland time to step back and he raised the machete, but all he could do was stab her with it – driving it deep into her chest, pulling it free with a sick, wet sound. He plunged it in again and again.

The woman didn't seem to notice the wounds flowering in her chest. She bent forwards, still trying to reach him with her teeth. Stacy grabbed her hair with her other hand, trying to keep clear of McClelland's flailing blade. She let go of the woman's slimy hand and instead she pushed her as hard as she could.

Stacy expected her to go down but she was strong, this woman, her feet rooted like a tree trunk, and she only swayed back against the tiled wall. It was enough. McClelland quit stabbing with the machete and pulled the shower curtain across in front of her once more. Stacy stepped out of the way, leaving him clear to swing wide. The curtain bulged outward under the woman's clawed hands as she fought, but it did not tear until McClelland cut a swath through it. The meaty crunch as the blade met flesh made Stacy flinch.

Now the woman did go down, but McClelland did not stop. He kept striking down with the blade until the shower curtain was in ribbons and, beneath it, the woman's flesh was too. Stacy caught unwelcome glimpses of her torso, her throat, her face, as the plastic was flayed.

At last the woman lay motionless, but still McClelland's arm rose and fell. He was like a man possessed. Stacy leaned against the wall, all the life suddenly gone from her limbs. She wanted to sink to the floor and close her eyes and let it all go. To sleep; and to hope that sleep was dreamless.

Then she roused herself, because the splashing of metal in pulped flesh just wouldn't stop, and she found herself dragging on McClelland's arm. "It's done," she said. "It's *done*."

He sagged. The machete hung loose from his hand, the tip of its blade dripping red on to the once-shining tile. He didn't speak, just stayed there, dragging in heavy breaths, his shoulders heaving.

Eventually he straightened and they stared into the bath, at the thing that had once been a woman. He said: "Fucking psycho."

Stacy looked at him, startled, and then both of them were laughing, as if they were kids in the playground, as if they'd never stop. His machete rattled to the floor and they leaned on each other, all of their strength gone. Stacy felt McClelland's arms close around her back. Warm, living hands. She clung to him and laughed into his chest, her body shaking, and she couldn't tell when the laughter turned to tears, or when his tight grip turned to a gentle stroking of her hair.

He was the first to pull away. “Come on,” he said softly. “Are you ready to be a hero? We’ve got some hapless tourists to save.”

She leaned in to his chest, sniffed, straightened again. She stared down at her hands, at the stuff glistening on her palms. She grabbed a towel and wiped the putridity away. Then she went to the sink, washed them and rinsed for a long time.

“No scratches?”

She shook her head as she dried her hands on a fresh towel, dropping it to the floor. Then she picked up the woman’s perfume and squirted it behind her ears. It smelled like a meadow full of flowers.

“Now I’m ready,” she said. She picked up her machete and headed for the door.

Chapter Forty-Seven

THERE WERE MORE of them crowded into the conference room than Ethan had first thought. They stood slowly, as if not sure how to react. They didn't appear to have a leader, though some were clinging to broken pieces of wood or chair legs.

The room was large and full of seats that had once been ranked theatre-style, facing a platform with a podium on it, but they were now in disarray. Standing amidst them were people who looked as if they'd just rushed in from the beach or pool, which of course they probably had. Their appearance was belied by the shock and fear in their eyes.

There were elegant women and men gone to seed. A teenage girl, still wearing a bikini, clutched her own shoulders. A mother kept tight hold of a boy of four or five. There was the woman who'd grabbed Ethan in the dining room, back when this had all began, and he saw that she had picked up her handkerchief; she was twisting the scrap of embroidery in both hands. A man in uniform stepped forward and Ethan recognised him too. It was Hector.

He stepped towards them, raising his hand and pointing at Ethan. "Infected," he said. "Scratched!"

Ethan held Lily tightly in his arms, the backs of his hands in plain view. He couldn't hide them without dropping her, and he wasn't about to drop her. He tightened his grip and waited. No one else moved or spoke until Mick stepped to his side and clapped his hand on Ethan's shoulder. It only struck Ethan in that moment what an odd figure his friend cut; a young man in a messed-up waiter's uniform clutching a barbaric club with shreds of flesh still clinging to its obsidian blades.

"He is not what you say," Mick said. "He has been with me the whole time. He is one of us."

Ethan felt Lily shaking in his hands. "I got scratched before any of this happened," he said. "It wasn't one of *them*." And his mother hadn't been, had she? Not then. She'd left that mark on him before she became something else, before whatever made her *her* had gone.

The woman holding the handkerchief stepped forward and some of the others shuffled in her wake, as if stirred by her movement; like sheep. Like *zombies*. Ethan tried to remember her name. It had been like a flower, hadn't it? The last time he'd seen her, she'd had a crazed light in her eyes. She didn't look crazy now. She simply looked very, very tired.

"He's okay," she said. "I'll vouch for him. I – I saw him, before. He's telling the truth."

Ethan felt the tension draining from the room. Francisco let his gun fall to his side. Ethan knew that the woman was lying – she couldn't know how he'd been scratched – and he didn't know why but he shook his head, walked to the nearest chair and sat down. He balanced Lily on his knee and rested his head against hers.

The woman went to his side and took the next seat. He turned to her – Heather, that was her name – and she gave him a gentle smile, lightly touched Lily's hair. It was a simple human gesture and it made him want to cry. He blinked the tears back. He couldn't afford to give in, not now. This woman wasn't his mother; he had seen his mother die, could still see the way his dad had kissed her but not kissed her. He couldn't afford to be a little kid any longer.

Mick's eyes glowed, but the fight was draining from him. He let the club slump to the floor and then he saw someone in the crowd who was wearing a uniform like his own. He greeted him by name – Miguel – and they began to speak in rapid Spanish.

At that moment a loud crash rang across the room as the door on the opposite side burst open. Ethan leaped to his feet, pulling Lily with him, and everyone turned, expecting a ravening horde to spill into the room. There was no horde. A man and a woman stood there, their clothes grimy and their faces drawn. They were holding machetes, but they lowered their weapons as relief spread across their features.

"You're alive," the woman said. She sounded surprised, as if it wasn't what she had expected; as if that wasn't the norm any longer. She looked around, taking them in or possibly counting heads, Ethan wasn't sure.

"Everyone," she said, "get your things together. We're leaving."

The man she was with turned to her. His expression was grave. "No," he said, softly. "No, we're not."

Chapter Forty-Eight

STACY STARED AT McClelland in disbelief. She knew she should say something, that everyone was waiting to hear her words, but she couldn't speak; she had nothing left. All she could think of was that subterranean passageway, the weapons and the control room that should have been there but weren't; the way she'd been lied to.

McClelland looked back at her. Suddenly she dropped her machete to the floor. She flew at him, her fists flailing, beating at his chest. "Get out," she said. "If you're not with us, get the hell away, you bastard."

A part of her knew he was still holding his own machete, that if he'd betrayed them she might at any moment feel it puncture her ribs, find her heart. But he didn't raise it, didn't fight back. He just dropped his own weapon and grabbed her hands.

"Listen to me," he said. "Look, tiger! Just listen."

She stopped struggling. No one had come to help her; didn't they understand?

"Stacy," he said. It sounded odd coming from him and she realised it was the first time he'd called her by her first name.

At first she couldn't meet his eyes, but when she did their expression was warm.

"I'm not going with you," he said.

She shook her head, confused.

"You are," he said. "You're getting out. That's your job now, Keenan. You have to get these people away and safe."

"So what the hell are you talking about?"

"I'm going back." He looked upward, indicating all the floors above them. "I can't run away. Don't you see?" He took a deep breath. "I hid once. I'm not going to do it again. We have to close these things down, before they spread. Before they make the whole world like them."

"But that's not what you did; you didn't hide. You survived. You didn't rush in, you didn't try to fight a battle you couldn't win..."

He let go of one of her wrists and put his finger to her lips. "Someone's got to fight. I'm a hunter, Keenan, so they say. Well, I'm going hunting."

"You can't. You'll die." She thought of the hotel room upstairs, the way she'd feared he'd want to hole up until everything had passed. How could she have been so stupid? Now she wished that was exactly what he was doing.

He gave a wry smile. "Another place, another time, Keenan. We might have been good friends, you and I."

"We are." She choked. "You fucking *idiot.* We are."

He laughed and pulled away from her, turned to address the group that stood watching them. "Sorry for the show, folks. This is your head of security, Ms Keenan. She's going to lead the way out of the hotel – as soon as the way is clear and she can do so safely. You need to go with her and do everything she tells you to do." He met Stacy's eyes again and smiled. "It's your best chance."

"We should stay here," someone called out. It was the

woman with the child. "Help will come. I called the airline when this started. They'll be here soon."

"Lady, I busted through your barricade without taking a breath. And what are they going to do, send a rep with a six-pack to make it less painful when those things eat your face?"

The woman subsided, but someone else piped up. "Well, where are we going? What is she going to do? I don't see—"

"You can stay here and die if you want, sir. It's entirely your choice. But I suggest you do something to save your skin, because really, no one else gives a—"

Stacy quieted him with a hand on his arm. "No one's coming," she said, calmly and clearly. "I called the police at the start of all this. They can't help us. We can't panic about that, but we do need to get away, because this place is overrun. Frankly—" she glanced at McClelland – "staying here is madness. We need to help ourselves now. We have to go."

No one else spoke.

"And you," Stacy said in a lower voice. "You need to come with us, Alec."

She knew he'd heard, but he didn't acknowledge her words. Instead he called out, "There's something else. I'm staying. I'm going to take as many of those things down as I can. Someone has to stop them, and I'm not saying I can do that, but I'll try my damnedest. If anyone else wants to stay and fight, you should come with me." He indicated the clock on the wall. "You've got a little time to think about it. But not too long, okay?"

"I'll come with you."

"There's one. Good man. The rest of you – start thinking."

He turned away from them, drawing Stacy with him. She exploded. "McClelland, what the fuck are you doing?"

"Let's not do this, Stacy. I'm too... I'm tired." He smiled at her. "Look, as soon as I saw those things walking along under the water, I had a feeling they knew where they were going. Understand?"

She frowned.

"And now, the way they're climbing the building – what's up there, Stacy? Do you know?"

She shook her head. "They're stupid. I don't think they're doing anything. It's all random, and you're going to die because you're too—"

"I don't think it is," he said. "Sure, this thing, this disease, whatever it is, it's outside too. It's spreading across the city as fast as they can bite people. Some of the zombies aren't from the sea and they're not from this hotel – they're from out *there*. But I think there's something here that's drawing them to it." He looked at the clock again. "They're heading upward. Hell, I don't know, Stace. Maybe they've formed a cosy zombie suicide pact and they're all going to jump from the top. That would be nice. But I do know we've left the door of this room open – might as well have put a sign out saying 'lunch is served' – but none of them have come, have they? Because they've all suddenly got somewhere better to be.

"We should have a little time – we can rest up here, gather our wits. If they keep on going up towards the top, that leaves the way clear for you. There are lots of ways out of this place. And they'll all be above us, when we attack. We can work our way upward—"

She shook her head. "I'm coming with you."

"No. No, you're not." He stroked her cheek and she barely felt it, didn't even want to; she knew it was his way of saying goodbye. "Look, Keenan, these people will go with you. That's your thing, right? You know how to keep them calm and you'll keep them safe. You never got the chance to do your job, did you? Not really. Now you do."

She looked around. "McClelland – I don't know what the

hell I'm doing. I don't even know where we should go."

"Yes you do. You'll check it out, see if it's safe. Maybe the army will have come; maybe it'll be okay. If so, you stick with the men with the big guns, right? And maybe send them in this direction. If not, Keenan – if things are bad – you're starting along the coast, right? Where it's quiet. No good rushing headlong into God knows what."

"That's what I had in mind."

"Good. So, if Acapulco has fallen, you keep on going down the coast."

The idea of the city being lost made Stacy feel dizzy, but she couldn't think of that now. She just looked her question at him and he mouthed the answer. Her eyes widened.

"It's still there, Keenan – all of it. Full of food and hopefully fuel, all of it just dropped there, ready to pick up again."

"But the zombies—"

"They left it." He grinned. "I saw them, remember?"

"Maybe not all."

"No. Then you deal with that. Look, if this thing is as bad as it could be, there'll be chaos out there. People will have tried to get away. They'll have taken boats, cars, buses, any damn thing they could. You take what you have to too. Worst case, you might have to make a raft. But it's all still there. That thing was built for a couple of thousand. The supplies should last you for months. And you can get away, wherever you want to go. Maybe even as far as Australia. The contagion may not have spread there yet. I'd like that, Keenan. I'd like to think of that, when—"

She leaned forward and kissed him.

"I like that too," he said, the smile spreading across his face. "You know, Keenan, I have a good feeling about this."

She shook her head sadly.

"Remember, people will be running about all over the place. The roads will be clogged; the airports closed down by now. But there's no way that anyone will head for the plague ship. There's no way they'll want anything to do with the RFS *Demeter.*"

Chapter Forty-Nine

ETHAN STARED AT Mick. The waiter seemed like a stranger to him again. His dark brown eyes were aglow, but not in any way that Ethan could recognise. Lily fidgeted on his lap, and for once he ignored her. "What are you doing?" he asked.

Mick shifted his focus from something far distant and met his eyes. "I am going to fight," he said, and the words were so simple and direct that Ethan knew there would be no changing his mind.

"But why?"

"Why? You need ask me why? You know this."

And Ethan did, though Mick had never told him. He'd seen the zombies coming from the city. He remembered the way that Mick had stared out of the window into a young man's dead eyes as he clambered up the outside of the pyramid, so close and yet so far away.

"Your brother."

Mick smiled. "Take care of her," he said, nodding towards the child squirming on his lap. Then he reached out, slowly, and shook Ethan's hand.

Francisco moved to their side and he too looked down at Lily's golden hair. "She is a good girl," he said. "I thought she was rich. And maybe she is, no? Richer than us. She has a good brother."

Ethan shifted uneasily. What on earth did they think he was? He was just a kid and all he'd tried to do was find his sister, and he'd failed at that, hadn't he? He'd given her up for lost. He wrapped his arms more closely around her. He would never let that happen again.

"I am also going back," Francisco said. "It will give you a chance to get away."

Ethan shook his head. "No one should go back. Not for me, not for anyone else. Not for anything."

Francisco shrugged. "I have a gun. I should fight." He looked about, as if he could see dead men walking all around him. "Those things – I do not know what they are. Or *how* they are. I only know that you do not defeat your enemies by force only. I know this better than many." He paused. "First, you defeat their minds. You make them fear. That is why – the gangs in the city, that is why they do terrible things." He glanced once more at Lily, but she showed no sign of listening to his words. "They take the heads of their enemies. They take their faces, cut them into pieces and leave them where they will be found. So it sends a message, no? I believe that someone is doing this. They conquer men's hearts then eat their flesh. Someone has unleashed death among us."

"But why?" Mick asked.

"I do not know. But I wish to find out."

They fell silent for a time, each lost in his own thoughts. Ethan looked at the scattered survivors. The doors had been pulled closed closed once more and chairs stacked in front of them. It wouldn't be hard to break through, but at least they'd hear them coming. Anyway, no one had come.

Someone had broken into a cupboard behind the podium

and found a small supply of food: biscuits, wrapped pieces of cake, even some fruit. Heather brought some over to him, unwrapping it so that he didn't need to let go of Lily. His sister ate a little and then she slept in his arms, her breathing becoming sweet and deep. No one said anything. There didn't appear to be anything left to say.

After a time Ethan found himself nodding off. He supposed he must have slept, but he woke when a stir ran through the scattered survivors. The man with the machete stepped forward.

"It's time to go," said McClelland. "We'll make our move together. That way, if there's any trouble, we can draw it away. Who's with me? Mick?"

Mick walked to his side. He seemed to Ethan to grow in stature as he went. He held the *macuahuitl* and it looked as if it belonged in his hands. And then he started pulling at his shirt and he tugged his name badge loose. He let it drop to the floor. "My name is not Mick," he said. "It is Iktan."

McClelland nodded. Then Francisco stepped forward and stood on the other side of him. He had drawn his gun and held it loosely, pointing at the floor. No one else moved.

"Last chance," McClelland said, and grinned. He scanned the room. Ethan found himself looking around with him. No one else looked inclined to volunteer. He saw Hector and remembered the way he'd brandished the fire extinguisher. The man seemed to sense his gaze and met his eyes before looking down at the floor. He gave an almost imperceptible shake of the head. Miguel, next to him, shifted his feet.

Ethan stood. He wanted to do something, to say something, but then Stacy called out and the moment was gone. "The rest of you, come with me." The group re-formed around her. She looked at McClelland and he looked back.

"So. We go," Stacy said, walking towards the doors. She gestured and a couple of people started dragging the stacks of chairs away from them once more. No sound came from the other side.

While they worked, Heather pulled away from the group and went up to McClelland. Ethan saw her pull something from her pocket – a whole bunch of those silly embroidered handkerchiefs – and she thrust them into his hands. He looked bemused, but he nodded wordlessly and stuffed them into his own pocket.

"They might be lucky," Heather said. She stood there a moment longer, as if she was trying to think of what else she could do for him, and then she walked away.

They swung the doors open, revealing an empty corridor. The way was clear. Stacy walked passed Ethan, ready to lead them. As she did, Lily stirred. She had tucked her thumb into her mouth; she removed it now, and for the first time in a long while, she spoke. "You smell nice," she said, and Ethan grinned in surprise. Then he saw Stacy's face and the smile faded.

She took her place at the front of the group, her machete in hand. She did not look back at the three men heading away in the opposite direction. And Ethan tried to pretend he hadn't noticed that the woman who had come to save them was crying.

Chapter Fifty

IT SEEMED ODD to be under the burning sun again. Ethan had a sense of disorientation, almost as if he'd expected it to be night-time, or if he'd thought he could close the door on the nightmare and wake up again in England. Or maybe it was just that he'd expected everything to be restored, as if he'd stepped out of a magical wardrobe and back into the real, sane world, like in a children's story.

Everything was quiet. It was a perfect afternoon. Bees buzzed around extravagantly purple bougainvillea spilling from a pot. A light breeze flicked at the edges of palm fronds. The sun baked the earth and melted down on to Ethan's head and sparkled on the surface of the pool, where a small cluster of zombies circled the place where the slide entered the water.

Something that vaguely resembled a human being was clinging to the top of it. He looked like a squatting toad. His skin looked like a toad's too, and Ethan saw that it was blistered and burned and peeling. He had thinning hair and his scalp and his shoulders were a pink that deepened in places to crimson. Flaps of skin had flaked away, revealing raw, painful new skin that had burned in turn.

Slowly, he turned his face towards the group that had emerged from the hotel. He blinked as if he couldn't understand what they were. His eyes were tiny in his swollen flesh and his lips looked furred. They had burned too, furrows peeling from them so that they looked twice their natural size. He looked like what he was: a man who hadn't had a drop of water to drink since the zombies came, a man who'd been trapped in the full glare of the sun with nothing to shield him from its rays. He looked desperate. The sight of him made Ethan's head ache.

Stacy hefted her machete and signalled to the others to stand back. She started to walk towards the pool. The remaining zombies hadn't seen her yet, but the man at the top of the waterslide did.

Slowly, as if his muscles wouldn't respond properly, he shook his head. Ethan saw that he was still alive but there was little in his face that was human any more. It had been seared out of him. He shifted now as if he didn't know what to do, still clutching the handrails at the top of the slide, and then he let go.

As he dropped, he crossed his hands over his chest. There was barely any chance to see his eyes, the way they looked up at the featureless, indifferent sky before he hit the water. Droplets flew high, brilliant in the sun, *like holidays*, Ethan thought, and then the zombies were on him. The pool exploded into splashing and thrashing, the zombies fighting each other in their efforts to reach him. The bright spray gave way to blood. Its deeper hue spread through the water, a pink foam forming on the surface.

Stacy had frozen. She took a step back.

Ethan caught a glimpse of wet and rotting faces dripping with pool water and blood, stinking of chlorine and death, their teeth ripping at the easy meat. He supposed there must have been screams, but he hadn't heard them. Why had the man just let go – had he simply had enough? Perhaps he'd only been waiting, after all, for someone to witness his end.

Another thought came to him, something about whether zombies preferred their meat ready roasted, and a bubble of laughter rose to his lips. He pressed his face into Lily's hair to keep it inside.

"Quick," Stacy whispered. "Before they finish."

The group kept close together and quiet as they made their way along the side of the pool and on to a narrow path edged by sweet-scented jasmine. The sea came in glimpses and then they started down the steep stairs towards it.

Ethan stepped off the patterned concrete and into deep, dry sand. The ocean was before him, wide and featureless, and he remembered the exact way he'd felt when he'd last stood in this place; he wondered how everything had changed so quickly.

He shook his head. The hotel's jagged shadow stretched in front of him. Stacy didn't pause, just stood aside, glancing around. She motioned them along the beach, pointing the way. Soon Ethan reached the edge of the hotel's shadow. He could make out the small blocky ruin that marked its top and he stepped over it, on to pale yellow sand, and it was behind him.

That's that then, he thought.

The cliffs were a dark line ahead of them. Somewhere beyond them, plumes of smoke dirtied the clear blue sky. The last time he'd been here, the sea had been full of people. They had been laughing, bouncing their kids in the waves, cooling themselves.

Ethan kissed the top of Lily's head. "We're going home," he whispered, and he walked with the others, wondering if it was odd that there seemed to be no one on the beach for as far as he could see.

Chapter Fifty-One

THE STAIRWELL ECHOED with the sounds of the dead. The walls looked new, the freshly painted shaft rising upwards, stairs wrapping around it, but every instinct told Francisco that it was really something else. He could sense the resonance of it, as if lines of ancient power lay somewhere behind the things he could see. It also stank like a tomb.

He peered upwards and saw that the handrail was smeared with some unthinkable substance. He snatched his hand back from it, taking in a breath of warm air laced with the trapped stench of rotting flesh.

"Nice," McClelland sniffed. He rounded the corner up ahead and Francisco heard him cry out, saw him stagger back a step before hurrying onward, and there came a muffled thump followed by another. An object rolled out in front of him and he blinked. He had seen such things before, left by roadside tombs – offerings to the dark saints of *Los Fieles.* He had no trouble in recognising it and yet, somehow, it was different now. *He* was different.

The thing was a girl's head. She was maybe ten years old. Her dark brown hair was tied back in two long plaits and her eyes were open and very pale. They appeared to be looking straight at him.

Francisco remembered something that El Calaca had told him once – that the eyes of the dead continue to see, even after their last breath is spent. He looked away from them.

Family, he thought. Had he really needed to find one so badly? But he was alone now. There was McClelland and there was Iktan, but each of them was alone. They would likely die alone too. He found himself wondering how long each of them had, wondered if the difference in their remaining lifespans could be reckoned in seconds or minutes. Perhaps that, after all, made them brothers of a kind.

At least Lily and Ethan had each other. They would be outside, somewhere under the open blue sky, and free. He hoped they'd stay that way. He gave a bemused smile at his own thoughts. He hadn't thought such things in a long time. Still, he had wanted to feel such things again, hadn't he? Now it seemed he did.

"Upward," McClelland murmured. They started off once more. This time McClelland stood back at each corner, peering around before continuing. Francisco still held his gun loosely in his right hand. He had some spare bullets in his pocket, but there couldn't be many left. How many tourists had been in the hotel? He supposed there must have been a lot.

Ahead, McClelland gave a warning cry. Then he staggered back into the wall, almost fell. He brought his machete up just in time to shield his arm from ravening teeth snapping closed just short of his skin. Francisco jumped to his side and fired, without hesitation, into the zombie's face.

A hole appeared in the woman's greenish-tinted forehead and she jerked back before collapsing. Francisco looked up to see others behind her, a cluster of them shuffling towards the three of them.

Iktan stepped to Francisco's side. McClelland recovered

himself and turned. They stood shoulder to shoulder as the zombies came. McClelland took a bare-chested guy under the chin with a meaty crunch, and it checked him without dropping him. Francisco shot him through the eye. It spat viscous fluid and he fell, barrelling into McClelland, almost taking him down. The next one was smaller, a young guy of about seventeen, every rib visible under his skinny chest and a hole the size of a coconut in his belly. Intestines hung like tangled string. In places they'd spilled open and Francisco could almost taste the stench of it, felt bile burning the back of his throat.

He fired a shot but the lad didn't even twitch. He lined up another, this one right between the eyes – they were placed a little too close together – and he felled the boy, heard the fragile sound of his bones cracking against the edge of a step.

Iktan buried his club in an older man's throat. Francisco could see that it was hopeless. The boy must have been crazy to come here with such a useless antique. He started to line up another shot and then Iktan wrenched back his arm, forcing the blades back and across, and the next thing Francisco knew he was dodging the man's head as it tumbled down the stairs towards him.

Iktan finished the last of them, a girl with hair that was strawberry blonde or streaked with blood, Francisco wasn't sure which. He did it in mere moments and then stood there catching his breath, not seeming to notice the gouts of crimson dripping from his club. Francisco regarded it again. Its blade was black and keen. It looked hungry. He nodded his respect at the younger man.

Then he looked down at the bodies. They didn't look like people he would ever have expected to fight. One of them – the older man – even seemed familiar, as if he might once have seen him on television. He frowned. That was why these people were brought here, wasn't it? Because they had money or fame or influence. And those things were all the same in a way, weren't they? Because they all added up to one thing: power.

Now someone had called them here, just as death began to walk the Earth. Why? To demonstrate their own power? To take those who held the respect of millions and see them laid low? Or was it simply for the pleasure of seeing the world come down?

Francisco suddenly found it hard to imagine what might be left behind, or indeed what kind of a man could ever wish to rule over it – these empty husks inhabiting a grey, dead world. But then, he had known men like that. Men who wanted only to be in control, who would tear apart everything they touched if that was what it took; men who were dead inside already.

He reloaded his gun, checking the bodies to make sure they did not twitch. He had always been a believer in life after death. He had been told it was something beautiful, something better than anything in this world. Now that he could see it with his own eyes, he could scarcely credit that he had ever believed in anything at all.

Chapter Fifty-Two

McCLELLAND LED THE way onward at a slower pace. No one had been scratched or bitten yet, but if this was how it was going to be, it would be a miracle if nobody was. Then they'd have one more of those things to deal with, and he didn't want to think about that. He was starting to wonder if he should have explained to Francisco and Iktan that he'd never had any expectation of getting out alive.

But there wasn't time to think. He rounded the next corner and saw what it held and he stopped dead. A writhing mass of bodies blocked the way upward. This is where the sound had been coming from, a moaning so muffled it had seemed to be coming from somewhere much further away. The zombies had struggled so hard to cram themselves up the stairs that they'd become wedged like a cork in a bottle. Bloated arms and legs twitched and dragged at each other, putting McClelland in mind of a fisherman's box full of maggots.

A boy crammed into the mass, his head hanging loose on a broken neck, saw them coming. He started sniffing for them and tried to turn, but he couldn't pull free. Francisco pointed his gun at the child's head but McClelland snapped out a hand

and motioned him back. They had no way of telling how far the blockage went. If they cleared it, what then? The whole stairway might be packed with them, right to the top of the pyramid. The thought of it made him feel faint. Where the hell were they all going?

Iktan pulled on his arm, motioning the way down. A few steps away there was a door, leading on to one of the hotel's lower levels.

McClelland nodded and started towards it. If the zombies were packed in here, maybe they didn't have to take them all out one by one. Maybe there was another way.

Chapter Fifty-Three

ETHAN WAS DRENCHED in sweat by the time they reached the end of the beach and Stacy called a halt. Lily was fractious, wriggling in his arms, her hair plastered to her head. Where her weight lay upon his chest, sweat pooled against his skin. It gathered too on his forehead, just above his eyebrows. A drop breached the barrier, stinging his eyes.

"You okay there?" Stacy peered at him.

Ethan couldn't bring himself to answer. He simply nodded. There was no way he was going to hand off his sister for someone else to carry, but he had never imagined she could ever feel so heavy. He wanted to set her down on the sand, to sit there with her while the waves rushed towards them and washed everything away. The sharp salt tang of it was in his nose. He would be happy to stay like that, breathing it in, as long as the rest of the world would just keep away from them.

The Hotel Baktun, from here, looked incredibly quiet. Peaceful, in fact – a haven. The sun had begun to lower in the sky behind it, bathing all it touched in gold.

"We need to head upwards" Stacy said, "on to the cliffs. We

should be able to see out over Acapulco from there. Then we can decide what to do."

"You don't know?" Hector looked petulant, but no one met his eyes; no one else asked questions. They simply followed Stacy as she led them on to the rocks.

The path was narrow and edged by jagged boulders. At first it was slippery and there were crabs that scattered as they clambered towards them. Ethan heard the odd clicking sounds they made under the noise of the waves. Here and there, tiny white flowers clung and danced in the breeze. Now that the land was edged with teeth, the waves looked rougher. They rushed in fast, turning to foam that whipped into a spray.

If it wasn't for the heat, Ethan could have fancied himself to be somewhere on the coast of England. And then he looked down and saw the body in the water, lifting on the swell before sliding down the glassy side of a wave. It looked as if it had once been a man. It floated face down, staring at who knew what. Its hands floated wide, as if he were reaching after something he could no longer grasp.

"Come on." Stacy spoke softly. He turned away, his feet gritting on the path. He wasn't sure the others had seen the shape in the water. Thankfully, they were leaving him behind; the body was below them now. Whatever it was that the dead man was looking for, at least he wouldn't be able to reach out and touch them.

The path levelled out and they clambered one by one to the top of the cliff. Stacy had been right, they could catch glimpses of the city, tessellated pieces of rooftop and the jutting towers of high-rise hotels hugging the coastline. In the distance everything gave way to murky green mountains. Parts of Acapulco were burning, but Ethan couldn't hear any sirens. The city had fallen silent.

He turned and looked back at the Hotel Baktun. He could see it all quite clearly, its twelve jagged steps blurred by the shapes clinging to them. He could easily make out its flat rooftop, its glass-topped bar and the ruin behind it.

He heard Iktan's soft voice, as if he whispered in his ear: *The* Monumento que Canta *is here. It is also called the* Tumba que Canta – *the tomb that sings. Did you know that?*

And Ethan caught his breath as a spotlight speared out from the top of the hotel, piercing the evening sky.

Chapter Fifty-Four

McCLELLAND LED THE way back outside and towards the gardening hut he'd visited with Stacy so long ago. The day was drawing to a close, the shadows lengthening. He didn't like going back instead of onward; it made him feel every bit of the tiredness that was dragging at his bones.

He went straight up to the door of the outbuilding, but hesitated before he opened it. He could smell what was inside. The dead thing had smelled bad enough before he'd killed it for a second time. Now it was worse; the air was thick with it. He tasted the death in it, could feel it creeping into him.

"*Guácala*," Francisco muttered, wiping his mouth. "You are sure about this?"

"Wait here." McClelland didn't have time to stand and think about it. If he did that, he'd never go inside. He pushed open the door and a sliver of light gleamed back from what looked like a foot-wide slug trail. The body was slumped on the floor where they'd left it. It didn't look as if anything else had tried to eat it during the intervening time, but it was difficult to tell.

Iktan came in behind him. McClelland didn't wait; he just stepped over the body and started searching, not for machetes, but for the thing he should have found in the beginning. A row of cupboards with plain metal doors lined the back wall. He opened two of them before he found what he sought: a canister of petrol. He could tell it was almost full from the weight as he lifted it over the edge of the cupboard. He shook it and heard a dull sloshing. He suddenly wanted to breathe it in, to banish that other stench with its sour-fruit aroma, but instead he straightened.

"We should put that on," Iktan said.

McClelland frowned, turned to him, and saw that the Mayan boy was still staring down, not at the petrol, but at the dead body. "What?"

"It might hide us," he said. "If we wear its skin – the god of death might pass over us, when he comes."

McClelland stared down at the slowly drying yellow-purple mess spread out on the floor. He felt quite sure, suddenly, that he was going to vomit.

"Fuck that," he said, and pushed his way ahead of Iktan, outside, back into the fading day. It wasn't until he looked upward that he saw the beam of light scanning the sky, like a beacon shining from the biggest lighthouse in the world.

Francisco watched it too, his head tilted back. "Don't know what they doin', man, but all the *desollados* in the world going to see that." He said it conversationally, as if he'd just commented on the weather; or as if he didn't care any longer.

"We should get moving," McClelland said. "Whatever they're doing here, they're doing it *now*." He looked gravely up at the light. It swept one way and then the other, like a huge signal. "Wait – what's the date today?" But he knew the answer to the question before he'd finished saying the words. It was the day everyone had come here for; the one they had all been meant to celebrate. It was the day the Hotel Baktun officially opened.

"It's the ceremony," he said. "The opening ceremony, only

no one's here to celebrate it any more. Those lights must be automatic. They were meant to be part of the show."

"There is someone here. Just not who they were expecting, is all." Francisco jabbed a finger upward, to where dark shapes pressed against the rail at the edge of the pyramid's flat top.

McClelland saw that he was right. The roof of the hotel was already becoming crowded. "Christ. We need to get a move on, while they're all trapped up there." He started to walk back towards the entrance, Francisco moving with him. Only Iktan remained where he was, staring upward with eyes that did not blink. McClelland wasn't sure he liked the expression on the boy's face. It was as if he was barely seeing what lay in front of him at all.

"Come on, kid," he said, and at last Iktan turned.

The blank look passed. "I am not your kid," he said, and he brandished his club. He grinned lovingly over it, the lowering sun gleaming off black blades and white teeth.

McClelland didn't answer. He suddenly didn't have any words. No, the Mayan boy was not his kid. He could see that; he could see it in the madness shining from his eyes. With an expression like that, McClelland could almost permit himself to hope that they might just bring this off after all.

Chapter Fifty-Five

INSIDE THE HOTEL, all was quiet and all was dark. In the intervening time, the main lighting had switched itself off; only emergency lights pointed the way with their greenish glow. McClelland wondered if it must have been planned as part of the entertainment. The show hadn't just been intended for the guests; the hotel was meant to be seen. The spotlight shining from its roof must now seem brighter than ever. Still, it wasn't difficult to make their way back to the stairwell. The sound of zombies guided them.

As soon as they reached the place where the dead had blocked the stairs, McClelland unscrewed the top of the canister. The smell of petrol was a welcome relief from the zombie stink in the enclosed space. He splashed it across the writhing, moving bodies and their cries rose in volume.

When he stood back, Francisco was already holding a match in front of his face. He grinned. "Get ready," he said, and McClelland leaped back down the stairs as he threw it at the petrol. He heard the *whump* of ignition behind him and a flare of heat seared the back of his neck.

The moaning deepened, was interspersed with the high-pitched whistle of air hissing through fat. They crouched down low as thick smoke crept down the stairs and over their heads. Iktan started to cough.

"Shit," McClelland said. "They're packed in too tight. We have to go lower." As if in affirmation, a drift of blackness passed in front of his eyes. The zombies were burning, but there was nowhere for the smoke to escape, nowhere but down. And zombies didn't need to breathe, but they did. He shook his head in frustration. He wanted them to burn, for the whole hotel to burn if need be, carrying all its demons to whatever Hell was waiting for them. But there was no air up there, not past the first layer of bodies. The fire would quickly go out.

"Get back," he called, his chest wheezing. "We have to find another way. This isn't going to fucking work."

Iktan stood there, his shoulders shaking, and McClelland realised he wasn't coughing but laughing. "What the hell is it?"

The lad met his eyes. "At the beginning," he said. "In the kitchens. I switched off the flame. I did not want everything to burn. A pity, no? Now—"

McClelland gave him a shove, got him moving. They started back down the stairs, McClelland's chest growing tight. He could almost feel the zombies above him, hundreds and hundreds of dead presences, waiting for them.

I'm coming, he thought. And then: *I'm sorry, Stacy.*

He led them from the stairwell and along a corridor that looked the same as so many others. There was another staircase along here, wasn't there? And then Francisco caught his arm, bringing them to a halt.

McClelland stared at what he had seen. They had reached the lifts, all of them with their doors closed, no lights on to indicate they would ever move again. But next to them stood another, smaller lift. He didn't recall having seen it before. He only had a vague recollection of one of those small, blank black doors that wouldn't open. It was open now. The light inside was on and as they watched it flickered, as if in invitation.

Chapter Fifty-Six

STACY STARED HARD at the Hotel Baktun. She couldn't believe McClelland was still in there. What the hell had he been thinking? He would die, and that death would be needless, and it would solve nothing. The zombies had come and they were making the world anew in their image. She could see it in the way the whole pyramid seemed to glow, taking on a bloody hue as the sun spread itself along the horizon. The ruin at its top was alight.

He should have run. He should have run with *her.*

The boy with the pale face and the old eyes stood at her side. She knew he was exhausted, but she also knew he wouldn't let her help. He wasn't that kind. He placed his sister gently on the ground. The woman – Heather – crouched in front of the child, stroking her cheek.

"He might make it," Ethan said. "We all did."

"We weren't idiots." Stacy hadn't intended to spit out the words so bitterly. "We didn't just decide to kill ourselves."

The boy didn't reply, and she cursed herself. She was supposed to be leading these people, giving them hope, not terrifying them. Not making everything worse. She drew in a deep breath, trying to think of how she could soften her words, and time stretched out between them. She could think of nothing.

Ethan's face drew into a look of concentration.

"What is it?"

He didn't answer. He only narrowed his eyes, leaning forward, as if that would help him see better. She followed his gaze, saw the glowing pyramid with the light bursting from its top, and she frowned. "What is it?"

He pointed. She still couldn't see what he meant, but then she did. Something had changed at the south-easterly corner of the pyramid. As the sun sank away in the west, deep shadows were spreading from its jagged edges. It had started at the topmost step – two clear triangles had already formed. Another was almost complete.

"The serpent," he whispered.

"What do you mean?"

"Mick – *Iktan* – my friend would have known," Ethan said. "It was in my mother's guidebook. She told me about it at the airport."

She waited for the rest. As she did, a fourth shadow began to creep downwards from the pyramid's edge.

"It makes a serpent," he said. "A shadow serpent, and it creeps down the pyramid. Not here – it's not supposed to be here. It happens at Chichen Itza, the Mayan – the Maya site. It means..." his voice faded.

"Tell me. What does it mean?" Stacy's voice was urgent. It suddenly seemed important; as if a story from a book could mean something now, as if anything could.

"It's the feathered serpent. Kukulkan, they called it. Twice a year, at the equinoxes, its shadow slithers down the pyramid and goes to the sacred well."

Stacy stared at it. There was no equinox and no well here, not that she knew of. There was only the ocean, giving rise to its constant whisper.

"The serpent allowed men to talk to the gods. But..." he paused. "Only where there was sacrifice. Bloodletting, was the way they put it."

McClelland, she thought, and his name was like a pain in her chest. She put her hand to the place and felt her heart under it, beating fast. What was this boy saying? Dreams and visions, that was all. They were only words. They couldn't mean anything.

The shadows seemed to be travelling quickly now. The shape they formed was almost perfect, though it didn't put her in mind of a snake; it was more like the ridges of a dragon's back. But what had he called it? *The feathered serpent*. Maybe that was what they had meant.

"The serpent could also mean something else," Ethan said. "Besides communing with the gods."

"What?"

He didn't meet her eye. "War," he said softly.

For a while, they didn't speak. They simply watched as the serpent came. It had almost reached the base of the pyramid. The colour of its shadow was taking on warmth; the setting sun had touched it with crimson.

Stacy cried out. The single beam of light shooting upwards like the gaze of a baleful eye had given way as more illumination snapped on, this time lighting up the whole rooftop. It made the surface of the pyramid as bright as day and revealed the horde that had gathered there.

They stood and watched as a single figure stepped up on to the top of the ancient ruin that had been waiting there all along. He stood tall before them, and he raised his arms up high in a gesture of triumph.

Chapter Fifty-Seven

THEY SQUEEZED INTO the lift together, McClelland feeling a wave of displaced reality. The machete in his hand spoke of basic survival, but now he reached out and pressed the lift's single button, as if he were a pampered hotel guest off to take a shower. Immediately, the lift began to rise. No one asked where they were going. There was no way of stopping it anyway.

McClelland felt, more than ever, that they were being manipulated, that everything around them was falling into place just as someone had intended it to, and then the lift came to a gentle halt.

The sight that met them as the door slid open made McClelland's insides turn to ice. He had never imagined that death had claimed so many. They stood now shoulder to shoulder, their decay exposed to the setting sun. There were the drowned and the diseased, the young and the old, men and women. All of the new and ancient dead seemed to have gathered together in this one place.

Thankfully their backs were turned and McClelland realised that they were all looking towards the thing that stood outlined against the bloody sky: the ancient Mayan ruin. Its old stones echoed back the sound of their keening. It seemed to echo and amplify the mournful chorus of death.

As McClelland watched, spotlights ignited all around them. For a moment every dead man or woman was haloed in a bright white light. He flinched, blinking away the after-images that danced before his eyes, and then he saw a shape standing above the rest. It was a man. He had stepped up on to the Mayan structure at the top of the pyramid. His features were cast into darkness by the shadows of last rays of the failing sun. He stood there a moment before raising his arms to greet the onrushing night.

Another light snapped on, as if in answer to his summons, revealing the man's face.

Even from across the rooftop McClelland could see that he was old. His cheeks were hollow, his eye sockets sunken, his skin as dry as paper and as wrinkled as a prune. He looked as if he'd stepped out of a gas-lit Georgian street in his black frock coat, which was ragged and covered in what appeared to be dust or mould. A white kerchief was ruffled at his neck and it alone looked fresh, accentuating the greenish-grey tinge of his skin. It was obvious that the man was dead.

McClelland remembered something that Stacy had told him, that the owner of the hotel was a descendant of Thomas Moreby, the black magician and architect who had died back in London in the early 1800s. Now he had no doubt that the man himself was standing before him.

As if in answer to his thoughts, Moreby turned and met McClelland's eyes. His direct gaze took in the three of them, standing there isolated among the dead, holding weapons that seemed pitiful in the face of the host. He gave a slow smile. Then he pointed in their direction and all hell broke loose.

The zombies turned as one and began to shamble in their direction. Some were quicker than others; those wearing the once brightly coloured clothes of tourists were first to reach them. Others followed on behind – those with sea-bloated flesh or withered husks that looked as if they'd spent years or decades in the ground. Francisco fired his gun and one of them dropped. It didn't stop the others, who simply stepped over their fallen comrade, raising their hands to reach for them.

McClelland braced himself, and on each side Iktan and Francisco turned so that their backs were covered. McClelland's machete claimed its first throat and a low gurgle was cut short. The zombie fell to its knees and was trampled underfoot.

Iktan's blade was hungrier still. It swept a zombie's head from its shoulders, catching another on the backswing. Blood – or some kind of cold ichor – spattered McClelland's face. He shook it away, scything through another of their attackers. Francisco fired again and again and then came the sound McClelland had, on some level, been waiting to hear: a dry click.

At once, Francisco threw the gun into a dead man's face. He pulled a thick-bladed knife from his pocket and stuck a middle-aged woman through the temple. He tried to pull it free, yanked again harder, almost falling when it came loose. McClelland could see what was going to happen. The knife was powerful, but it wasn't clean. Francisco would have to pin the zombies down and saw the heads from their bodies before death came. There was no way to do that here.

A dry scratching undercut the rustling and wailing rising from the army of the dead, and he realised it was coming from Moreby. He was laughing. The laughter went on and on, as if it were trapped inside McClelland's brain, and he suddenly knew that he had heard the man's voice before, when they had been standing in the basement.

Let them spread our glory across the Earth . . .

But they weren't spreading glory. The living were going to lose. He made a desperate lunge forward, covering Francisco.

They were being pushed aside by the press of bodies. The zombies did not give way in the face of fear or anything else. They would simply keep on coming until there was nothing left to stop them. Then they would be free. They'd spread their plague across the world, making everything their own. Soon McClelland would fall. Perhaps, before he did, he would see his friends – his *brothers* – fall first. It wasn't something he wanted to witness.

He fought on because there was nothing else left to do. His arm rose and fell and claimed more of the creature's heads. Bodies were piling up and they retreated behind them. At least it was something to slow the onslaught.

They fell back, towards the edge of the roof. Iktan swept a man's head clean off his shoulders and it tumbled from the pyramid, making a sick thudding noise as it bounced downwards. The boy he'd met, with the wan smile and bent stance, had become a warrior. McClelland could feel the battle hunger that burned from his friend and he redoubled his own efforts.

The machete stuck in a bony neck and he tugged it free with a wet sound. He turned and saw a figure that was little more than a skeleton coming for him. What appeared to be a corroded cutlass dangled from a loose, sea-faded leather strap. The thing didn't use the cutlass, didn't even seem conscious that it was there. It reached for Francisco with the hook it had in place of a hand, painting a deep scratch across the Mexican's face.

Francisco stabbed out with the knife but McClelland was quicker. Their weapons struck in mid-air with a clang, then metal struck bone. The pirate's head went the same way as the other, clacking its way down to the balcony below. The torso, released from whatever occult power had been holding it together, collapsed and clattered to the deck like jackstraws.

Others stepped forward and took its place, apparitions with

grinning teeth and rotting cheeks and the flesh flayed from their bones and missing fingers and sunken eyes and their endless, insatiable hunger and, always, the smell of death. McClelland went on slashing and cutting. His mind was shutting down. Such things had never meant to be seen in this world, and there was nothing to do but fight against it; and so he fought.

Chapter Fifty-Eight

IT WAS A hopeless sight. Ethan looked on anyway as the tiny figures were pushed ever closer to the edge of the pyramid. The man standing on the ruin simply watched.

Ethan glanced at Stacy. She showed no sign of wanting to keep moving; it was as if she too needed to see this. Tears had sprung to her eyes and she did not stop them or wipe them away. The three who had gone back to fight were hopelessly outmatched. It was clear to Ethan that soon, they would fall.

As he watched, something did fall from the building, bouncing down from one level to the next. He narrowed his eyes. He couldn't make out what it was, but he thought he knew. It was a decapitated head, flung from the flat top of the pyramid. That chimed with something else he'd read in his mother's book, such a short time ago and yet it felt like a thousand years.

What should have been an opening celebration for a fabulous new hotel – a grand new achievement, wrought by man – was now a sacrificial bloodbath. He half-closed his eyes, picturing the ancient Mayans cutting the heads from their offering's bodies and flinging them from their pyramids.

It came to him that their gods must have been hungry too, that perhaps, as Iktan had once suggested, they would always be unsatisfied. Perhaps that was the thing with sacrifices; they only made the gods hungrier still, as if their appetites were only increased by the more they were given.

Chapter Fifty-Nine

FRANCISCO BATTLED ON with the only weapon he had left, slicing through a boy's throat. This was the end, the only chance he had to make his life count; after this there would only be death. He wondered what that death might hold. He wondered how long it might last. *One bullet*, he thought. *Why hadn't he kept just one?* He might have had time to send it through his own skull before they took him. Maybe that would have given him peace.

McClelland took off an old woman's head; half of her nose and cheek were already bitten away. She fell before she could reach Francisco. The man was covering him.

Farther off, Iktan let out a cry at once full of rage and exultation. They were being driven back. The knife wouldn't stop them. Francisco stabbed wildly, catching hands and arms and chests. He got a good swing, managed to embed the blade in a zombie's head, and that one went down though it nearly dragged the knife from his hand. Then he saw what was coming for him through the crowd of the dead, and his heart failed in his chest.

She was taller than the others and wearing only the shreds

of a thin, green summer dress. She had lustrous long dark hair, embedded with seaweed, and the flesh had been almost entirely stripped from her. She smiled as she advanced. Her teeth were white and her bones glowed through what remained of her flesh. She was a living skeleton and yet she was beautiful. The remnants of grace clung to her, undefeated even by death. Francisco could see the shape of the skull beneath her skin and it held nobility in it. He did not know how he knew that, how such a thing could even be possible; he only knew that it was.

She cut through the crowd and they parted around her. Francisco's hand fell to his side. *La Poderosa Señora*: Our Lady of Death. She was here before him, and she had eyes only for Francisco.

His gaze dropped from hers. He couldn't look at her; she was too beautiful. He could see her heart through her ribs. It was there, but it did not beat. The sight of her stole the strength from his legs, from his arms. It was as he had said, and the words returned to mock him: *You do not defeat your enemies by force only. First you defeat their minds. You make them fear.*

He trembled as she approached and he felt something grab him from behind, its sharp teeth closing on his shoulder. His eyes narrowed in pain. *It begins*, he thought. *The thing that was waiting all along.*

He had thought he would be able to feel the infection going into him. He had thought it would rob him of life before it took his soul, but actually the pain was oddly sweet. So long he had waited and now it had found him, and it was like seeing once more the face of an old friend.

He had eyes only for her. He had denied her for so long, his Lady. Now she came towards him. She was smiling; she could do nothing else. She stood before him in her finery. No: there was no finery, only her ocean-stained rags, her necklace of seaweed, but she carried it about her anyway. Her greatness

clung to her like robes. There was no doubt in his mind that here was something approaching a god.

He touched the medallion at his throat, picturing for a moment the image of his namesake. It felt like a cold, lifeless thing in his hand.

The Lady reached out towards him, and Francisco realised something odd. The zombies weren't attacking him any longer. If anything they seemed to be drawing away. Perhaps they knew he was already one of them; but then, he *wasn't* one of them, not yet. Even as he thought the words, the start of coldness began to spread upwards from the base of his spine. *No*. It couldn't be. He had only wanted to feel again, to feel – *something*.

He stepped forwards, towards her outstretched hand. He had no choice. There was a buzzing sound somewhere deep in the back of his skull, and it was like a thousand humming mosquitoes. He almost felt there were words in it, that if he only knew how to listen, he would understand what they said. A part of him – the part of him that was still Francisco – somehow knew that it wouldn't be long before he did.

He groaned, pulling away from her. The other zombies were moving aside, giving them space. The Lady – *La Flaca* – stepped backwards and Francisco followed. He no longer knew how to do anything else. He walked through the tide that had parted before him and he approached the ruin. He could feel its age now, sense the power humming through its ancient stones. He narrowed his eyes and noticed a strange thing; a cloud of insects hung over the monument, hovering there like a crimson cloud. The man in the black coat was almost hidden at their heart.

The woman turned at last, stretching her jaws wider into a rictus grin, and she bowed before the man standing on the ruin. *Husband*. The word was not spoken but Francisco heard it anyway, in words as dry and lifeless as desert sand.

Wife.

The edges of Francisco's sight were turning black, his vision narrowing to only their faces. Distantly, he thought he could hear someone calling his name; perhaps they were calling him home.

He began to turn and then a third figure stepped forward, taking his place at the lady's side. It was a figure Francisco knew. It was someone he had once called brother.

He too was skinny and wasted. He too looked as if he was grinning, his gold teeth flashing through an almost lipless mouth. He bared them at Francisco.

It was El Calaca, the Skeleton, now truly one of the dead. And he was coming for him; for one of his own. He walked towards him and Francisco wanted to run but found he could not. His legs would not move. Everything he had sown was returning to him. He had sworn fealty to this man and soon, truly, he would be *Los Fieles*; he would be one of the faithful. He would have no mind left, no choices to make that were his own. There would be only cold death and the voices in his mind and nothing of himself remaining at all.

He kept his eyes open. He had wanted so little of the time that remained to him. He thought for a moment of the child with the golden hair, now hopefully far, far away from him. He had wanted a family, yes, but not the one that had come for him. He had wanted to *feel*, but not like this.

Now he did feel it as El Calaca reached out and sunk one sharp claw deep into the wound in his shoulder. The centre of it was numb, but the rest burned like fire and Francisco opened his mouth to scream. He felt it as El Calaca leaned forward as if to kiss his forehead, and instead pinched his teeth, so delicately, around the skin. He felt it as suddenly, sharply, those teeth ripped downwards, tearing the skin from his face. He felt it go, as delicate as paper, and the pain was exquisite.

He felt it as El Calaca closed his embrace around him, moving in as close as a lover, biting down once more on his scalp, tearing the skin down his forehead to his nose. It hung from El Calaca's golden teeth for a moment before he sucked it down.

He felt it as El Calaca leaned in once more, bringing with him the stench of decay, this time biting at the tender skin below Francisco's eye. Distantly, he knew that he was screaming. And the knowledge came, bringing with it certainty: soon he would feel nothing at all, and so he relished it, cradling it to his heart like some golden treasure, feeling everything in the world in ways he never had before.

He smiled as the skin was torn from his face, becoming a *desollado* at last, understanding everything, and he opened his eyes one last time to see El Calaca looking deeply into them, his expression one of love.

It was always so, Francisco thought, as the darkness rushed towards him. *They always did the most terrible things to those they once called family.*

Chapter Sixty

IKTAN BELLOWED HIS rage. The zombies all around them had stopped, had turned to face the man on the stone, as if awaiting orders only they could hear. Francisco was screaming in pain. McClelland was trying to cut his way through to their friend but the zombies had closed ranks, shoulder pressed to shoulder, and they were packed in too tight. He couldn't even swing the machete.

Iktan raised the *macuahuitl*, swinging it around his head before taking aim. Its hunger drove down through his hand and along his arm, into his heart. It was as if he and the weapon were one. He struck another head from its dead shoulders and the zombie in front of him fell. Iktan did not know if it had been a man or woman and he did not care. It barrelled into him, taking him back, and he staggered into something solid and yet yielding. He felt the dampness of suppurating skin on his arm and he pushed it away in disgust.

Now he couldn't see Francisco, but he could still hear him. He wished that he could not.

He couldn't see McClelland either. Every instinct told him to be silent in case it brought all the zombies to him, but he forced himself to call out for his friend. There was no answer, only a smothered cry ahead of him and away to the side, which told him that his friend was being dragged away. It was truly over, then. Death was everywhere and there was no one left to cover their backs and yet, for now, the zombies were not attacking.

They had simply stopped, as if whatever force was driving them had gone. Then something nudged his arm and Iktan nearly screamed. It was a child, a girl of about seven with honey-coloured, blood-streaked hair. She held out her hand.

Fighting back his revulsion and moving as if in a dream, Iktan took it. Her hand didn't look so bad – the skin was discoloured but whole – and yet it was so cold, a chill that was bone-deep. He shuddered but he did not let go. He only tightened his grip on the club with his other hand, wondering if he would still be able to bring himself to take her head if that was what was needed. Then the crowd parted around them and the little girl led him across the roof towards the ruin that dominated it all.

Iktan stood before it. The white stones were inflamed and bloody against the darkening sky. The man in the ragged black clothes looked down upon him. And Iktan realised that, although the zombies around him were silent, their moaning ceased, the *Tumba que Canta* continued to sing, spilling its mournful sound into the night air.

That noise made Iktan think of lost places, lonely places. He glanced around and realised that, from here, he could see everything. Acapulco looked more peaceful than he had ever seen it. There was no hum of traffic, no angry beeping of car horns, no music crashing from the beachside bars lining the Costera road. It was quiet; for once in this world it was quiet, and the mountains all around them were dark.

Above them was only the endless indifference of the sky and here were only the man in black's eyes, staring so deeply into him it made Iktan feel as if the man could see everything; every small and hopeless thought or word or dream Iktan had ever had in his life.

The wailing coming from the ruin intensified. It sounded like pain, echoing from the depths of the world.

The man smiled. He spoke in a voice that was little more than a whisper and yet Iktan heard him quite clearly. "He is hungry."

He stepped down from the ruin and stood in front of Iktan. He was gaunt and tall and his nose was pinched and aquiline, his skin dry as old parchment. His eyes were the very palest of greys.

Iktan could not bear the thought of the man walking up to him, maybe even touching him, and he took a step backwards. He looked down to see that his hand was empty; even the little girl had gone. He stood alone, with this man who was an empty hole in the world, and he shivered.

This is where everything would end. He remembered the way he had looked up at the pyramid when he'd first come to the Hotel Baktun. He had looked upon it and imagined it would have incensed the gods. Now he was not so sure. Perhaps this is what they wanted all along; perhaps they were never so much angered as hungry for the human flesh they had for so long been denied.

The man in front of him nodded, as if he had seen the dawning of understanding in Iktan's eyes. Then he turned his head and looked away and across, scanning the air itself, as if there was something else he wanted Iktan to see.

He followed the dead man's gaze and saw they were not alone on the rooftop. A dark cloud of insects – mosquitoes? No, they were fleas, he realised, huge red fleas – hung over them all, and suddenly he could hear their high-pitched droning. He watched their progress as they moved across the top of the pyramid, then circled back towards him.

He shook his head as if in denial, but it wasn't any use. The first of them came, then all of them, landing on his arms, thick and brown. He swiped at them as they began to bite. He couldn't feel them, not really, but his skin prickled anyway as they redoubled their attack.

Suddenly he was itching everywhere: along his hairline, in the line of sweat across the back of his neck, inside his sleeves. He writhed. He rubbed at his face. When he took his hand away it was streaked with blood. One of his eyelids had begun to swell. He couldn't feel any pain, but his vision was starting to narrow. He cried out in disgust. He had never seen so many fleas; had there ever been so many?

The man laughed. And just as suddenly as they had descended, they left him.

Iktan watched in disbelief as the cloud formed once more. It hovered, then moved away towards the *Tumba que Canta*. There, they landed. No: he realised they didn't land. Instead they sought out the gaps between the stones, the narrow slots. They were disappearing into the structure itself.

The wailing sound intensified and turned into something else; a sound that filled Iktan with dread.

"My dear friend," the man said, smiling still. "Why do you believe it to be called a tomb?"

Iktan stared. He could not reply. He only watched as the man turned and gestured towards the ruin.

As one, the zombies shambled towards it. They covered it with their bodies, stumbling into each other in their efforts to obey. Then the first of them were pushing outward once more, this time carrying ancient white stones in their hands.

They flung them from the rooftop and Iktan heard them crashing down below. The zombies fell back and were replaced by others, carrying more stones as they disassembled the structure that had stood for so many centuries, first on the sea shore and then in this place. Iktan tried to see what lay within.

A body, old as time, perhaps still with tufts of hair clinging to its head and wrapped in rags? Gold... treasure?

The zombies fell back, staggering away from the ruin as a deafening cry rang out. Then the thing that had been hidden inside the tomb slowly rose and towered above them all.

Iktan's heart failed inside him. He fell to his knees. The monstrous god had risen, and he wanted only to bury himself into the earth, to hide himself from its gaze. It wasn't a desiccated cadaver; it was real and vital and dead.

Its eyes glowed with some unholy fire and its chest was bared, every rib visible beneath the putrescent skin. It wore a headdress of bright feathers and a circlet of jade, while a conch shell, split in half, hung about its neck. A human skull, the empty eye sockets gaping, adorned its crown.

It was taller than any of the walking dead, much taller than Iktan. He cowered before it, found himself sobbing. He frantically searched for the club that was no longer in his hand, scraping his knuckles against the empty ground.

He tried to hide his face as it cried out once more. There were no words, but Iktan knew what it wanted. The sound resonated through his chest until he thought his ribs would vibrate into dust. And suddenly the memory came to him and he knew what he had to do.

He let out a moan, inarticulate and loud. Then he wailed as if in pain. He remembered the gentle gaze of the friend he had discovered in the midst of death, Ethan's blank look as he had told him of Ah Puch, the god of death.

Howl, Iktan had told him. *Moan. Scream. Ah Puch will think you are troubled by demons already. He will pass you by. If he thinks you are one of the dead, he will not drag you down to* Mitnal – *to the lowest level of Hell.*

Iktan groaned again, already knowing that it wasn't any use. He had heard Francisco's dying screams, his cries of pain. His own cries were nothing like that.

Not yet.

A heavy step came towards him and he covered his head with his arms. Soon he would be moaning for real. He would be moaning, but he would no longer be troubled by demons; not then. Iktan had the feeling that soon he would be troubled by nothing at all.

His insides felt light, as if he were floating. He wished, more than anything, that he could do that now, simply rise up and away, leaving all of this behind. He waited for the crushing blow, the death blow, the ripping of teeth; it did not come.

He lifted his head. *Iktan, you are a man. A warrior.*

He raised his head the rest of the way. He did not know where the words had come from – somewhere deeper inside him than he could name – but he knew that they were right. They had to be right. Slowly, he drew himself up, unfolding from the ground. He stood and looked into the eyes of the beast. It looked back, blank and indifferent as the sky. Fleas whirled and hummed around its head.

"He was hungry." It was the man who spoke. "So very hungry."

The thing opened its mouth, revealing sharp, pointed yellow teeth. As if bidden, the fleas flew inside and the thing swallowed them down, the insects and the blood they carried.

"His servants have sustained him."

Iktan stared. So that was it. That was how the thing had slept, down through the aeons; with the blood of men still feeding its fevered dreams. And now it had been awakened again.

When he looked at it, he knew that the world was lost. No one could or would stand against it. The old gods would join with the new, and men would flee before them. They would hide in terror and they would die. Worse, they would bow down and worship.

But Iktan refused to bow down now. There was no club in his hand to give him strength; no family remained to him. But he stood before it and he did not flinch as it bent towards him.

The baleful god stared into his eyes. Iktan felt as if it was examining his soul. Then it tilted its head to one side, as if considering.

When it reached in towards him and he understood, Iktan could not stand tall any longer. He was a child again. He wanted to hold his brother's hand. He wanted his mother.

The god's hands reached for what it needed and its touch was cold on Iktan's face. Tears spilled from his eyes as its fingers felt for their source, probing the hollows, and then turned to claws that pierced the warm meat, gouging and closing around the thing they sought before ripping it from Iktan's head.

Iktan screamed. It was a real scream now; he couldn't help it. Half his vision had gone dark. He saw the god as it brought its treasure towards its own face and at the same time, like a veil drawn over the world, he saw blackness. It was both things at once, and it was pain. He reached towards his eye, the one the monster now held in its clawed hand, and he touched his own ravaged face, stopping just short of the bloody wound which was all that remained.

Ah Puch cradled the eye, bringing it closer. Iktan expected it to open its mouth, to close those yellowed teeth on the still-glistening orb, to see the juice spurt from the sweet fruit. Instead it raised the eye higher, towards the headdress it wore and the skull that sat atop it. Then it pushed it into the empty socket.

The god looked at Iktan once more.

Iktan started to shake. He no longer felt fear, only an emptiness he knew would never leave him; that, and a bone-deep resignation. He thought it might be shock, settling into his body. A chill sweat broke out across his forehead.

The god reached for him once more and Iktan closed his remaining eye, as if that could protect it, as if it could protect *him*, and he let out the unrestrained sob of a child as darkness came to swallow his world.

Chapter Sixty-One

LOOKING AT THE ROOF of the Hotel Baktun, Ethan could see the zombies for what they were; a swarm, come to subsume everything. It had been hopeless from the beginning. As their friends ceased to carve their way through the colourless crowd and disappeared among them, he knew that all was lost.

He just wasn't sure that Stacy had realised it yet. She stared out towards the hotel and her eyes gleamed with moisture. The pyramid blended into its surroundings, darkness creeping up from the ground and spreading all around it, claiming it for its own. The city too was fading into night, becoming one with the encompassing mountains. Only the top of the pyramid shone, a beacon that would surely be visible for miles.

Was that why it had been built? To demonstrate to all who could see it the power of the new world that was to come?

Stacy roused herself and turned from the scene. She looked in the opposite direction, out on to the darkening sea. Its colour had deepened to a dull purple, save for a pale fringe that showed where the sun had once been.

She stared intently down the coastline. Ethan realised that

the sea wasn't empty; a small yacht was skipping across the waves. Beyond that, further out, was something larger still.

"There," she said, pointing. "That's where we're going."

Ethan shivered; he did not know why.

"It's abandoned," she said, and the word felt right to Ethan, as if she'd spoken some truth of which she hadn't even been conscious. Abandoned; yes, they were all abandoned now.

Stacy waited, as if she expected someone to object, but nobody did. Their faces were exhausted or resigned or blank with shock. No one had any objections left.

"We should go now." She spoke firmly, but no one moved, not even her. She turned to look once more at the hotel. Ethan had the feeling that the only person she was trying to persuade was herself.

Chapter Sixty-Two

McCLELLAND COULDN'T SEE a way out. He was hemmed in by the stinking dead. He knew that he'd never rid his lungs of the scent of them; he'd die with it still in his nostrils. His skin crept with revulsion. Still, they were no longer intent on attacking him. He hadn't been bitten or scratched. But he had seen Iktan go down, taken by the thing that had emerged from the ruin, and he knew that he would be next.

His hand was slippery on the machete. He tightened his grip anyway. There was nowhere to hide, even if he'd wanted to. But he didn't want to; all he wanted was more death.

He looked across the roof at the creature that had sprung from a nightmare and he saw Iktan's eyes looking back at him. They looked doleful, as if they could see everything and understood what it meant – the end. The apocalypse, perhaps even the one the Mayans had foretold, arriving not at the end of the baktun but here, at its hellish namesake.

He knew it didn't matter if he became one of them; there was nothing else left. Still, a part of him did not want to call the zombies' attention to his presence. If he did, they would scratch. They would bite. They would separate flesh from bone with their teeth and they would swallow him down.

It didn't matter.

What mattered now was not if he was turned. What mattered was how quickly.

Silently, he counted how many of the dead stood between him and Thomas Moreby, the man who had orchestrated the death of his friends and the wreck of all that he could see. There were a lot of them. The nearest looked as if it had been dead a long time. Its skin was mummified and its clothes were rags; impossible to tell what kind of costume it had once been.

McClelland brought his hand back and impaled it through the neck. Its head came away, hoisted aloft on the blade's point, and he flung it across the crowd. McClelland let out a cry that was part disgust and part exhilaration.

The zombies turned to face him.

It felt right. It had always seemed to him that it would come down to this. He struck out at the next macerated face, slashing at it, but it did not do what McClelland had expected; it reached out and grabbed his arm, as if to detain him while awaiting further orders.

McClelland stepped back and felt bare toes crunching under his boots. Another hand grabbed his and he flailed with the machete, unable to bring it down. He wrenched free, ducking low and forcing his way between them. For a moment his face was buried in someone's mildewed ribcage, its smell of old churches and time and dust, and then he was through. He glanced up and saw Moreby. The man had stepped up on to what remained of the ruin once more and he was quite still. He watched McClelland as a white-clad scientist might observe a rat navigating a maze, and he smiled.

That smile told McClelland what he already knew: he was going to lose.

Where would Moreby go after that? Egypt, the land of the pharaohs? Or Peru maybe, that of the Incas? Would he raise more gods, more armies of myth to do his bidding and terrify the world into submission – to make sure mankind lost the battle before it was even begun? Perhaps they would all join him, these emblems of death and power, to be the generals in his new world order. They would rule together and they would feed.

It was hopeless. McClelland had managed to clear a little space, was able now to wade into the lumbering bodies, but if he did he would be up close again; too close. He wouldn't be able to swing the machete. They would close in behind him and the first time he showed a hint of weakness they would fall upon him.

He looked around, but he knew no one was coming to help. Everyone was either gone or dead, standing before him in their new, perhaps final forms.

Spotlights continued to shine down on the scene, warming the top of his head, as if it was being heated by the sun. Suddenly that seemed the worst thing of all – that they were blocking out the sky; he wouldn't even be able to see the stars before he died.

He lunged suddenly in a new direction. He couldn't hope to take out Moreby. All he could do was make a stand, cover his back and cut as many of them down as he could.

He moved towards the bar, its glass structure glowing and shining back glints of light. He struck more heads from their bodies, feeling the shock of it running down his arm. He had a passing thought that it would hurt like a bastard tomorrow and pushed it away. There wasn't going to be a tomorrow for him.

He struck down harder, cutting clean through a woman's soft and rotting neck. He sliced through the cheek of a skinny man wearing nothing at all, widening his mouth into a lopsided grin. Another blow and the man fell. McClelland kept on going. The bar was in front of him. He could at least get behind it, shield himself for a little longer. But still, the nearest zombies hadn't attacked. In fact, they seemed to be parting around him, leaving a line clear across the roof; a line leading in the wrong direction.

McClelland paused, looking through the passage they'd left. At the end of it he saw not Moreby but the horror he had raised from the tomb.

The thing was looking straight at him. It looked hungry. It began to walk towards him.

McClelland's belly turned to water. He knew that he didn't have long. He shoved another zombie aside, shouldering it without fear. He didn't know how, but Moreby was holding them back somehow. He was going to feed him to his favourite pet.

He stumbled and pushed himself up. Only a single zombie stood between him and the bar. He grabbed hold of it, threw it down. He could no longer remember why he had even wanted to reach it in the first place. *A dying man*, he thought, *that must deserve one last drink.* Laughter was on his lips as he pushed his way towards the bar. It was not a good laugh and it did him no good to hear it. His heart thudded. He wondered if it would still be beating when the Mayan god ripped it from his chest.

He fell once more, putting out his hands, and he felt cool glass beneath them. He pushed himself up and got his back to it after all. There was a transparent wall behind him, a smaller one in front concealing shelves of glasses and rows of bottles. His eyes widened when he saw what was waiting there.

Every kind of tequila or mezcal was stashed under the bar: blanco, gold, reposado, añejo, pineapple flavour, melon flavour, chilli flavour, the bottles fat or slender or wearing miniature fucking sombreros, for God's sake. McClelland threw himself to his knees and grasped for them. The first bottle under his hand had a slim neck with what felt like raised lettering. He didn't care what it said. He smashed off the lid and half the contents went with it, the liquid slopping across his hand. He threw it at one of the nearest zombies, patting at his pockets, finding the small shape tucked inside with a flood of relief.

The zombie had turned towards him, its eyes blank. It was only then that McClelland recognised him as the singer – Colton Creed – they'd brought in to do their fancy show. The thought of it made him bark out laughter as he gripped the machete between his knees and fumbled with his cigarette lighter. He tried to strike it and it whirred, spluttered. He cursed, tried again, forcing himself to strike it more gently.

A flame rose. He drew in a deep breath, wishing suddenly that he'd just drunk the fucking stuff, and then he half-threw himself across the bar towards the zombie. Creed did not move. He just stood there while McClelland held the lighter to its arm, and there was a fizzling sound as the flame met the liquid darkening its shirt.

Not enough alcohol. This had looked so much easier in the movies.

The Mayan god was walking slowly but steadily towards him. There would not be any more chances. McClelland grabbed the machete, threw himself down and reached for another bottle. He snatched at the one that looked the most evil, the smallest, and he wrenched open the top. He realised too late that it was half-empty, but he could feel the burn of alcohol vapour at the back of his throat. He fumbled in his pockets once more, reaching for something else, something he had never thought to need.

They might be lucky, she had said, and McClelland had wanted to laugh, but he did not laugh now. His fingers were too big and too clumsy, but he pulled it free: a small white handkerchief, a purple flower sewn on to it.

He shoved it into the top of the bottle. Then he struck the lighter once more.

The cheap fabric went up almost at once. He threw the bottle and it exploded across the ground, spattering glass and liquid, and flames burst upwards.

The nearest zombie, withered and desiccated, was enveloped immediately. The one next to it, however, looked as if it had been in the water for a long time. Chunks of oozing flesh still clung to its bones, though much had sloughed away. Just as McClelland was thinking it would never burn, that it was hopeless, the greedy flames found its clothes. They must have dried out in the sun and the fire licked around them, the flesh beneath beginning to sizzle.

McClelland caught a trace of salt in the air, mingling with the smell of the drink. *Tequila fucking slammer, you fucker.*

The zombies had no direction but they stumbled, not thrashing or trying to put out the flames. Without aim, they barged into each other, and fire spread from one to the next. McClelland felt a thread of hope work its way deep inside him. Four of them were burning now. Creed stood in their centre, the flames lapping at him too, and he was keening: a new song without words.

Then he began to move. The singer was intent on something – no, someone – ahead of him. McClelland squinted against the bright points of light licking the zombie's ragged hair. His step was faltering but he kept on moving, and then McClelland realised what it was: a dead woman who looked as if she had come from the sea.

Pearls in her hair, he thought, but of course it wasn't like that. He couldn't see her so clearly – he only knew that she held the impression of regality in her bearing, despite the ragged garland of seaweed she wore.

Creed made the last few stumbling steps towards her, fell, and his outstretched hands grasped her about her neck.

He held her close; closer. She did not scream as a living woman would. She merely looked into his eyes, as if there was something there she should know, something she should see, as she too began to burn.

McClelland tore his gaze away. The two were being consumed together by the flame, the light so bright it dazzled him, and he found he did not want to see. It was as if he was intruding on something intimate, something that was for them alone. Then he heard the man in black's outraged shriek and he half-closed his eyes against it.

He reached for another bottle, wondering if this one would fuel the fire or only put it out. He smashed off its top and shoved a handkerchief into it, this one bearing an improbably green flower. He looked up and saw Moreby. His face was written with fury and his hand was spread in an unmistakeable gesture: *Stop.*

The zombies had stopped. They stayed where they were, turned to flickering pillars of light, forming a rough square around him. McClelland could make out no expressions on their faces. They simply burned.

Only one figure was still moving. McClelland did not want to look at it. His legs felt weak as he straightened and turned to face it. The Mayan god loomed tall over him. It regarded him with two sets of eyes and when McClelland looked up, seeing the warm brown gaze of his friend looking back at him from amid the old bone, he thought he would go mad.

The bottle with its pitiful handkerchief fell from his hand. He flailed, finding instead the now-familiar handle of the machete, and he knocked it to the floor.

A part of McClelland wanted to throw himself to the ground after the blade. He wanted to let it all go, to fall to his knees before this thing and wait for such mercy as it might give. And he knew that was the way it would be: men would fall before it, giving themselves in willing sacrifice to the beast in their eagerness to cling to something – anything – that might save them from its glare.

And its glare was terrible. McClelland couldn't meet it, but neither could he look away as it reached for him. It smelled of age and time and carrion, and McClelland squeezed his eyes tightly closed as it leaned over him.

They snapped open again as a ragged scream pierced the air. Someone else was moving after all, running across the rooftop towards them, and he saw that it was Iktan.

His friend had found his club. His eyes were like dark stars, almost-black blood tracking down both cheeks. He stumbled through the gap the zombies had made for Ah Puch, and he did not stop when he reached them. He opened his mouth in a grimace or a snarl. Then he drew back the club and swung.

Ah Puch reached out with one hand, the movement casual and without a trace of fear, and he caught it. Iktan did not try to fight. He murmured, "You're in my *mind*," and he threw himself to the floor. The obsidian blades ripped through Ah Puch's hand, and fingers toppled from it as they were severed.

McClelland did not hear the creature make a sound but Iktan flinched, putting a hand to his head, as if pain had shot through it. It did not stop him for long. He hefted the club again, this time aiming low. He buried its black teeth in Ah Puch's leg, then dragged the cutting blades through the limb. Ah Puch wavered. The great beast lumbered forwards, falling to one knee. The thing opened its mouth and a howl of fury rang out. McClelland clamped his hands over his own ears but Iktan only swung the club again, tugging hard to drag the blades through the thing's neck, and its cry became a high-pitched shriek.

It was not a sound that any human throat could make. It rang in McClelland's ears until he couldn't bear it any longer and then it was silenced as Iktan struck again. The creature's head flew from its shoulders and Ah Puch crashed to the ground.

The skull it wore came to a rest between them. Iktan's

eyes were still embedded in its sockets and they looked up, expressionless and blank.

"I see," Iktan whispered. "I can *see*." He raised his blind face to look at McClelland. "I don't have long," he said.

McClelland picked up his machete, his shock giving way to a new resolution. He had seen a blind boy strike down a god. If Iktan could do that...

"No," he replied. "You have all the time in the world, Iktan. I will get you out. Even if I have to kill them all." But the zombies weren't attacking. And in the spaces between McClelland's words, all he could hear was Moreby's crazed and mocking laughter.

Iktan half-smiled. "That is not what I mean, my friend. I am turning."

"No, you're not. We'll find a way..."

"I feel it. I'm becoming one of them." Iktan frowned. "I can still hear his thoughts."

McClelland shook his head, confused, but he thought he knew who Iktan meant. He glanced down at the body of the god. It did not stir.

"He is—" Iktan struck the side of his head – "Inside me now. They all are. But him most of all."

"Iktan, no." The machete felt like a dead weight in McClelland's hands. He nearly let it drop from his numb fingers.

"He is only waiting." Iktan half-turned towards Moreby, as if he could see him. The dark man was watching them. He was shaking with mirth or rage, McClelland couldn't tell which.

And then Iktan swept downwards and picked up the headdress of Ah Puch. He tilted his head as if he could look into his own eyes, and then he set it upon his head. He adjusted it so that his dead eyes were pointing straight at McClelland.

Iktan smiled. It was a cold smile.

McClelland fell back a step; he couldn't help it.

Iktan's expression changed once more, softening. "Please," he said. "You have to help me. He's *inside* me."

"What can I do?"

"My friend. You know already what you must do." As Iktan spoke, the colour began to leech from his skin.

McClelland shook his head. "I can't."

"Then you will die." There was no inflection in Iktan's voice. It was flat and dead and empty. "And soon. It will be soon. My master is waiting. This, he wishes to see."

Tears sprung into McClelland's eyes. He could see Iktan tightening his grip on the club that had always seemed to belong in his hands. He was drawing himself up, seeming to grow taller as McClelland watched. His face was reconfiguring itself into angular lines as the humanity faded from him.

It was too late. There was nothing left that McClelland could do. He let the machete fall from his nerveless fingers. He wondered, briefly, if this was what it would be like, as a slow numbness spread up through his spine and along his arms.

Iktan drew back his lips from his teeth. Saliva dripped from them, mingling with the blood mask he wore. It almost looked like a smile.

McClelland shook himself as a single image rose before him, sudden and clear as daylight: Stacy's stricken face. He leaped back, snatching the machete from the ground once more. There was no time left – Iktan was raising his club. There was only one thing he could possibly give to his friend, while any semblance of his friend remained, and that was the thing he had asked for, the thing he craved. A true death.

He lashed out, hard and accurate, and he severed his friend's neck. Iktan stared at him for a shocked moment, the sockets that had held his eyes brimming with darkness, and then his head fell from his shoulders and rolled across the ground, coming to rest face to face with the ancient god.

Then the zombies attacked.

McClelland was forced back, slashing and hacking at the hands that reached for him. There were too many of them. Even the zombies that were burning were slowly turning to face him and shuffling in his direction, stirring up sparks that danced into the night sky. He thought he caught a glimpse of Moreby's face, contorted in fury, and for a fleeting second he saw why: the older zombies, the ones that were little more than bones, were falling all around him. And he felt a sudden lightness passing through the air, as if some dark power had lifted.

He shot a look at the fallen god. *It's gone*, he thought, and he did not know why. He only felt, somehow, that it had been controlling them, the most ancient of the dead, and now its power had passed, possibly never to be raised again.

But there would be no victory here. He had seen that in the faces of his dead comrades. Now there was only survival. Every instinct he possessed awakened and he fought, his blade flashing everywhere, claiming heads and arms, and he saw in the blank faces around him all that remained. There was only hunger, now and forever. Soon there would be nothing else left.

He swiped wildly, taking a woman's head from her body. Once she might have pushed in front of him at the buffet or flirted with him at the bar or asked him to rub suntan lotion into her skin. Now she died.

And he realised that there were no others behind him, only Ah Puch's collapsed servants reduced to piles of dusty bones littered with the remnants of armour and cutlasses. The way was clear, right to the rail that ran around the edge of the pyramid. He turned and ran, and launched himself towards it.

Chapter Sixty-Three

STACY SQUINTED INTO the almost full dark. She could no longer see the sun, but the streetlights had switched on across the city; from here, she could almost believe that normality had been restored. Some of the lights weren't quite right, however. The ones shining on the Hotel Baktun looked almost like pillars of fire.

She could hear distant sounds and they were most definitely not normal. She had heard a man screaming and she had thought it was Francisco, but then she wasn't sure; it might even have been some kind of animal. Or perhaps that was only a yarn her mind had spun to comfort herself.

Then there had been other screams. She did not know who had made them, but she feared.

The breeze was coming in cooler and she shivered. The others stood in loose clusters, waiting for somebody to do something. Emptiness spread its cold fingers inside her. There was no hope left, but she supposed she would go on anyway. She had to. These people were counting on her. Harder still – they trusted her.

Then she saw something moving beneath a chain of light, leading away from the Hotel Baktun.

She started and took a step towards it. For a moment all she could make out was the straight thread of a well-lit road, and then she caught her breath. She had been right – a shadowy mass was moving beneath the lights, heading inland, away from where they stood.

The boy – Ethan – came and stood next to her. He watched. "Survivors?" he asked.

She shook her head, wishing she could lie. "I don't think so."

The crowd – so many – moved slowly. It was difficult to make out any detail, but they did not appear to be in any hurry and they carried nothing with them. They simply walked with a single intent, as if they had finished what they came for and now had somewhere else they were supposed to be.

"Where are they going?" Ethan asked.

Stacy shrugged. She had no way of knowing; and then she remembered the maps she'd studied, back when she was a different person, living a different life. "That's the main highway," she said. "It leads to Mexico City. They call it the *Autopista del Sol* – the Route of the Sun."

Ethan did not reply. He simply watched them go.

After a while, Stacy spoke. "It's time we left."

"Wait," he said. "There's something else."

He was right. One of the lights shining over the hotel appeared to be moving, growing brighter. In the same moment that she noticed it, Stacy heard the sound of its approach – blades chopping at the air. A helicopter.

A ray of hope shot through her. She had a vision of a huge Sea King descending on the clifftop, everyone with her ducking at the wind in their faces while crying with joy at their rescue. Some of these people were rich, weren't they? Perhaps one of them had got the word out that they needed help and the cavalry had finally arrived. *Too late*, she thought, even as the dot grew larger. Spotlights shone from it, stabbing downwards, looking for something. And then, too quickly, it started to descend.

It wasn't coming to the cliff. It was descending towards the pyramid, and there it seemed to hover, just above the flat rooftop. It did not look like a rescue helicopter: it was small and black.

Stacy half-closed her eyes. She could almost feel the breeze of it anyway, so close that the sting in her eyes mocked her. She could just make out the figure of a man stepping into it. She thought he was wearing an old-fashioned black suit, but she could not be sure.

No one else boarded. After another moment the craft began to ascend, spinning around and heading back in the direction it had come, following the line of the highway that led ever onward beneath it, like a general overseeing its troops.

Stacy took a final glance back at the hotel as she checked that the machete was still hanging from her belt, and she caught her breath.

"What's up?" Ethan asked.

She didn't answer. She only took another step towards the hotel, staring. Her heart felt as if it was trying to shake free from her chest.

"There!" She pointed.

Ethan frowned; then he too moved closer.

Stacy felt a smile trying to break out on to her face. It was stupid, she knew. The small shape climbing down the side of the pyramid could have been anything. It could have been one of *them*, and yet, she didn't think it was. It was moving too smoothly, too carefully. When it reached the edge of a balcony and lowered itself over the rail, it hesitated before it dropped.

"What is it?" Ethan asked again, and she heard something new in his voice.

She turned back to the view before her. "I told him," she said, and then she couldn't stop herself; she laughed. "I told him it was a security issue, for God's sake. The hotel – the way it's built in steps, not so easy to climb, but..." Her voice tailed away. She simply watched as the distant figure made its way down the side of the pyramid.

A hand tapped her on the shoulder. Stacy turned and beamed into the face of a worried-looking woman.

"We wondered – I mean, shouldn't we be going?" She looked around nervously. "It's dark."

Stacy's smile turned into a grin. "You know, we should." She called out more loudly. "Everyone, get ready to move. We're going to head down the coast. All of you, stick together and keep a lookout. Any zombies – don't keep it to yourself, okay?"

Ethan raised his eyebrows. "Aren't we going to wait?"

She put her hands on her hips, leaning back, grinning towards the pyramid. She couldn't see the small shape any longer – he must have reached the ground, been hidden by the softly waving palm trees – and she shook her head.

"He can handle a hotel full of zombies," she said. "I think he can manage to catch us up, don't you?" And she moved around the group, checking that everyone was all right, instructing them on how to watch all bases while they went; making sure they were ready for whatever came next.

Chapter Sixty-Four

LILY UNCURLED HERSELF in the bottom of the boat. She frowned as if puzzled by the sound of waves slapping the side of the rib, the eddies rippling away beneath them. The boat scudded across the waves as if happy to be out on the sea.

Ethan let the breeze whip his hair away from his eyes, feeling the salt sting of spray, grabbing a handle on the boat's inflatable side as it tilted. The engine missed and the prow began to turn as Larry, the American, pointed them more directly into the oncoming waves. They couldn't afford to capsize, Ethan knew. They couldn't mess this up.

They'd found the boat, deflated and covered in old ropes and a layer of salty dust, in a broken-down boathouse off a small rocky inlet on the south edge of the peninsula. They had only come across two such structures and the first had been empty, only a broken oar discarded against its side. This one had seemed deserted too. There was only a lone pelican floating at the edge of the sea to witness their approach.

They'd travelled along the cliffs far enough to be able to see Acapulco's wide harbour in the distance, its tacky shops and the gaping mouths of its bars empty. The port had looked empty too. There was no one waiting there to rescue them. Ethan hadn't really expected that there would be. There was only the wide blue curve of the ocean, and no boats as far as they could see. They must have long since sailed; perhaps many had been stolen in the panic to get away. Ethan tried not to think about that. He tried not to think of someone coming along to recover this one, all set to make their escape, only to find it gone. But then, perhaps no one would come. He didn't want to think about that either.

Stacy and McClelland sat close together at the prow. Occasionally they looked at each other and grinned. McClelland had caught up with them just as Larry and Miguel had been fixing some final patches to the boat's worn sides. He hadn't said a word when he'd arrived, hadn't had the chance; Stacy had flown at him.

It had startled Ethan, half-thinking she was going to attack him – he didn't know why, but some part of him must have become so inured to reasonless violence that he'd come to expect it – but then she had been kissing him, and he'd had to look away. They weren't kissing now but each time they grinned at each other, Ethan couldn't help grinning too.

McClelland had fought and he had come back. He was proof that there could be a life again, after.

Ethan wasn't sure what *after* there would be. Hector wanted to head back into the port, to find the *federales* and make a complaint, but no one was listening to Hector. Larry wanted to head for the States; no one had responded to that, one way or the other. Ethan imagined that meant they were seriously thinking about it. He imagined that some of the others, like him, were thinking of their home in England. It seemed an impossibly long way off. He could feel his separation from it in the way the sun sparkled off the sea, its clean briskness, the view of nothing but the ocean with its depths and distances and strange shores.

Lily giggled as Heather pushed herself up and picked her way over a pile of supplies from the boathouse – rope, nets and other fishing gear – and crouched down next to her. She dangled something in front of her; another embroidered handkerchief. Lily crowed and grabbed for it with her chubby hands. She waved it in front of her face, letting it flap in the breeze, and then she let it go.

Ethan tried to catch it. It flew by the tip of his fingers, over the back of the boat, vanishing beneath the foam they left in their wake. He turned to Heather to apologise, but she was laughing, making a fuss of his sister. *Simple things*, he thought. Perhaps they were the only things worth treasuring.

He turned and faced forward as their destination grew closer. In all the wide-open sea, the *Demeter* alone broke the smooth horizon. Its white edifice loomed tall, jutting proudly above the ocean. It was modern and white and alone. Ethan kept casting glances towards it, but he did not think there was anyone on its deck. Soon there would be. He wasn't sure how he felt about that. He had no idea what might be waiting for them up there.

He looked away from the ship, focusing on the scratch on the back of his hand, his last gift from his mother. It was already healing over. Soon, perhaps his memories would be forgotten too; there would only be what lay before him and his old life would finally be gone.

He shook his head, roused by the sound of Lily's laughter. No, it wasn't all gone. There must be something left that was good in the world, and with that ship at their command, they could go anywhere; they could surely find it. One day, perhaps, he might even find his way home.

Epilogue

SABATINA SAVAIN STOOD on the rocky outcrop where her father had once taken her fishing, before the bad times came. When her sister had disappeared she was sure that was as tough as things would get; she hadn't known there could be bad times and worse times. Now, she supposed, the worse times were here. She wasn't sure where her father was any longer. He hadn't said goodbye. None of them had.

She had brought his old fishing net with her, but as soon as she'd seen the wildness of the waves she knew it wasn't any good. She did not have the strength to wield it as he had. The rocks were slippery and there were no boats left. If there had been, she wouldn't have known how to row.

She let herself fall to the sand and felt its grit coating her skin. Variola would have been ten now. Variola would have known what to do. Maybe she still did, but no one knew where she had gone. They didn't even think she was on Tortuga any longer. They said she was far, far away, spirited from her father and mother and her sister in the night, and Sabatina could hardly bear to think of it because she knew it was her fault.

Variola was always the one who had new clothes. She didn't

have them often, but then Sabatina never had any at all. Old clothes, old shoes; old, old, old. Everything she wore had her sister's smell on it. When the pretty red dress began to be too small for Variola, though, she didn't care; and Variola saw.

Sabatina remembered the way her sister had twisted each of the pretty buttons from the front of the dress, her smiling face not troubling to cover her spite. Sabatina had cried all night. She had pushed her face into her bunk and she had wished the thing she had wished, and she could not take it back. The next morning, when she had woken, Variola was gone.

She would do anything, now, to have her sister back again; or anybody. The whole village had emptied, though it wasn't like her sister. No one else had simply vanished, like her. No: first, they had changed.

She shivered, though the day was hot, the sea already blood-warm where it splashed around her ankles. There were plenty of fish in it, though men had grown tired of catching them. There was easier meat.

She remembered the way her mother had sat by her bed and taken Sabatina's hand in her own strong fingers. She told her that Variola had been taken by the *bokor.* She said that Haiti had once been a land of slaves, and now people wanted slaves again and so the *bokor* must have worked his magic. He had taken her sister's *little good angel*, the part of her soul that made her *her* – and Sabatina had screwed up her face thinking of it, unsure that her sister could ever have had anything good inside her – and that she was a *zombi* now.

She had been taken from her family and her home and she would work and she would never even miss any of them. Her mother had said that in a soothing voice, as if it was a good thing, a comforting thing. *It is only the living that miss the dead*, she had repeated, stroking Sabatina's cheek.

Sabatina had not believed any of it. She knew what had happened. She had wished her sister gone and then she *was* gone. It was as simple and strange and complicated and magical as that, and she did not know how she could begin to undo it.

But now, the dead were coming back. The *bokor*'s magic had somehow escaped and roamed free. Some said it was a disease, that it had spread from an aeroplane or perhaps a ship, but Sabatina knew that wasn't true. It had come from inside her. The badness had been let out and now the dead were different. They were blank as the dead had always been, but now they were hungry too. Like the *loogaroo*, the demons of nasty tales, they thirsted for blood.

Sabatina ducked down lower, behind a rock scabbed with barnacles. The men stood a little distance away, where the sand gave way to sparsely planted sea grape trees. As she watched, a broad, brittle leaf fell and rolled end over end as the breeze carried it towards her. It brought the smell to her too, the one she could never become accustomed to; the one like the rubbish heap at the back of the market where the butchers threw their bones.

There were many of them now. They seemed to be surrounded by a cloud of insects, almost invisible unless she turned her head a certain way. The insects didn't seem to trouble the dead. Maybe that was a nice thing about being like them; that and the not caring and not missing and not feeling anything at all.

She felt a stab of longing and breathed deeply, forcing herself to become a blank, like the waves washing footprints from a beach.

Nothing. She must think of nothing. Just as if there were no little good angel inside her either.

Maybe then the *zombis* wouldn't want her. *Zombies*, she reminded herself. That's what they were now, a different kind, and that was a comfort at least. Wherever Variola was, she was not like these men, like their neighbour, old Gedulien, who had snapped at her with half his front teeth missing; like her father, his eyes bleached by the midday sun. Like her mother.

Sabatina shook her head violently, then bit her lip, peering down the beach. The dead were good at seeing movement. They were good at seeing meat.

She was lucky this time. None of them moved; instead they stood together as another shambled towards them. This one was in a bad way. It lumbered, its back malformed, just like the Sack-Man her mother used to tell her of, the monster who came to carry off naughty children.

Her heartbeat quickened, even while she told herself it wasn't real. She had no use for bedtime stories now. Not since the worse things had come, and stories walked under the midday sun.

Anyway, the Sack-Man didn't do anything. He just stood with the others, looking neither to the left nor right, as if he had simply stopped. There were more of them now, and more were coming, a group of men of different ages, different kinds, some that would spit from their fancy car windows as they drove through the village, others that would sit by the dusty road playing backgammon with chips of bone.

Whatever their differences, they walked together, each clumsy step bringing them closer. Some of them were bloated, their flesh puffy-looking, as if they'd been left too long in the sea. The smell grew stronger. Sabatina wrinkled her nose, but she did not dare move further away. They might see her. Perhaps they could smell her too. She knew her skin smelled of salt and sweat and the beach. She hadn't washed in days. She hadn't been home; home wasn't a safe place to be any longer.

But the zombies were doing something strange. Some of them were lying down on the sand, head to toe and toe to head, just like the family who used to live down a rough track at the end of the village, the ones who only had one bed between six of them. The Sack-Man shuffled forward and she realised he wasn't misshapen, as she had thought. He wasn't even carrying a sack. He had coils of rope looped around his shoulders and now he let them fall.

A wave rushed in, bubbling under the line of feet and heads and more feet, and they lifted in the swell. The heads darkened, turning to fetid-looking matter. Sabatina pulled a face. How did they breathe? And then she remembered.

More of the zombies were lying down on the sand. They didn't discuss it or look at each other or hesitate. They simply did it. Those who remained picked up the rope and started to walk between them, bending and straightening by turns.

Sabatina frowned. She could not see what they were doing. There seemed to be no use in it and yet their actions spoke of quiet intent, as if their blank faces had something inside them after all.

The tide was turning. Didn't they know? But they were just lying there. Hope leaped suddenly inside her. Perhaps the dead were really dying now. They had walked the earth, unnatural and unwelcome, and now they were simply going back to where they belonged.

She was so intent on watching the zombies with their ropes that at first she didn't see the dark figure making his way down the beach.

He wore a top hat and a long black jacket that looked ragged at the bottom. He carried a cane with a large bulb on the top and then Sabatina realised that it wasn't some carving, wasn't a decoration – it was a human skull, still with shreds of meat attached, and he bit into it as he approached, just as if it were a hot potato on a stick.

She could see his skull too. The apples of his cheeks had rotted away, leaving behind only the gleam of bone. He did not seem to mind. He did not lumber like the others. He strolled; he swaggered. She could see a shine in his yellow-rimmed eyes and, even though he didn't smile, she had the impression that a smile was not far away, that mirth was dancing just behind those eyes.

Then she knew who he was.

She forgot the need to be still and her hand shot to her mouth. She ducked down lower, found herself sprawling flat on the sand, her chin pressed into the sun-warmed grit. It was another story walking the Earth, but this time she knew that it wasn't pretend; it didn't just remind her of something. It was real.

The man was Baron Samedi, and now he stood over the zombies on the beach. They continued to lie at his feet without moving. Then he raised a hand over his eyes, as if he was looking for her.

Sabatina pressed herself deeper into the sand, wishing that she could burrow into it, just keep on going until she reached the middle of the Earth. He must be able to see her. Surely such a god would see everything.

She heard her mother's voice, as if she whispered at her ear. *When we are gone, child, we will never be alone. The Baron will come for you.* She had smiled, gently, when she said those words. Tears had been shining in her eyes; tears for a missing daughter, a missing sister Sabatina knew was never coming back.

No one need stay dead, child, for the Baron will come for them. He gathers them all from their graves and he brings them to Heaven. She laughed, then, a laugh that had sadness in it, something that Sabatina did not understand and wasn't sure she wanted to. And then her mother said, *Unless they have offended him with their life. Make sure you do not do this, my dove. For those he does not bring to Heaven – why, them he will make zombi. But he will surely take your sister, Sabatina. He will not let her suffer. He will not let her be that way. It is only those who have displeased him who will be made his zombi slaves, forever and ever.*

She had rested her chin, then, on Sabatina's head. It had hurt a little, but she hadn't complained. She hadn't been able to see her mother's face and she hadn't wanted to see it, hadn't wanted to look at the pain she'd caused.

Displeased him, she thought. *Offended him.*

She turned her face into the ground and felt the sand pressing against her eyelids, drying her lips, tickling her nostrils. She couldn't breathe. She lifted her head, expecting to see the Baron's face peering into hers with those cold dead eyes, but he was not there; he stood with the others, and now he was looking out across the sea, towards the mainland of Haiti.

Others were coming. More men, tall, but not so tall as the Baron – no, not nearly. They too carried canes, though these were longer, more like walking sticks. They did not walk as if they needed the help of a stick, and then she realised what they were: oars.

She gasped, looking at the zombies lying on the ground. Those with the ropes had finished and stood back as if awaiting new orders. She could see the insects, a red-brown cloud buzzing about their heads like evil thoughts.

Another wave rushed in, higher this time, and she saw what they had done.

The zombies had been lashed together into one big mat, one that was half-afloat. It flexed and moved and as it did they moaned, a mournful sound that made tears spring to Sabatina's eyes. She could hear the sea echoing in their throats and their gullets and their wounds. The water was claiming them for its own, and yet they did not sink into it; they lifted and fell as it carried them, and the Baron moved forward and stepped on to their bloated bodies.

Those carrying the oars did the same. They trod on the bodies of their comrades, those that did not need to breathe, and they pushed away from the shore.

The raft floated. And as it did, it sang its notes of despair and hopelessness and loss.

Sabatina bit her lip so hard that blood came. Horror mingled with hope. The zombies were leaving. Perhaps, soon, they would be all gone.

She closed her eyes, breathing in the air, trying not to think of the shore away to the south where thousands of people lived and worked and ate and loved. Familes, just like hers. She tried not to think of what they would feel as the raft came closer; their surprise. Their curiosity. Their fear; their despair.

As the raft diminished into the sun she straightened, brushing the sand from her skirt. She did not move from the shore for a long time. She watched the zombies until they were nothing but a dark shape, a little like a new island that had appeared on the horizon, and she wondered if it would be better not to feel anything at all.

Acknowledgements

Many thanks, as usual, to Duncan Proudfoot, and to Clive Hebard and Emily Kearns, Joe Roberts, Michael Marshall Smith, Jo Fletcher, Christopher Fowler, Reggie Oliver, Sarah Pinborough, Mark Samuels, Jay Russell, and – for those who know – Bram Stoker and Stephen King. Special thanks to Alison Littlewood for making sure that this book will never make comfortable reading while you are relaxing on holiday. —SJ

A huge thank you to Stephen Jones, whose invitation to add to the growing *Zombie Apocalypse!* world led to more writerly fun than should strictly be allowed. Thanks also to the writers who have helped create that world and its characters, some of whom found a Mexican connection just in time for more zombie mayhem. Thanks to Jo Fletcher, for adding enthusiasm to a great project. As ever, love and appreciation to Fergus – I bet you never imagined where that trip to Mexico would lead. And finally, this one is for the Birdland gang. You know who you are . . . —AL

Alison Littlewood is the author of *A Cold Season*, published by Jo Fletcher Books, an imprint of Quercus. The novel was selected for the Richard and Judy Book Club, where it was described as "perfect reading for a dark winter's night". Her second novel, *Path of Needles* – a dark blend of fairy tales and crime fiction – has recently been shortlisted for a British Fantasy Award. Her third, *The Unquiet House*, is a ghost story set in the Yorkshire countryside. The author's short stories have been chosen for inclusion in *The Mammoth Book of Best New Horror* and *The Best Horror of the Year* anthologies, as well as *The Best British Fantasy 2013* and *The Mammoth Book of Best British Crime 10*. She lives in Yorkshire with her partner Fergus, and you can visit her at: www.alisonlittlewood.co.uk

Stephen Jones is the winner of three World Fantasy Awards, four Horror Writers Association Bram Stoker Awards and three International Horror Guild Awards, as well as being a multiple recipient of the British Fantasy Award and a Hugo Award nominee. A former television producer/director and genre movie publicist and consultant (the first three *Hellraiser* movies, *Nightbreed*, *Split Second*, etc.), he has written and edited more than 135 books, including *The Art of Horror*, *Horrorology: The Lexicon of Fear*, *Fearie Tales: Stories of the Grimm and Gruesome*, *A Book of Horrors*, *Curious Warnings: The Great Ghost Stories of M.R. James*, *Psycho-Mania!* and *The Mammoth Book of Best New Horror* and *Zombie Apocalypse!* series. You can visit his website at: www.stephenjoneseditor.com